JUDITH
WANTS
TO BE
YOUR
FRIEND

JUDITH WANTS TO BE YOUR FRIEND

ANNIE WEIR

Matador
9 Priory Business Park,
Wistow Road, Kibworth Beauchamp,
Leicestershire. LE8 0RX
Tel: 0116 279 2299
Email: books@troubador.co.uk
Web: www.troubador.co.uk/matador
Twitter: @matadorbooks

ISBN 978 1785890 048

British Library Cataloguing in Publication Data.
A catalogue record for this book is available from the British Library.

Printed and bound by CPI Group (UK) Ltd, Croydon, CR0 4YY
Typeset in 11pt Aldine401 BT by Troubador Publishing Ltd, Leicester, UK

Matador is an imprint of Troubador Publishing Ltd

For my husband, John.

PROLOGUE
Hexham, Thursday 12th November

Chloe looked over her shoulder a couple of times. Normally she would have headed straight for the waiting room, the one with the big, black marble fireplace. Even when it wasn't lit, it seemed warmer than the other one. She didn't want to be trapped in there today. Seeing Judith at the door, she hastened on. She glanced back over her shoulder again, then stumbled and tripped over her own feet and fell from the platform onto the tracks. A horn sounded as the goods train from Newcastle to Carlisle trundled through, sending a blast of cold air around the building. Then there was a screech of brakes and an alarm sounded. Station staff rushed to the line and waiting passengers stood and stared at the spot where Chloe had been moments before.

Judith stood and watched the scene. It appeared to her that the world had suddenly become silent, a sort of calm before a storm or a picture frozen in time. She turned and walked back to her car where she sat for a few moments struggling to comprehend what she had just witnessed, then she switched on the engine. As she approached the exit from the station car park, she had to wait to allow the ambulance and two police cars through.

CHAPTER 1

Carlisle, September 2009

Monday 14th September 2009

While I wait, I note the changes they've made here. Now it's all tile flooring, rustic plaster and orange lampshades; last time I was here it was plastic tables and cardboard cups. The blackboard is still by the door but it looks more in keeping. This is getting boring. I study the back of the waitress's head instead. *Head-instead. Redhead-instead. Hurry up and get off the phone, Redhead.*

She dials another number.

'Emma, it's me. Can you work this evening? Oh please. You-know-who has let me down again and I'm stuck here and I should be…,' Silence while she is interrupted. 'OK, never mind. See you tomorrow.'

I wonder where she wants to be so desperately this evening. If I were her, I'd shut up shop and go. It can't be worth staying open just for me, and I'm not even going to pay. Suddenly she's facing me and I hear an echo of my mother's voice. *Don't stare, Judith! People won't like you if you stare.*

'Sorry, I didn't see you there.' A forced smile. 'What can I get you?'

'Latte please.' I offer the voucher torn from the local paper.

'I'll bring it over.'

She brings the coffee to the round, scrubbed pine table right opposite the counter, a smile firmly fixed on that freckled face that so typically goes with red hair. I feel a bit sorry for her actually and smile back. Heaven knows I don't need to make enemies here as well. The coffee's as good as the rich smell that draws people in; it should be after the noise and effort that goes into making it. A recording of a Spanish guitar plays quietly in the background. I think I might come back to this café-bar tomorrow. We'll see.

I don't go straight home. Home, that's a joke. I haven't got my beautiful flat in Hexham any more. Even in a town of that size I couldn't hide after all that business; well, after the misunderstanding. I suppose home is my rented one-bedroomed flat, which used to be half of a decent-sized house, two doors down from the Crown Inn. There's nothing to go back there for anyway so I walk around the city for a while, window-shopping by street light, then have a BigBurger Meal and read my book until ten o'clock when I know the café bar will be shutting. I walk back along English Street. Sure enough, Redhead's preparing to lock up. I hold back. It's not dark enough so I look in the window of House of Fraser and watch her reflection turning the key and pulling down the shutter. She strides on down English Street on her way – where? A car park? The bus stop? The station? All in good time. God knows I have enough of that. I turn back the way I'd come, back past BigBurger.com, down Scotch Street, through the rancid underpass that smells of old cabbage and which is decorated with not very witty graffiti, and I walk up the half a mile of hill to Stanwix.

Tuesday 15th September 2009
It's quiet in the cash office once the change has been run through the counter. Maureen starts the shift by allocating the jobs then we just get on with it. It suits me quite well actually. I like things to be right. Checks and balances. I don't like Maureen watching everything I do, though. Oh God, she's speaking to me.

'How are you enjoying working here, Judith?'

'OK thanks,' I say, lying.

'Yes it's a good laugh, isn't it?' she says.

Laugh? I can't remember the last time I laughed but it certainly wasn't in the cash office at Cost-Save. It's easy enough work though. Count the money from the tills, balance the cash with the readout from the computer, sort the cash and prepare it for banking. It pays the rent and the discounted grocery bills. It'll do for now. I'll go back to that cafe bar later. Cafe Bar Sierra. I wonder what the redhead's called – Lucinda? Eleanor? Bridget? No, I bet it ends in 'a'. I like names that end in 'a'. *Pay attention, Judith! People won't like you if you don't listen to them.* Her voice again, I'm trying hard, I really am. I turn back to my supervisor.

'Do you balance?' Maureen reverts to type, discarding the friendly chat in favour of jobs-worth. 'Securicor will be here soon and the cash needs to be checked and bagged-up.'

'Yes, I balance.' Balanced ten minutes ago, actually. Better not let on. 'I think I've got it right.'

I'll be home soon; a brisk five minutes' walk past the new car showrooms – did I really used to own a BMW? – and down Scotland Road, clogged with traffic as usual. I don't know whether it's a good thing, living quite so close to work. It might be better to be a bit further away. At least then I'd get some exercise walking to and from. Too much comfort food and not doing anything except sitting on my bum in the cash office is not good. I wonder what Redhead does to keep so trim. All that Mediterranean fare in the café-bar must be a temptation. I considered the Penne Carbonara yesterday evening but a BigBurger.com Meal suits my budget better these days. Maybe she goes for a run around the park every day, or to a fitness class twice a week. As I said, all in good time.

I'm back at my bijoux half-house and it's just after five. I don't mind it here really. The embossed wall paper, magnolia of course, is clean and the white curtains actually look quite classy in pale contrast. I'm not supposed to put any pictures on the walls so I have rebelled and hung up an Indian-style rug instead. The lease didn't say 'no Indian-style rugs'. The bathroom is small and new, as is the kitchen with timeless white fittings. It's warm enough and furnished minimally. It's fine for one person.

I wonder what the best time will be to walk into town for my soon-to-be regular early evening latte. By the best time, I mean when Redhead won't be too busy. I must engage her in some conversation today. I take a long shower to wash away the smell of musty old bank notes. As I lather myself with grapefruit-scented body wash and the hot water pours over my head I imagine our conversation; she remembers me from yesterday and I say the coffee was lovely and that I hope it wasn't too much of an inconvenience for her having to work last night. Then she tells me where she should have been and I get the first piece of the jigsaw. I put on a clean pair of jeans, a white t-shirt and take a light jacket. These autumn evenings are lovely at the moment but get nippy when the watery-blue sky darkens and the sun goes down. Hopefully I won't be home too soon. Walking down the hill over the bridge spanning the River Eden, I spot the old man walking his Jack Russell. I'm feeling rather good and smile at him. He nods and smiles back at me. *You see, Judith, it's not so difficult after all.*

Approaching the café-bar I find I have slowed down. I'm not nervous, of course, just enjoying the anticipation. Come on, don't hesitate now. I push the door open and stroll in, pretending to study the coffees listed on the blackboard on the wall just inside the door; Americano, Flat White, Cappuccino, Mocha, and on and on – how many choices of coffee do people

4

need? – and hope Redhead spots me and makes conversation first. Nothing. I turn towards the counter. A tall, slim young man dressed in black, his long shiny hair tied back, patiently waits for my order.

'Where's the lady who was here last night?' I blurt out.

'Joanna? Day off. What can I get you?'

'Latte please.'

The latte is as good as I remembered, and worth the money as well as the time and noise. It's very quiet in the cafe again tonight. I take my coffee and go to sit in one of the deep leather armchairs near the window and read the local paper that someone has left behind. As I leave I ask whether Joanna – it does end in 'a' – will be in tomorrow.

Friday 18th September 2009

I'm back at BigBurger.com again, this time the one near Cost-Save and the new car garages. I could eat at Cost-Save if I wanted to, in what they laughingly call a restaurant but after being there all day I prefer to go somewhere else. The discount would be handy though. It's a struggle living on my lousy wages. Five-thirty is a dreadful time to be here. There's a party of screaming kids squabbling over balloons and crying for more of the clown; or is it because he's terrified them? Two young Scottish couples on the next table are nearly as loud. The girls look like clones of each other with black boots and leggings and black and white dresses over the top and belted cardigans over the dresses. What happened to individuality? Actually I don't think they are couples now; one of the boys is very effeminate, screeching and gesturing to be the centre of attention. Oh, just clear off! I used to like going to BigBurger. com in Hexham. It was a kind of inverted snobbery buying a BigBurger.com Meal wearing a business suit then working on my laptop while I ate in. I've noticed a lot of business people meet in BigBurger.com these days. I never noticed how loud and incessant the pop music is. They never play anything I recognise.

I really must do something to keep my mind sharp. If I could find out what Joanna does when she's off-duty I might do it too. It would show we had something in common. My next mission, should I choose to bother, is to find out where she goes on the evenings when she isn't working. Concurrent mission, which may be easier, is to take Maureen-chief-cashier-witch-woman down a peg or two. I hate being told what to do all day. It won't be too difficult. She's not that bright. She's not that much of a witch either, just really irritating and enjoys being in charge and being perfect. And anyway, she deserves it after today. The kids and the Scots have gone, thank God.

Oh yes, today was my three-month review with the ghastly Maureen. Who does she think she is? I've never been late or asked for time off. I learned the tedious job within a few days and there have never been any discrepancies. But is that the important thing?

'Well yes,' I said to her, 'it is.'

'But you're not a *team* player, Judith.' She stressed the word team. Obviously play doesn't enter into it.

'No. I'm not,' I replied evenly. 'I didn't know that was part of my job description.'

That threw her, mentioning the job description. I pulled out my copy and suggested we went through each part in turn. Her counter-move was to pull out the person spec. There was plenty about being flexible, willing to work extra hours, being reliable and accurate, but nowhere did it say I had to be jolly and join in with her bloody childish conversation and buy raffle tickets for her village's latest good cause. It's a job, for God's sake. I'll come in, I'll do the job, I'll stay late, I'll cover if someone's off sick or skiving. But I will not creep around *you,* Witch-woman, and you will regret trying to make me conform and become one of your coven. I can cast a few spells of my own.

She recommended that my position become permanent and we signed the appropriate documentation for Personnel.

Saturday 19th September 2009

Well, well, well! A piece of the jigsaw walks past my line of vision. I have answered the buzzer and opened the hatch between the cash office and the checkouts. One of the supervisors needs change. We only did a change-run twenty minutes ago. They should make sure checkout operators understand the concept of getting what they need when it's offered. As I hand over a bag of pound coins in exchange for a twenty pound note, Joanna walks past. In the snapshot of five seconds I see her catch the hands of a small boy and swing him up into her trolley. Keeping hold of his hands and nudging the trolley along with her stomach, she bends forward to rub noses with him. It is so obviously a familiar and intimate mother and son gesture that the matching red hair and freckled faces are incidental. How lovely to be so at ease with someone, so sure of reciprocation and so unforced. If only I had been able to keep… oh never mind all that again. She seems so nice; capable but vulnerable, responsible but needing support. Another thought strikes me; what if she has a husband and other children? How else could she work in the evenings? Maybe on Monday night she just wanted to get home to watch TV.

I am still standing there by the little window when Maureen's voice breaks through the density of my inner conversation.

'Judith. Judith?'

I stand there a little longer, deliberately of course.

'Judith, what are you waiting for?'

'Nothing. I'm done.' I close the wooden shutter to isolate us from the outside world.

'What did they want?'

'Pound coins.'

'Why did that take so long?'

I look the unlovely Maureen right in the eyes. 'It didn't take that long.'

She doesn't know what to say to that so she reverts to what she always says.

'Have you balanced your cash?'

The buzzer goes again. This time it's the duty manager wanting to be let in to sign the banking. I release the outer door so that he can come into the lobby, and when it locks again I let him into the inner sanctum that is the cash office. It reminds me of visiting my mother at Mill View Care Home in Hexham. That was all buzzers and lobbies and having to be let in and out. Maybe that's why I don't like Maureen; she's too much like the manager at the care home telling me what I can and can't do. The oblong room here, fortified on all sides with only three small windows, seems to fill up. God knows it's claustrophobic enough with four of us working in here. He (Mr. Wilson, but call me Ken) sits down in front of ten wire trays each containing bundles of bank notes amounting to £15000. Maureen brings over the scales. He does a test-weigh then proceeds to quickly weigh and initial each bundle. I wonder, not for the first time, at the accuracy of the scales; that they show up a missing note or a piece of Sellotape sticking a torn note together. No hitches. The banking is signed off ready for Securicor. Maureen presents the breakdown of the cash office float; the total being the money held in the safe and excluding what is in the tills at that moment, and of course the banking ready to be sealed and collected. That is the moment I start to hatch my plan to trap her.

Monday 15th September 2008

Judith looked at the embossed invitation and thought it was about time that the shop re-opened. It had been closed for nearly six months and there were rumours that when it opened, it would be 'really nice', whatever that meant. Hexham could do with a 'really nice' antique shop, she thought, as opposed to the endless row of cluttered junk shops that merely pretended. She looked around the minimalistic décor in her flat deciding what she might like to go where. She RSVP-ed after office hours on their answer-phone.

Friday 26th September 2008

'That damned clock! I wish it would tick more quietly!' Chloe spoke aloud even though she was by herself for a few minutes. The caterers had been in and arranged the canapés on a trolley in her office adjoining the sales area, and the champagne flutes were on another one ready to bring through when people started to arrive. The bottles, already chilled, were in buckets of ice by the back door. Chloe stood up and peered out of the huge square window; from her vantage point she could see up to the market place to her right and down the hill a little way before the road curved around to her left. There were plenty of people hurrying through the rain but none appeared to be waiting for the grand opening of Phoenix Antiques. It was only just after five and Louise, her long-time friend and member of staff, wasn't back yet. There was still nearly half an hour to go. The grandfather clock in the corner ticked on, counting down to five-thirty. Chloe stood up and moved from one carefully placed antique to another. She minutely adjusted the position of the ceramic statue on a stand in the centre of the room. There were no prices visible on anything. She studied a picture on the wall, went to straighten it, thought better of it, and then looked out of the window again. Not much change. Still raining. Phoenix Antiques read backwards from where she stood; she had already grown used to that. She heard the back door open and Louise called out as she shook out her umbrella and hung up her dripping coat.

'We'll need to make a space for people's coats. It's tipping it down outside.'

'Good idea. I need something to occupy me anyway. This waiting is killing me.'

'Relax, will you? I saw a couple of people when I was out. They're really looking forward to this.'

And soon the grandfather clock tastefully chimed the half-hour, and Louise swept her outstretched hand towards the door as if to say 'It's your moment. You do the honours.' And she disappeared to find another coat stand from the store room and a basket for umbrellas.

At eight o'clock Chloe and Louise finally sat down and Chloe retrieved the last bottle of champagne reserved by them for them to either celebrate or commiserate. It was time to celebrate.

'The time has flown past,' said Chloe as she poured champagne and sat down.

'Yes, and imagine selling a carriage clock, a painting and even one of the coat stands that wasn't really ready.'

'We made some good contacts too. Do you know that woman with the tan? Dark hair and really smart? Judith, I think.'

They chinked glasses.

'Judith Dillon. She's an accountant; has her own business

around the corner in Market Street. I don't really know her, but her sister was in my year at school.'

'She seemed really interested in the paintings; said she would have bought that seascape if it hadn't just been sold. I said I'd keep a look out for more and call her when I had any. She said she'd pop in now and again as well. She seemed really nice.'

She got up again to adjust the painting. It was a little high for her petite stature.

'Do you think this looks like a Seurat?'

'Only in the use of dots; not the subject matter or what the people look like.'

'Mmm, I suppose. Or Signac?'

'Same comment. Anyway, about Judith Dillon, I think she keeps to herself a lot. Some people find her a bit strange. You did well to bond with her.'

'Oh you know me! Bonding is my middle name. And anyway, if she's an accountant she's bound to have money to spend.'

Chloe refilled their glasses and refused to think badly of a potential customer, not tonight anyway.

Back at home, Judith considered the evening a success. The champagne and nibbles were good, and the shop was very much to her taste. Chloe and her assistant had been friendly and that ghastly painting being sold was a stroke of luck. She was able to say how much she liked it. It gave good reason to keep going back, though nothing Chloe would produce for her to see would ever be just right. It would provide on-going entertainment through the long winter months ahead now that Alison had suddenly gone back to London to live. She noticed her phone flashing with a message. Sod it; whatever it was, it would have to wait until the morning.

Saturday 27th September

The phone was ringing before Judith had got out of bed. She let it ring. The message cut in.

'Judith? Are you there? Oh, answer, for God's sake! I need to talk to you now. Right now, Judith. Answer the phone.'

Judith turned over and snuggled back into the duvet. Fiona could wait until she was ready. She was getting really rather bossy. *Right now, Judith. Answer the phone.* She knew what it would be anyway. Their mother would be worse. Fiona always said that. 'Mother's worse, I can't cope (and why should I?), it's not fair on Rosie having to be a part-time carer for her granny, and we need a serious talk about it.' Fiona and Rosie got to live in Granny's house though, and they didn't complain about that.

After a long soak in the bath and two cups of coffee, Judith called her sister back. Their mother was worse, Fiona wouldn't be able to cope for much longer and it wasn't fair on any of them. Not quite on script but close enough not to have bothered.

'Where were you last night, anyway?'

'Out.'

'What, all night?'

'None of your business, but no actually.'

'So you could have called back last night. Why didn't you?'

'God, Fiona, have I rung you back to get the same speech as every other time and to answer a barrage of questions as well? I'm going; I've got stuff to do today.'

'You have not. You never have anything to do on Saturdays. I need you to come over and talk about Mum. Apart from anything else, it's not fair on Rosie…'

'Change the record, Fi. Heard that one.'

'No, she really is worse. Please come over. Come for lunch and let's have a proper family meeting. You haven't seen her for weeks; you don't know what she's like now.'

Missed that one – the fourth in Fiona's quartet of stock phrases. 'OK. I'll be round at lunch time.'

At midday Judith pulled into the leafy avenue where she had lived as a child and noticed a bag lady sitting in the bus shelter. It looked as though she had a dressing gown on over clothes, and slippers on. Judith wondered what on earth this neighbourhood was coming to. The woman's hair was a mess and as Judith slowed down to look at her more closely, she got up and stumbled into the road in front of her car. Judith slammed on the brakes and leapt out.

'Mother?'

The woman looked through her then turned to leave.

'Mother! Come back! What are you doing out here dressed like that?' She looked round to see whether anyone was watching. Nobody, thank God. 'Get in the car. I'll take you back home.'

'God, Fi, that was so embarrassing. Our mother was sitting out there in the bus shelter in her dressing gown and slippers.'

'Embarrassing? Is that what you call it? My, God! You get worse. It isn't embarrassing, it's impossible to deal with. I've had her assessed and she has dementia. She needs specialist help. She needs help all day and every day. It's not embarrassing; it's our mum; it's sad; it's it's…' and Fiona's voice started to break up under the weight of dealing with it by herself for so long, for not being able to ask for help, for trying her best, for being absolutely exhausted. She sobbed.

Judith looked at her. 'Where's Rosie, anyway? Isn't she here helping you?'

'Why should she? She's seventeen. She needs her own life. She's struggling to cope with it as well. We barely even talk about it. We just do what we have to, what we can, trying to be normal.'

'Well, you both live rent-free in Mum's house. That's one reason.'

'You are totally heartless. Piss off. I'll deal with it without you then.'

Fiona didn't usually swear and Judith softened her tone a little. Maybe she hadn't given Fi enough support lately. It wasn't Fi that she resented. It wasn't Fi's fault the she was their mother's favourite blue-eyed girl. To be fair to Fi, she had never appeared to notice. Judith had found it hard to concentrate lately and she knew she was falling behind with her work. Alison suddenly deciding to leave the area had put her off kilter and the pressure of it had built up.

'You don't have to deal with anything. She can go into a nursing home. We'll get power of attorney, sell the house then we'll both be free of her and each other. You do make a meal of everything, you know.'

When Fiona looked up from a fresh bout of sobbing she saw that Judith had already identified suitable care homes from the Yellow Pages, and was dialling the number for one.

'Mill View,' she said, 'that place is fine. It's only a couple of miles from here and has a good reputation. I've got a client there. I've been out a few times to see him. The manager is a client as well actually. It's a good business. Leave it to me.'

'Ok, thanks Judith.'

After a brief conversation Judith hung up and said, 'Great news. Someone died a couple of days ago so they've got a spare room. Some people wait for years.'

Leaving her sister's house without staying for lunch, Judith appraised her car. It's a pity, she thought, that she hadn't smashed into a lamp-post when she swerved to avoid her mother. She could do with it being written off and replaced on insurance. She called in at the BMW showroom on her way back home while she pondered how she could make it happen.

A woman in her position should have a sporty little number to be seen around town in. Sod the over-priced poncey antiques that no one would ever see. She needed a new car.

Sunday 28th September 2008

Fiona and Rosie sat down to Sunday lunch. Granny had refused to come down when Fiona asked her and by the time Rosie had gone up to try, she was asleep on her bed.

'So Judith thinks Granny should go into Mill View?'

'Yes. What do you think?'

'I do too, really. My friend Moira from school works there at the weekends. She says it's OK.'

'Hmm.'

'Don't you agree, Mum? Granny needs to be looked after better than we can do it.'

'Hmm.'

At two o'clock Judith arrived at the BMW garage for her appointment with the salesman and spent the afternoon test-driving a selection of models. She knew she should be in the office catching up with her work. She prided herself on doing a good job but needed something to distract her completely. She took a 3-Series out towards Mill View. Yes, that would be an ideal place for her mother to live. Fiona had always had her own way when they were growing up and had got away with everything. It was time that she was forced to see sense over this, even if she didn't like it.

Judith realised that the impossibly fresh-faced young salesman was waiting for her to answer him. *Pay attention, Judith! You really must learn to listen to other people.* Her mother's voice echoing in her head was as loud and clear as ever.

'Sorry?'

'So, how do you like this model?' he repeated. 'Any better than the others?'

Of course he didn't know that it was all a charade. She knew exactly which car she would have; the red Z4 from over an hour ago.

'Not sure. I'll drive the Z4 again. What time do you close this afternoon?'

'I'm due to finish at five, but we can go out in it again if my boss will stay open for a bit longer.'

'I'm quite sure he will,' said Judith.

She knew these people; anything for a sale. Poor lad probably wanted to get home for his tea before going out on the town. Tough. He'd be on a good commission.

Monday 29ᵗʰ September 2008

Judith's day had not got off to a good start. There was an answer-phone message from a client complaining that she hadn't returned his call from the previous week. She picked up the phone to ring him, but put it back down with a sigh. She would open the mail first. Her secretary was away and it was easier to deal with things that didn't talk back. The first letter was from that same client saying that he was taking his business elsewhere. Oh well, he was one she could do without; always complaining and demanding attention. She would get Kate to sort out his files next week then that would be one less thing to worry about. The rest of the mail didn't bring much more cheer. There was a letter from HM Revenue and Customs demanding money. Cobblers and their children's shoes syndrome kicking in – an accountant who couldn't get her own tax return right. Well after buying her flat and furnishing it all in the last year, she didn't have any cash to pay it. And she had ordered a BMW Z4 the day before, which would need thirty-three grand. She spent the rest of the morning planning how to dispute the tax demand.

Judith realised that she was hungry and glanced at her

watch. Nearly two; no wonder she was feeling tired. She had her coat on and was about to leave when the phone rang. She debated answering it but decided not to. As she left, she heard Chloe's voice, the owner of Phoenix Antiques.

'Hello Judith. I'm ringing round the people who came to the opening last week. Just to say thanks for coming along, and feel free to pop in any time for a browse and a coffee – unless I'm run off my feet – ha ha. Seriously though, any time. Bye.'

Oh, thought Judith, *how nice. But not today. Need to keep the tax man at bay today. Tomorrow afternoon.*

By the time she had returned, there were two more messages. One was from a client chasing something which could wait until Kate got back, and the other was from Fiona. She wanted to go and see Mill View and meet the manager before agreeing to their mother going to live there. She had phoned this morning and they could all go this afternoon. If Judith was too busy, she and their mother and Rosie would go without her. Their appointment was at four.

God, she couldn't let them go there without her. Fi would probably change all the plans. She might even chicken out altogether and cancel the place that Judith had reserved on Saturday. She would have to go. She typed up her letter of appeal to HMRC, wrote some notes to Kate and had a general tidy up. She wasn't expecting any clients in that afternoon.

Mill View looked stunning in the late afternoon. The low orange sun sparkled through the last drops of rain left on the already-turning leaves and the old Georgian mansion looked washed clean and burnished in the light. Judith hoped that Fi and Rosie would be seduced by it. She had been there on dark rainy afternoons and, frankly, it looked gloomy in those conditions. Inside was warm and neat, once you got inside that is, past the security buzzers and double-locked doors.

Judith hoped that this was a quiet time for the residents; hopefully dosed up to the eyeballs by now to give the staff a break before yet another meal to fill the endless days. It was quite disconcerting when these mad old people appeared and demanded that you took them home, or sat with you making unintelligible conversation. She prayed that none of that would occur this afternoon. She had arrived before Fi and Rosie deliberately to head off any such problems. She was in the manager's office drinking coffee when the buzzer went again. The office was directly off the reception area and Mrs. Walters went out to let Fi in.

'I thought you were bringing Mum and Rosie?' Judith launched in without even saying hello then remembered Mrs. Walters. 'It would have been so nice for us all to look around together,' she continued in a softer tone. Fi looked tearful.

'Mum won't get out of the car. She says she doesn't like it here.'

'Let's you and I go and persuade her together,' said Mrs. Walters with a kind but firm and determined smile. She handed her a tissue and Fi was putty in her hands from there on in.

Later, back at Fiona's house over yet another cup of coffee, she enthused about Mrs. Walters, Mill View, the beautiful rooms looking out over the river and the staff. Judith sighed with relief and decided she could afford to be magnanimous.

'Life will be so much easier for you and Rosie now. It's the right decision. You'll see.'

'Yes. Thank you, Judith. I knew you would help sort it out if you knew how bad it had got. In a way, I'm glad that Mum escaped on Saturday morning and you found her.'

'Did you let her go deliberately? So that I would find her?'

'No, of course not! How could you say that?'

'Just a joke. Lighten up, Fi.'

'A joke! Your jokes are not at all funny, you know. Anyway who was the bloke that jumped out when we were in the dining room?'

'Henry Lloyd. He's a client. Actually, you must remember him. He was friendly with Mum and Dad way back. I was at school with his nephew Martin who fancied me.'

'Vaguely. He never came round here, though, did he?'

'Not that I remember. Anyway Tina Walters said he wanted to see me about something. It's always about nothing, actually, but I charge him every time I go out there. He's loaded, and I could do with the cash. We'll need to get this place sold as soon as Mum's settled at Mill View. I'll sort out power of attorney with the solicitor tomorrow.'

'Stop talking like that Ju, insinuating that I let her wander off so you'd see the seriousness of it and talking about her like she's already dead. Anyway this is mine and Rosie's home. I don't want to sell it.'

'You'll have to. We'll have to find fees for Mill View. I can't afford it. Can you?'

'You know I can't. And Rosie will be away to uni soon. That'll cost a fortune.'

'Exactly. We all need the cash and you won't need such a big place. We'll get it sold really soon before the recession kicks in any further. Anyway, I'm off. I need to get back to the office for an hour. I'll let you know what the solicitor says.'

CHAPTER 3

Carlisle, October 2009

Monday 5th October 2009

Well, after all my preaching to Maureen, I went down with flu (with complications) for two weeks. I bet that pissed her off just after recommending my permanent contract. Still, back now. Working here is more boring than being ill on my own and watching day time TV. It's good to be feeling better, though. I'll go down to Cafe Bar Sierra after work and have a latte. It'll do me good to have a walk.

It's easy walking into town because it's downhill all the way. There's no rush so I decide to take a different route to try to get to know the town a bit better. I find myself near Trinity School just off the main road. The No. 76 bus pulls up, and Joanna gets off. The driver waves to her as she darts across the road then she practically runs past me and up the steps into the school. I wonder whether her son or maybe an older child attends there. I stroll down after her and see the Adult Education board outside. An evening class, now there's an idea. I pick up a brochure from the display stand and flick through. Most have already started, but only just. I wander up the steps to enquire as to which courses are on now. The reception area is empty so I have a walk about. Room 101 appears to have some sort of first aid thing going on. I hope that's what it is anyway, with people adjusting other people's positions on the floor. The next room has about ten people all walking around shaking hands with each other. I check the timetable; Room 102 is Spanish. That makes sense after all, and as I look up again, I see Joanna shake hands with a middle-aged man and stumble over her words. Even though she is concentrating, she's laughing and the tutor comes over to offer help. Spanish; perfect! I go back along to reception and ring the bell several times to attract attention. A young woman is happy to take my details and my money and enrol me onto Spanish for Beginners. She suggests I wait for the coffee break to meet the tutor and then to make a start this evening. Sorted.

Joanna doesn't recognise me, of course. She must see loads of people in her cafe bar, and it was over two weeks ago that I was there. Not to worry. All in good time. I claim to know a little Spanish, I know quite a lot actually, but better not let on. I dutifully repeat the phrases we are taught about what we are called, where we come from and where we are planning to go for our holidays – Spain, of course – why else would we be there? It's alright; better than spending the whole evening alone as usual. I sit behind her and to one side so that I can watch her, see who she talks to in particular (no one) and how well she picks up the phrases (not particularly well). When nine o'clock comes round I leave with everyone else and walk back up towards the city. She walks that way too, but turns left. I don't follow. One step at a time. I need to take things slowly this time round. *Honestly, Judith! Don't rush into everything. You scare people!* Yes, Mother, coming through loud and clear.

Tuesday 6th October 2009

Oh joy unconfined! It's Maureen's day to do her team briefing to us all. Work stops while she enjoys the sound of her own squeaky voice for twenty minutes. I look at her throughout and concentrate hard. She will never catch me out. Boring though it is, I remember everything. Just as she is drawing all the exciting store news to a close she says, 'And don't forget I'm on holiday next week. I'm helping with the refurb of our village hall. I've still got some raffle tickets left if anyone hasn't bought any. We need all the funds we can get.'

I had forgotten. I must be slipping. I suppose with being off for two weeks I just hadn't given it any thought. Still, that's good. That sounds to me like an opportunity.

'Anita will take over as chief cashier while I'm off. Can anyone do any extra hours to help cover?'

Discussion ensues about childcare responsibilities and bus times. I don't take any part in the discussion until Maureen goes on her lunch break. Only then do I look up at Anita and smile.

'I'm happy to help out while Maureen's off,' I say quietly, 'just let me know what you need me to do.'

'Oh, thanks Judith. We know so little about your life outside Cost-Save, we didn't like to ask.'

'I'm fine next week. Anything you need.' And I smile again. Maureen won't believe it when Anita tells her about it later – not about offering to help but about me smiling, twice!

It seems that Maureen had received a telling-off over lunch for not conducting a return-to-work interview with me yesterday so we go somewhere private to go through the tedious and predictable process, the WARM process as she calls it. She formally **W**elcomes me back (that's the W) and tells me that I had been missed as I was now a valued member of the cash office team. She moves on to the A, the **A**bsence itself to make sure I had really been ill and not faking or being stressed. She reminds me that I have a contractual **R**esponsibility to be at work (like I don't know that) then we agree to **M**ove on with positive action. This is where she is supposed to tell me what I have missed and how I will catch up. It's irrelevant because all I've missed is counting money and getting it ready for banking. It didn't look to me as though that had fallen behind. I smile at the thought of the cash office bulging with notes because I hadn't been there for two weeks, and Securicor men queuing up outside.

'What's so funny?' she asks, clearly not confident in her own ability to conduct this interview. She thinks I am laughing at her.

'Nothing,' I say, and leave it at that but I maintain eye contact.

She looks back at me for a few seconds before looking away and, I think, deciding that I am not worth the effort. 'Let's get back to work then.'

'I haven't had my lunch yet.'

'Oh, you haven't, have you? Sorry Judith. We could have done this later.' I believe we could have done without it altogether, but say nothing. 'Go now.'

The staff canteen is almost empty. I get a sandwich and coffee and settle down to read *The Time Traveller's Wife* when Mr. Wilson (call me Ken) sits down with me. Oh well, it can't hurt.

I smile. 'Hello Ken.'

'Hello Judith. How are you now? I hear you weren't well.'

'No I wasn't but fine now. How are you?'

'Oh fine.' He hesitates, 'I was thinking…' but mercifully I am spared his thought as She-who-must-be-obeyed comes to whisk him away. Mary Morris is the General Store Manager, and is not to be trifled with.

I pretend to read but actually I am thinking about Ken. Not in that way, well yes, sort of in that way. He may be useful some time. I know Chief-Cashier-Maureen likes him. In fact she flirts with him outrageously at times. If nothing else, it'll annoy her if he and I get friendly. She can't do anything. She's married with two small kids, and I'm free as a bird. Sort of, anyway. Let's see how this one develops.

It's another nice evening. I take my usual route to town over the bridge. Actually, as far as I can see, it's the only route to

23

town. This time the man with the Jack Russell says hello to me. I say hello back and bend down to stroke the little dog. I hate dogs but I am full of goodwill towards the world just now.

'T'were an accident,' he said.

'What was?'

''is leg.'

And it was only then that I noticed that the dog had a leg missing. I pulled my hand back involuntarily. I can't believe I lost control like that, and immediately put my hand back on its head.

'Poor thing. Anyway, must get on.'

'Aye. 'night.'

I hurry on less full of goodwill than fifteen minutes earlier. I feel that I could do with something stronger than coffee but I can't afford the prices in the bars. I might stop at Bargain Booze on my way home and get a bottle of cheap plonk. I never thought I'd see the day. As I push open the door of Café Bar Sierra I hear a voice that sings out, '*Hola*, Judith. *Cómo estás es ta noche?*'

'*Hola*, Joanna. *Estoy bien, gracias. Cómo estás?*'

And after we exhaust our conversational Spanish, I order a latte and we chat in English until she has other customers to serve. Result!

Friday 9th October 2009

I am back at work after two days off. I tend to work at the weekends as the other staff have families they want to spend time with. God, wait until they grow up; they'll want to spend as little time as possible with them then. I prefer days off in the week anyway. The buses and trains are more frequent, which is a big consideration now that I haven't got a car. My trip to Newcastle by train on Wednesday was good. Anywhere is good that isn't here and isn't Hexham. I was tempted to get off when it stopped there but resisted. Too soon.

'How were your days off, Judith?' Anita is making an effort. It's Maureen's day off so I make an effort back.

'Fine, thanks. I went across to Newcastle to see some old friends. We had lunch and went to an art gallery.'

'An art gallery? Nice!'

Maybe I should have said that I had gone to the cinema, or something else more normal. But then I would have had to have known something about the film. No, better stick to something only just outside the sphere of knowledge.

'Do you like art, then?'

Be civil. 'Oh yes, my late husband was the one who was really interested and I suppose a bit of it just rubbed off. I'm not an expert or anything.'

'I know what you mean. You know what you like!'

Keep smiling – it's really not that difficult making stupid small talk. 'Ha, yes exactly. I know what I like. I can't afford to buy what I like, that's the problem.'

Anita suddenly looks serious. 'Did you say your late husband?'

'Yes.' I look away. I don't know where that idea came from but I will need to think it through for a while. I try to give the impression that I don't want to talk about that, and go back to counting cash. 'I'd better get on. Securicor will be here soon.'

Anita doesn't mention the dead husband thing again but I can tell that she is thinking about it. She is looking at me with big eyes and with a great deal of sympathy. She'll tell the others later and they will all start to be more understanding of my strange moods and behaviour. Yes, that was a stroke of genius. People always keep away from a bereaved person, but when they have to be near them, they are always very nice.

The evenings are drawing in already and soon the clocks will go back. Spring forward, fall back. It'll be dark when I walk into town then. I've left it a bit later tonight so that I don't see the man with the dog. It's just after six when I approach Cafe Bar Sierra, and I see Joanna leaving with a cheery '*Ciao*' to the staff and customers. She turns and hurries down English Street like she did the first time I saw her. I pick up speed and follow her round the corner, across the road and into The Crescent. I hang back. She speaks to a couple of people, obviously a regular here, as she waits for the No. 76 bus to pull round. She gets on, takes out a book, and settles down for the journey home. No. 76. I must look up where that goes to. I walk back to the café bar and order my usual latte. I'm feeling the after effects of the Bargain Booze cheap red from my days off so decide to drink up and go back home for an early night.

Saturday 10th October 2009

Maureen's last day before her holiday. I try to be as off-hand and difficult as I can without the others seeing. It's not that easy in such a confined space so I stop that game and concentrate on being perfect in my work. Ken is duty manager today and when he comes in to sign the banking he smiles at me.

'I never told you what it was I was thinking about the other day, Judith,' he says with what can only be described as a twinkle.

I smile back. No one misses a moment of this. 'And I haven't been able to sleep for wondering what it was.'

His pager buzzes and he is once again distracted. Maybe Mary Morris fancies him and wants him where she can see him, but more likely that she has found some out-of-date produce or some tins facing the wrong way on the shelves and is waiting to give him hell when he gets out of here. He quickly signs the banking and leaves, but before he goes he says to me, 'I'm still thinking the same thing.'

'I'm still wondering what it is,' I reply.

Maureen's eyes are boring into the back of my head. I don't turn round for a few moments, just to wind her up a bit more. At that moment the Securicor man buzzes from outside, it's time to do a change-run for the checkouts and do a till reading, and sadly there just isn't enough time for her to ask me about it. She will have to go off on a week's holiday thinking about me and Mr. (call me Ken) Wilson and what developments there might be before she gets back.

I don't walk into town on Saturday evenings. It's too sad even for me to be out on my own when everyone is at least fifteen years younger than me and being noisy and jolly in crowds. *Strictly Come Dancing* and *X-Factor* are enough to keep me occupied. I picked up a copy of the bus timetable. I think the No. 76 starts from somewhere around here in the area they call Stanwix. Then it stops at West Tower Street; I know where that is, close to the smelly underpass, and the next stop is The Crescent where I saw Joanna get on. Next is Grey Street, which I look up on my map and find off London Road, then on to Durranhill. I've never been out in that direction. It's quite close to the motorway so must be in the general direction of Tesco. If I had a car I'd go for a drive round when she was at work. It looks too far to walk so one day soon, I'll catch the very same bus! That was a satisfactory piece of research. I settle down to await the judges' comments and the audience vote. I don't know why I enjoy these programmes as I am not interested in music or dance. It must be the ritual humiliation.

Monday 12th October 2009
Life in the cash office is quite dull without Maureen to bait. It also has a good atmosphere. Everyone does what they have to, chats occasionally and it's altogether more relaxed. We take our breaks separately as there are fewer of us working more

hours than usual. That suits me better. I still haven't given enough thought as to how my husband died. Falling down the stairs is my preferred story – because he wouldn't eat the poisoned mushrooms – but I had better not joke about it. I think an unexpected heart attack is least controversial. I can say that he was a bit older than me. I had better tie it in with leaving Hexham as well. I needed a fresh start but it isn't as easy as I thought it was going to be. I need a lot of time to get used to it. As I ponder over the details, should any be needed, I see Ken approaching. Oh, no! I'm not ready for a date yet.

'Judith! What I was thinking the other day, you remember, was that as we're both on our own maybe we could go out for a drink one night, or a meal, or to the cinema. What do you think?'

I am tempted to say that he has no idea whether or not I am on my own, then remember that he has probably heard about my dead husband.

'I'm on an early finish today. How about tonight?'

'Sorry Ken. I would like to go out sometime but I'm busy on Monday evenings.'

He has to go back to work but says, 'Yes, let's do it,' and fairly skips through the door.

Monday night is Spanish night. Nothing will interfere with that. I make sure I am outside in plenty of time, and then hang around until I see Joanna walking along the road. She's dressed in black so I guess that she's come straight from work. I make out that I have just got there too and we walk into the building together and sit together. The teacher mixes us up for conversation practice but I have a base next to her. We practice what we learned last week and laugh at our pronunciation of the words. Senor Rossi comes along and gently corrects us, praising wildly when we get it right. At coffee break someone suggests going for a drink. I say I would love to but have to be at work early in the morning. She says she would love to but has to get home for the babysitter. She asks where I work and I ask how old her children are at the same time.

'*Usted puede pedir a los demás que en español,*' says Senor Rossi, so we laugh and try it again in Spanish.

So she has one four-year-old boy who has started going to school three half-days a week. Her mother usually babysits but she is out with friends tonight. I tell her that I work in the cash office at Cost-Save and leave it at that. The less she knows about me the better. This is a fresh start. What's gone is gone and we are where we are.

Wednesday 14ᵗʰ October 2009

I walk into town at lunch time and check that Joanna is at Cafe Bar Sierra. She is, so I walk on to The Crescent to await the No. 76. It arrives at 12.45 as promised in the timetable and ambles its way along London Road until its turning to the next stop. Twenty minutes later we arrive at Cumrew Close where we go round in a loop and head back for the town centre. A satisfactory trip and I decide to reward myself with Penne Carbonara for lunch. I know she will be busy but that's fine. Another piece of the jigsaw fits into place.

Friday 16ᵗʰ October 2009

This week is flying past. So much seems to be happening at the moment that I need to keep my eye on. My web of deceit is taking a lot of concentration. I must get all my stories straight so that I don't forget who knows what. Anita asked me today how long I had 'been on my own' and I went for nearly two years. That makes my prospective friendship with Ken acceptable. Maureen will be fed up because she can't have him and the others will say how nice it is after all this time that I have found someone I like to go out with. From Ken's point of view I can use it as an excuse for it still being too soon for a serious relationship, and when Joanna gets round to finding out she will understand why I don't like going back to Hexham; too many associations. Anita asks me if I have made friends in Carlisle and I say yes, I know quite a lot of people now. Well, I do know quite a lot of people; I just wouldn't call them friends. When Sal comes back from her lunch break, Anita and I are talking about *X-Factor* and how bad some of the hopefuls were. She joins in and we all share the laughing. Oh, if Maureen could see me now! I laugh a bit more, pretending I am still thinking about the fat girl whose dad makes her dresses.

I go for lunch dreading Ken coming in to press me for a date. I am really not ready for this yet but he is central to my plan for Maureen. He pops in to the canteen but it is to apologise to me. He is going away for a holiday with the lads. It seems they are keen golfers and it is a cheap time to go to Spain and they have the golf courses virtually to themselves. No kids running around, empty roads but enough bars and restaurants still open so they don't have to cook. Apart from the golf bit, I think it sounds rather good. I decide it's time that I give something to this conversation, well, and the relationship.

'Oh Spain, lovely. I go to Spanish conversation classes on Monday evenings. That's why I couldn't go out with you earlier in the week.'

'I had a few lessons last year,' he says, 'at Trinity School. But actually everyone speaks English where we go so I haven't used it. Can't remember most of it anyway.'

'That's where I go. I'm hoping to go to Spain next year sometime.'

I thought for a moment he was going to suggest we go

together but he said he would tell me all about it when he gets back. He asks for my email address to send some photos and I tell him I haven't got one. He looks surprised.

'I'll set you up with a hotmail account when I get back,' he offers.

Why is it that men think that if you haven't got something it's because you don't know how to get it? Of course I've got an email address; it's a computer and internet access that I haven't got. I'm not going down to the internet cafe to look at his drunken holiday snaps. I murmur something non-committal and hope he forgets.

Or maybe I'll win the lottery and be able to afford all that stuff again; a Blackberry phone, Sky Plus and a decent car – well, any car. He probably thinks I don't drive either and will offer to give me lessons. It's time to go back to the cash office and I decide to enjoy the last two days of peace without Maureen asking if I balance. She won't balance by the time I've finished, cash-wise or any-wise.

Tuesday 20th October 2009
Maureen is driving me nuts. I was going to wait a while before starting my plan but it's going to be today. It has to start somewhere. She keeps going on about her holiday, how they went on a city break to Rome that cost more than two weeks in Majorca. I thought she was painting the village hall all week. If I hear her tell someone about the Coliseum and the Trevi Fountain one more time, I'll explode. I'm not one for impulsive decisions but no harm in starting to sow the seeds of doubt. We have finished cashing up and have put our cash into trays ready for the banking. The buzzer goes at the window by the checkouts and Sal goes to answer it. The buzzer goes for the duty manager to sign the banking and Maureen answers that. While she waits the few seconds for

the outer door to close then releases the inner door, I whip a twenty pound note out of one of her bundles and drop it under her desk. The personnel manager, or HR as they call it now, sits down to weigh each bundle and to put her neat little initials on each one. Click, sign, click, sign, click, sign, click, sign, click, silence, click, click.

'Maureen, this bundle appears to be short.'

This never happens on Maureen's shift. She glares at us all.

'Whose signature is on the bundle?'

'Yours.'

'Mine? No way! I double-checked. I always do. Don't I?' she asks around generally. 'I'll re-count it by hand.' And as she moves back towards her desk she sees the twenty pound note on the floor. 'Thank goodness, there it is. How did that happen?'

'Indeed,' says the little personnel lady, 'how did that happen?' She fixes Maureen with a stare that says she is not amused.

I decide that the day has taken a turn for the better and that I will reward myself with a bottle of wine from Bargain Booze after my evening constitutional and latte.

Thursday 22nd October 2009

It's a beautiful day so I walk down over the bridge, but instead of going into town I turn right towards Bitts Park. I haven't really explored it before but I know from the local paper that things are always happening there. I think the next big thing is firework night. I'll be able to see the fireworks from my bijou half-house. Some people are playing tennis and others, much more seriously, bowls. As I understand it bowls is a vicious game. Maybe I'll take it up, ha ha. I set off to see what a Japanese Garden looks like in a town park but my attention is caught by two heads of red hair gleaming in the autumn sunshine. It's Joanna and son. Well, well, well.

'Come on, Mam. I want to feed the ducks.' Her little look-alike runs over and tugs her arm.

'What about our picnic? Aren't you hungry?'

'The ducks are hungry. Nobody feeds them in this park. Come on.'

She gives in, of course, young mums always do. I spot the picnic area and a kiosk selling snacks. Five minutes later I'm sitting at one of the wooden tables pretending to enjoy a gooey cheese savoury sandwich. I have my book as well, and pretend to read it while I await their return. I am fairly sure they'll come here. It really isn't warm enough to sit on the grass.

'*Hola* Judith! Look Ricky, it's my friend from Spanish class. Come and say hello.'

Ricky dutifully says hello then looks shy, then dives into their picnic basket, all inhibitions forgotten.

'Is it your day off today?' I ask.

'Yes, I usually have Thursdays off. You?'

'Yes, me too. I like days off in the week.'

'I do. But I'd like the weekends off with Ricky too. I have Sunday but I'm in the café from lunch time onwards on Saturdays. Luckily my mam doesn't work Saturdays at all.'

I venture a personal question. 'What about Ricky's dad? Does he see him?'

'No.'

Subject firmly closed so I move back to Spanish and what plans she has to go to Spain. I tell her that my friend Ken from work is flying out there at the weekend to play golf. She relaxes again as we leave Ricky's other parent behind.

'Come here, you,' she says as she grabs Ricky and wipes all manner of food from around his mouth. 'No table manners, that's your problem.'

'I have! It's not a proper table so I don't need them.'

'You always need them,' she says firmly and makes him ask properly before allowing him to go to the kiosk to buy an ice cream. Within minutes his mouth is covered again, this time with melting ice cream and chocolate. My God! Who'd have kids? It's only a matter of time before he gets tired and whiney and she decides it's time to take him home. I must say, I prefer our meetings without him. Well I don't actually say it of course.

As they wander off to catch the bus home she calls out that she will see me soon in the café and at Spanish. Oh yes, she will! A few words of Spanish float back to me as well, but I don't catch what she says and pretend that I am engrossed in my book. Better not appear too keen.

Thursday 2nd October 2008

It seemed to Judith that her phone never stopped ringing. She often wondered, and said on some occasions, that she didn't know what Kate did all day. *What do I a pay her for?* she sometimes thought, *she gets through so little in a day.* Maybe the phone was always like this and Kate shielded her from these callers who didn't stop talking then moaned when they got charged for the number of hours the practice had spent dealing with them. She looked forward to Monday when Kate would be back from holiday.

At midday the phone rang again. She answered it, resisting the urge to be short with the caller.

'Hello Judith. It's Chloe from Phoenix Antiques. Gosh, you've been busy this morning. I've tried ringing a few times.'

'The phone has never stopped since I got in,' she replied pleasantly. 'Still, all business is good business. How is yours going? I've been meaning to pop in but have had family stuff going on.'

'Not bad, thanks. Listen I've got hold of another seascape. You know you liked that one that I had on show at the opening? Well it's not the same, of course, but it is the same Seurat style. Would you like to come over at lunch time and have a look? I've got sandwiches and coffee if you'd like to join me.'

'Chloe, you are a life-saver. I really need an excuse to get out for a while. I'll be there in twenty minutes. One more phone call to make.'

There wasn't another phone call to make, of course, but Judith liked to play the game. Half an hour later she walked around the market place and down the hill a little way to Chloe's shop. Judith was seldom genuinely impressed by anything so it was easy to be enthusiastic.

'Chloe, it looks really good. I am so glad you didn't go for the cluttered old treasures look. There are a couple across the road from me that probably are full of treasures, but who could be bothered to rummage through and find them? No, this is really lovely.'

Chloe positively glowed. 'Thank you, Judith. Come through and have a sandwich then I'll show you the painting.' She led Judith through to the small, but again seemingly empty, office and offered delicate sandwiches on china plates and tea in china cups. Perfect, and all in keeping with the surroundings.

They chatted about their respective businesses for a while, then Chloe said, 'You said you had family stuff going on. Do you have children?'

'No I don't. I have an elderly mother who isn't well at all. My poor sister has been struggling to look after her for a while now. I do what I can, of course, but when you have a business to run there aren't enough hours in the day.'

'I know what you mean,' she agreed. 'I'm dreading when my dad gets to that stage, though he's pretty fit at the moment. I worry that he lives in Spain so I can't keep an eye on him.'

'My mum's physically fit, but she forgets where she is, who she is, who we all are.' She looked away and took a deep breath.

'Oh, Judith, I am so sorry. I didn't mean to upset you. I wouldn't have asked if I'd known.'

'It's OK. I'll have to learn to deal with it. We took the very difficult decision to put her into Mill View. I know the manager there so I know she'll be well cared for. We all went out there together on Monday; my niece as well. She's just seventeen so shouldn't have to be a carer at her age.'

'You sound like a really close family. That's so nice. Anyway Mill View is only down the road.'

'Yes we are, very close. It's such a comfort at times like this. It sort of helps to deal with the guilt.'

'Now you must not feel guilty. If you believe that Mill View is the best thing for your mum, that's the best you can do. It's lovely there, and you can go and visit any time you like. Now, shall we have a look at the seascape I bought at auction at the weekend?'

Judith spent a little while studying the picture. She quite liked it with its strange dappled effect with dots and shading but dreaded how much it would cost. She couldn't forget the tax demand, or the order for the new sports car.

'It's a little bigger than I really wanted,' she said eventually, 'although I do like it.'

'It's by Goquin,' said Chloe. 'He's French and not terribly well-known here yet. They love him in France and liken him to Seurat; what do you think? It's a really good investment at £750. It will probably be worth double that in ten years.'

Judith maintained the interested expression and thought about her next move. It was quite impossible to even consider buying it.

'It's about the right price range,' she ventured, 'but I'm just not sure it would look right in my sitting room.'

'Shall I bring it round so you can see it in place?'

God, this woman is persistent. 'That's a great idea, thanks. I really can't do it in the next week though, with having to deal with my mother. And you can't not offer it for sale. If you haven't sold it once Mum is settled, then yes, please do bring it round.'

'I am fairly sure it will sell quickly.' Chloe looked as though she were letting Judith down.

'Then you must sell it. You know what we said about

business earlier. And talking of business, I must get back to mine. Lunch on me next time.'

'OK, if you're sure?'

'Perfectly sure. I'll see you in a few days, and thanks again for lunch.'

Back at her office, Judith thought a good sort out was in order. She hated this untidiness. She pictured the seascape on the office wall. It would look really good in here against the pale jade paint. Then she snorted; £750! No chance. The phone rang again. It was the client from Monday who was taking his business elsewhere.

'Ms Dillon! I have been trying to contact you. As you don't usually answer your phone or return my calls, I wrote you a letter.'

'Yes I *have* received it.'

'Well, when are you going to send on my files?'

'It will be done when my secretary gets back next week. She's on holiday this week.'

'I think you could have called to tell me that. I feel as though I have to chase you for everything. And I think your last invoice to me was incorrect. I wonder whether you would check it. You've over-charged me.'

Judith sighed audibly. 'Certainly I will check it, but I doubt very much that it is incorrect,' she said with just enough of a hint of mimicry to make Mr. Sanders lose control.

'You should be struck off. Just send my books back as soon as possible. Please.'

Judith leaned her elbows on the desk and took the weight of her head in her hands. What was happening here? She had never felt work slipping away from her control before. Relationships, yes, almost always, but work was her one solid foundation, somewhere neat and ordered and constant. She thought about this date last month when Alison had told her that she was moving back to London, that Judith crowded her and she felt suffocated. Well, Judith felt suffocated now.

Saturday 4th October 208

'Fiona? Oh Rosie. You sound just like your mum these days. How are you?'

'Fine thanks, Auntie Ju. I'll get Mum.'

'Fiona. I thought I would come over this afternoon and we can pack up Mum's stuff, and decide what she'll take with her to Mill View.'

'Today's not very convenient. I need to take Rosie shopping for a winter coat.'

'I'll come and do it on my own then.'

'No, that's not a good plan. You don't know what she likes any more. You'll have to wait 'til I can do it with you. Come over tomorrow.'

'Her room's available from tomorrow. If we pack and sort out today, we can take her and her stuff to Mill View in the morning.'

'Stop it, Judith. Stop pressurising. This is her home. I don't want to push her out so quickly.'

Judith took a deep breath and grabbed the arm of her chair. 'Don't start again, Fi. We all decided. Mum even sort of agreed. There is no point at all in delaying things. I'll come over this evening then.'

'No, not this evening. Rosie and I watch *Strictly* and *X-Factor* together. It's our special time.'

'You watch that garbage? I don't believe you. It's rubbish.'

'I know it is but we like it. OK, come this afternoon. Rosie and I can go shopping another day.'

'And what do you mean, I don't know what Mum likes?

39

She doesn't know herself anymore. I'll be there after lunch. Don't make me any.'

Fi turned to her daughter who had a knowing look on her face.

'We'll go shopping next week. Ju's coming after lunch.'

'It's the best thing, Mum. I'll stay and help.'

'OK. I'll persuade Ju to come for lunch tomorrow to have a last meal, you know, all of us together.

There was no point in delaying what had to be done, and they knew that they could delay as long as they liked, but it wouldn't make the packing up any easier. They braced themselves for a long, fraught afternoon ahead.

Sunday 5th October 2008

Judith reluctantly arrived for the farewell family lunch and went straight through to the kitchen with the wine she had brought with her.

'Why are you here again?' demanded her mother when she saw her at the door to the sitting room. 'Do you live here now?'

'No, I don't, Mum,' *And neither do you after lunch.* 'I've come round so we can all have lunch together.'

'Why? You never come for lunch. Are you going to upset Fiona?'

'No, of course not.'

'You usually do. She cries when you go home.'

'Mum,' said Fiona, 'would you like some wine with lunch?'

'Wine? Why? We never have wine with lunch.'

'Today is special, Mum. That's why.'

'What's special about it? Just because she's here?'

'No, because…' and Fiona rushed to the kitchen to stem the tears before they poured out everywhere.

'Because, Mum, later on we're taking you back out to Mill View. Do you remember when we all went there last week?'

'Yes. I think so. Why are we going there again?'

'Because you are going to live there for a while. Remember? Mrs. Walters showed you that lovely room where you can look out of the window and watch the birds.'

'Live there? Fiona and Rosie as well? Are we all going to live there?'

'Shut up now, Ju!' Fiona was back and composed. 'Let's all enjoy lunch then talk about it later.' She fixed Judith with a stare that indicated it was not for debate. 'Will you come and help me serve up lunch?'

Judith followed Fi into the kitchen.

'It's no good pretending it's not going to happen, Fi. She has to know.'

'She won't know even if you tell her. She'll forget the conversation and we'll just have to do it all again. Trust me. I live with her, remember. Leave it now. Eat and make small talk and try to be nice.'

By the time they went back through to the dining room, Rosie had distracted her granny and it was as though the conversation had never taken place. At four o'clock she happily got into the back of Fiona's car with Rosie and they set off for Mill View.

Thursday 9th October 2008

Judith had told Fiona that she would tell her when she was going to see the solicitor about getting power of attorney for their mother, but actually she had no intention of doing so. She would have that power alone; that way she could push through the sale of their mother's house and sort out all their financial worries. It was rather bad timing with the talk of recession, but they could sell for below the market value for a quick sale. She would put enough money aside to pay the fees for Mill View for a good few years and share the rest with her sister. Fiona would soon come to see the wisdom of this plan. She always did in the end. Judith had intended to see Chloe again by now but she couldn't be bothered with the hard sell on the picture so she kept away.

'Judith, can I have a word please?' It was nearly time for Kate to finish for the day and she put down a pile of papers for Judith to sign, and which she would deal with next morning.

'No, sorry Kate. I've got an appointment with my mum's solicitor in a minute. I need to go out.'

'Are you coming back? There are messages there for you as well; people who need you to call them.'

'I don't know how you cope with that phone ringing all day. I struggled with it last week when you were off. I am so glad you're back. Yes, I'll be back later. It's just a preliminary meeting, to find out what's involved, you know?' As she spoke, Judith walked away from the pile of papers and messages and reached for her coat from behind her office door. 'Can it wait until the morning?'

'Yes, of course,' sighed Kate. She had been building up the courage to speak to Judith all afternoon and now she would have to wait for another day. *Oh well; typical Judith. She gets her way and you just have to wait.*

Friday 10th October 2008
Judith was busy signing the papers that Kate had left the afternoon before when Kate came in carrying another piece of paper.

'Is that something else for me?' she asked.

'Yes, sort of. You know I wanted to talk to you yesterday? Can I talk to you now?'

Judith sighed. 'Can it wait? There's loads of stuff here that I'll need to read before I sign. I'll give you a shout when I'm done.'

'No, Judith, now please!'

Judith looked up, pen poised in mid-air. Kate had never been assertive with her before, and Judith noticed that she seemed to be struggling to stop her hands trembling. She took a deep breath and opened her mouth but Judith got there first.

'You look terrified, Kate. Are you going to ask me for a pay rise? If you are, the answer is yes. I didn't realise how valuable you are to me these days until last week. Name your price!'

'No, it's not that.'

'Are you ill?'

'No, I'm leaving. This is my notice.' She put the carefully folded piece of paper onto the edge of Judith's desk, turned and walked back out of the office. As she reached her own desk, the phone rang, and with a 'smile-when-you-answer-the-phone' manner she lifted the receiver and said, 'Dillon Accountancy. How can I help you?'

Judith read and re-read the letter of resignation. Kate was leaving. How could she do this? They were a good team, weren't they? She wasn't bossy, let her work hours that suited her, and had just offered her a pay rise. Now Judith would have to find someone else and start again with training and hand-holding. She really enjoyed the freedom that working with Kate afforded her. She waited until she heard Kate finish her conversation, then she went through to reception.

'You don't give much of a reason for leaving,' she said.

'It's hard to put into a letter.'

'Perhaps you could explain then. Don't you like it here? The hours suit your children and I have just offered you a pay rise. We get on OK.'

'I know all that, but it's getting embarrassing.' Kate tried to look Judith in the eye but failed and stared at the phone on her desk instead.

'Embarrassing? What do you mean?'

'I've lived here, in Hexham, all my life. I know most of our clients and our suppliers. Everywhere I go people ask me why you haven't called them back, or why you haven't paid their bills. It's not fair that I have to make excuses outside of work as well as inside. It's part of my job to fend them off between nine-thirty and three-thirty but not at the school gate or in Marks and Spencer, or even in the pub. I've got another job. I went for an interview last week when I was off. It's not a job I want to do but I can't stay here as it is. Sorry Judith.'

So, that was it. Well, she could sod off then.

'Go now.'

'What? There's stuff to do, to finish off, to tidy up. I can't go now.'

'Yes you can. I'll pay you for the week. Just go!' And Judith turned and marched back into her office closing the door firmly behind her.

When she went through to make herself a coffee an hour later Kate had gone, leaving everything neat and tidy, and with a few notes designed to help Judith sort out the bits and pieces she had intended to do for her that day. Judith sat down at Kate's desk. *Oh my God*, she thought, *what have I done?*

Another hour later, Judith was on the phone to a temping agency arranging for someone to come in on Monday morning and to stay until she had recruited Kate's replacement. She considered contacting the job centre as it was a free advertisement, but decided the local paper was a better option. She had seen the types that the job centre sent. You couldn't trust them to make the coffee properly let alone speak to clients, or use initiative. She looked up the advert that Kate had replied to and arranged for it to be in the jobs page the following Wednesday. Half of Hexham would already know about the vacancy as Kate knew half of Hexham. That would be a double-edged sword. They would ask her why she had left so suddenly and no doubt Kate would tell them. At that moment, the temping agency called back. They said they would need to be paid before they would send anyone. Clearly someone there knew Kate and had done a bit of homework. Bugger! Bugger this town where everyone knew your business! Bugger, bugger, bugger!

Tuesday 14ᵗʰ October 2008

Judith had spent the weekend sorting out everything that Kate would probably have done in a couple of hours and so she was in reasonably good spirits when the phone rang. She had decided to try to manage without a temp for a couple of weeks. Ten o'clock and the only phone call so far was from Tina Walters saying that her mother seemed to have settled in at last and that they needn't worry about her any more. Judith hadn't worried at all but Fiona seemed to be on the edge. This time it was Fiona.

'Judith, I need to ask you a favour.'

'What is it now? I'm really busy at the moment with Kate having left. I can't do anything now.'

'No, not now Ju, later. Will you drive Rosie and her cello to her school concert, and stay and watch and then bring her home again?'

'Why aren't you going?'

'I want to. I might even come with you but the doctor's given me tablets for my anxiety and I'm not supposed to drive.'

'You were driving at the weekend.'

'I know. I don't take them all the time, but I really need to.'

'Can't she get the bus?'

'Of course not, not with a cello. Please don't be difficult. Please just say you'll do it. Please.'

'Oh God, Fiona, don't cry again. It's really irritating. OK I'll take her. What time?'

Judith continued opening the post. There wasn't too much but the next letter was from HMRC. It appeared they were not impressed with her appeal against the tax demand and gave her until the end of the month to pay before they prosecuted; and she had already incurred a fine. Bloody marvellous!

Her computer made a beeping noise to alert her to the fact that she had an email. Her new car had been delayed coming from Germany due to industrial action. It would be 31st October before it would be available. *One stay of execution, then*, she thought. Nothing to pay there for a couple of weeks. She couldn't afford the tax bill and the new car. The tax man wouldn't wait so she would have to buy the car on finance after all. Even finding the deposit would be difficult.

Tina Walters called again from Mill View and Judith's heart sank. She waited for the next bout of bad news about her mother's behaviour or wanderings but Tina just wanted to ask her to come out and see Henry Lloyd. She said he was becoming agitated about some money that he owed from some time ago. He would only speak to Judith about it. She agreed to go out to see him that afternoon. At least it would be a bit more income.

'Hello Henry,' said Judith and shook him warmly by the hand, 'shall we sit down in the lounge?'

'No! Too many people there. Private business, you know.' Unlike most of the residents at Mill View, Henry Lloyd stood upright and smart. He always reminded Judith of a major in the army with a clipped way of speaking, his head turning from side to side in considered sharp movements. Rosie would have described him as old school.

'OK, the dining room then. There was no one in there when I walked past.'

He hesitated as if making an important decision. 'I would prefer a private office.'

'We'll ask Tina.'

In the event, Judith was delighted that he had insisted on somewhere private because what he had to tell her was very interesting indeed.

'Miss Dillon, I owe money.'

'Yes, Tina told me you thought you did. Do you know who to?'

'To whom! To whom do I owe money? Is that what you mean? Don't let your standards slip, young lady! That's one of the reasons I employ you; you're not sloppy like some.'

'I'm so sorry, Henry, Mr. Lloyd. Of course, to whom do you owe money?'

He lowered his voice. 'Her Majesty's Revenue and Customs, I believe it's called nowadays. It's a crime not paying on time, you'll know that, and an expensive business if they catch you and investigate. I need to get it paid as soon as possible.'

'How much do you think you owe?'

'I know exactly how much,' he said and drew a cheque from his jacket pocket, '£28,052.' He had already made it payable to HMRC and signed it.

'I'll take your cheque and study your accounts when I get back to the office,' she said, 'just in case there is a mistake. I don't think you do owe them any money.'

'No mistake, Miss Dillon. I need your absolute word that you will pay it to them by first class post. In fact, promise me that you will post it this evening.'

'Very well. I'll write you a receipt now.'

'No!' He looked around warily, 'No receipt, no record.' He tapped the side of his nose. 'Hush hush, mum's the word and all that. Now off you go; and we never had this discussion.'

He opened the door of the small office and stood back to let Judith go first. She forced herself to go to see her mother who didn't appear to recognise her. That was OK. It was easier than her demanding to be taken back home. Then she called in to say goodbye to Tina.

'All sorted with Henry?'

'Yes, no problem, all sorted.'

'Will you be sending him an invoice?'

'No, he can have this one on me. It gave me a chance to have a little word with Mum.' And Judith practically danced to her car. A cheque made payable to HMRC, signed by someone with loads of money, and all she had to do was put her own tax reference number on the back. What a day this had turned out to be. Judith could not believe her luck. *There is a God in Heaven*, she thought as she looked out of the window at the clouds and offered a silent prayer of thanks. She tried to stay cool and collected. Mr. Lloyd valued professionalism above all things.

Judith's phone was flashing to indicate a message when she got in. She pressed the button and listened as she hung up her coat. It was Fiona again; really, that woman and her anxiety! It was to confirm that she needed to pick Rosie up at six-thirty and to tell her that the school wanted it to be a smart do, and could Judith make an effort? Judith, as it happened, was just in the mood to make an effort. She quickly showered and changed, then wrote her own tax reference on the back of Henry Lloyd's cheque and stamped and addressed an envelope. She had promised him that she would post it this evening, after all.

Rosie was ready and waiting when Judith arrived, and looked relieved that her aunt was in good spirits as well as being on time. Rosie was dressed in smart black trousers and a white sparkly top. She said that her mother had taken a tablet and was feeling sleepy so wouldn't be going with them.

'We all have to wear black and white,' she told her aunt on the way there, 'so we look like a proper orchestra.'

'What are you playing? Anything I'll have heard of?' asked Judith. 'No, actually, don't tell me. Let it be a surprise. I like surprises.'

'Do you? I thought you didn't.'

'Well, I don't usually, you're right, but I've had a good surprise this afternoon so I'm in the mood for them.' She pulled up next to a post box and hesitated before saying, 'Be a love and post that for me.'

Quite a few people had already arrived at the school hall and Rosie disappeared off to join the others in the orchestra. Judith took a glass of orange juice offered and picked up a programme. She saw Chloe standing by the entrance looking as though she was waiting for someone.

'Hello Chloe.'

'Judith! Lovely to see you. What brings you here? The music? Or do you know someone playing?'

'My niece is playing the cello. My sister was going to come as well but she's not feeling well so it's just me.'

'Sit with us, please. Don't be on your own. Louise's daughter plays the violin so we've come to support her. Here she is now.'

Louise came over with orange juice for Chloe and herself.

'Hello Judith,' she said. 'How's Fiona? I hear she's taken it badly, your mum going into Mill View.'

Judith was not surprised that people knew her business, but that didn't mean she was happy with it.

'Yes, she has taken it badly. She lived with her, you see, and I think all the years of stress have caught up with her. I volunteered to bring Rosie so she can have an early night.'

'Oh, really?'

Judith looked at Louise, expecting her to say more but somebody rang a bell to signal that it was time for the audience to take their seats so she let it go. She supposed that Chloe would have told her about their conversation. No need for bad feeling tonight. At the interval Louise went to talk to some of the other parents and Chloe apologised to Judith at least three times for the fact that she had sold the picture that she had shown her two weeks ago.

'Please don't worry,' she soothed, 'it's my own fault for not getting back to you but with everything going on, I'm afraid it's been the last thing on my mind.'

'I quite understand that. You are lucky to be part of a close family, though.'

'I know. Is business good?'

'Yes, I think it was the right thing opening here. Some people thought Hexham wouldn't sustain a shop like mine.'

'We're all delighted to have somewhere local to buy quality,' said Judith. 'As I said to you before, we have enough junk shops in the town.' She remembered to laugh as she said it to soften the sentiment. She meant it though.

The second half was shorter than the first, and it flew past. As Judith drove an exuberant Rosie home she reflected that the day had gone rather well.

The conversation in Chloe's car was somewhat different.

'Why did you have to invite her to sit with us?' asked Louise.

'Why not, she's nice.'

'She's a customer – that's all.'

50

'Meaning I can't talk to her?'

'She's not even a customer, actually. She hasn't bought anything yet.'

'Mum, don't spoil my night,' said a voice from the back seat. 'Don't talk about Rosie's aunt. Talk about the concert.'

'What's wrong with Rosie's aunt, Tash?'

'She's a bit strange. That's all.'

'I quite like her; well I don't dislike her.'

'Anyway, Mum, did you hear my solo? Chloe, did you? I didn't mess up one note!'

'I know, darling, you were brilliant. I loved it. I loved it all, and especially your solo.'

'Me too, Tash. You're amazing. I don't know where you get that talent. Your mum and dad haven't got any.'

'Cheeky! We have, just not musical talent, just not any talent that is obvious to anyone.' They laughed.

'Your mum has got talent, really, Tash. She could sell ice to Eskimos.'

'True, and coal to Newcastle,' said Louise.

'Sand to Silloth?' asked Tash.

'Oh yes, all that and much, much more. She's my best friend and my best employee.'

'I'm your only friend and only employee!'

'I've had a brilliant day,' said Tash as Chloe pulled up in front of their house. 'Thanks for coming to watch, Chloe.' She bent down to give her a kiss goodnight through the car window and went up to the house.

'Yes, thanks for coming, Chloe,' and Louise gave her friend a hug before getting out. 'It's all going rather well.'

Monday 20th October 2008

Judith was bored. Annoying though her sister was, she was more annoying when she took the tablets and slept all the time. Rosie had swapped caring for her granny for caring for her mother but she seemed OK with that. The BMW garage said that her car would be available to pick up on the first of November and she had been in to arrange the finance on the smallest deposit she could get away with. A few people had applied for Kate's job but the closing date wasn't until Friday so there wasn't much to be done yet. HMRC had confirmed receipt of the cheque and had also confirmed that she had over-paid by £6000. She had decided to leave that there to be deducted from her next demand. She felt a pang of guilt at what was effectively stealing from an old acquaintance of her parents, but it was done now. He had insisted and she needed the money more than him. Even the phone wasn't ringing as often as before. Judith was actually up-to-date with everything; well everything except the filing. She thought she might set that as a sort of assessment task for prospective employees and get it done that way. It was nearly lunch time. She picked up the phone and called Chloe in Phoenix Antiques.

'Hello Chloe. Judith here. I believe I owe you lunch.'

'Oh, that's OK, Judith. No problem.'

'I'll pick up some sandwiches and bring them round, shall I? Then I can have a look at any new pictures you've got in.

'Fine. I'll see you soon.'

Carlisle, November 2009

Monday 2nd November 2009

Last week was a long week. Half-term is tedious on so many levels. There was no Spanish class, for a start, and I must say that I missed it; not only Joanna but generally having some structure to what can nowhere near be described as a social life. I did miss Joanna as well. Ricky had half-term from his part-days at school so she had time off work and went away to Scotland for a few days with her mother. That meant that Cafe Bar Sierra was dull as well. The cash office was a madhouse as parents with kids in the store all week means loads of change to count. I haven't even had Ken for entertainment as he has been away. I wonder where he went in Spain that wasn't full of English kids on holiday from school. Surely lots of families go away then for a last blast of sunshine before winter sets in. Actually, considering the state of this store and of the town, most of them seem to be here.

The unlovely Maureen breaks into my thoughts as she leans over, probably to repeat what she has just said. Her bleach-blonde hair doesn't move with her head; it must be plastered with hairspray.

'Do you want to go for your lunch early or late today, Judith?'

'I don't mind. Whatever suits you,' I reply mildly. This gives the impression that I'm being helpful but actually I know it winds her up if people can't make simple decisions. She is a control freak but when she gives someone a choice, she expects them to decide. She frowns and turns towards me sharply then appears to change her mind. Maybe she is thinking about my fictitious dead husband.

'I'll go first then. You go at one o'clock.'

'Fine.' I don't look up but continue to concentrate on counting money and bagging and bundling it as appropriate. Since the incident with the twenty pound note she is doubly careful with her work and spends less time watching me.

The buzzer goes indicating that someone from the checkout area wants attention. Maureen gets up to answer it. It is Ken.

'Hi Maureen. Good holiday?'

'Yes thanks. Got a bit of a tan.' She flashes a brown arm at him. 'You?'

'Yes, really good. Is Judith there?' I could see him moving to one side to try to see past Maureen's head and shoulders. 'Oh, yeah, there she is,' and he stood and waited so that Maureen was forced to turn and tell me that Ken wanted a word.

'What time are you going for lunch?' he asked.

'One. You?'

'Yeah, I am now. See you in the canteen.' With that he disappeared and I quietly closed the shutter to once again shut Maureen and me off from the rest of the store.

'Are you and Ken seeing each other?' she asked.

'How do you mean?'

'You know, going out together?'

'No.' She doesn't get much out of me.

Sal buzzes to be let in to start her shift at midday and Maureen goes to do her shopping in her lunch hour.

Spanish class tonight is as good as ever. Joanna looks relaxed after her little holiday in the fresh Scottish air and comes and seeks me out to sit next to. Senor Rossi insists that all our casual conversations are in Spanish which means that they are limited but at least we are familiar with holiday stuff. Joanna asks when I am coming into the cafe again and I say tomorrow. That much we can manage in Spanish as well. The other people are nice too, but not interesting.

Wednesday 4th November 2009
I haven't been able to put Ken off any longer and have agreed to go with him to the pictures. I'm not a great fan of the cinema but at least I won't have to make conversation for two hours while we watch, and then we can talk about the film afterwards. I remember now why people go on first dates to the pictures. We spend a pleasant half-hour deciding what to see. I think he would have preferred *The Damned United*. My choice would have been *Amelia*. In the end we go for Michael Jackson's *This Is It*; it's topical and it will give me conversation in the cash office. I won't discuss it with Maureen, of course, but the others will have the benefit of the hot news that Ken and I have been to the pictures together. The film is alright actually. It gets on my nerves when people say about Michael Jackson, 'You either love him or hate him.' I don't; I can take him or leave him. We go to Cafe Bar Sierra afterwards for a nightcap just before it closes for the evening. Joanna is not on duty but the spotty youth with long hair tied back is there and sort of greets me like a regular customer. It feels good to be recognised; and to be going in there with a man. Hopefully that will give them something to talk about as well. I wouldn't want them to think I am some kind of weird loner. God no! Perish the thought.

Thursday 5th November 2009
I make myself a sandwich and walk down to Bitts Park. I wander around for a while then make my way to the picnic tables, surreptitiously looking around for Joanna and her mini-me. There is no sign. Eventually I eat my sandwiches and read my

book and start to feel a bit chilly. At least the sandwiches are better than the crap I bought from the kiosk last time. I walk towards the shopping centre, past men making preparations for fireworks tomorrow night. It's starting to get wintery and I decide to invest in a pair of boots. I haven't bought anything for myself since being here.

Debenhams is closest and on my way home so I look there first to get a benchmark of what there is, and then stop off at every shoe shop in The Lanes making comparisons as I go. I am admiring myself in a pair of black leather boots when I see a little redhead boy peering at me in the mirror. He is sprawled on the floor making a strange waving motion with both hands. God! Children are strange creatures.

'Hello Ricky,' I say to his reflection, 'is that you in that mirror?'

He giggles and nods then comes over to inspect my boots properly.

'Are you going to buy them?' he asks.

I see Joanna and decide that the way to befriend a woman is through her darling child.

'Not sure yet,' I say, 'what do you think? Do you like them?'

'Yes,' he says.

'Well they would look funny on you,' I say and he giggles again. He knows I'm teasing. 'I wonder what your mum would think. Is she here? Or are you on your own?'

This amuses him even more, and she comes over.

'What are you two giggling about?'

'Judith thinks I want to buy her boots and she thinks I go shopping on my own without you.'

By now we are all laughing, them at the joke, and me at how easy it is to fool kids. I thought they were supposed to be able to see through any insincerity. Anyway, job done.

'They look good, Judith. I think you should buy them for yourself. Ricky and I have already chosen his. Look.' Along with sensible and sturdy winter school shoes there is a pair of Bob the Builder wellingtons. I look dutifully impressed. They wait while I pay for mine and we go for a coffee before making our respective ways home.

Friday 6th November 2009
It is Maureen's day off, which means I get three consecutive days without her this week, and this puts me in a better mood than usual. I use the time to build up Strand 2 of my 'Annoy-Maureen' campaign. Strand 2 is my relationship with Ken.

'Did you have a good couple of days off, Judith?' asks Anita in the first lull of our work.

'Oh yes, very good thanks,' I reply. For once, this is a true answer to the question.

'Did you go over to Newcastle again?' she asks this a little tentatively, as though not wanting to pry but wanting to appear interested.

'No, I stayed in Carlisle,' I reply, then continue, 'I went to the pictures one day and shopping with a friend on the other day. It was really good.'

'Lovely,' she says then hesitates a long time before asking, 'Did you go to the pictures with Ken? Someone said they saw you out with him on Wednesday night.'

That was brave of her, I think. In fact, that was brave enough to deserve a full answer even though it irritates me that even I can't do anything in Carlisle without people knowing my business. I think I would rather know that people know than not know that they know, though.

'Yes, we went to see the Michael Jackson film, *This Is It*?'

'We were thinking of going tonight. Is it good?'

'Oh yes!' and I enthuse about it for a minute or two. This

will really wind Maureen up when Anita tells her about it. I never speak to her in that way; that being Strand 1 of my 'Annoy-Maureen' campaign, telling the others things but not her, not ever.

'We'll definitely go then. I'll tell Jack it's on your recommendation.'

'You'll love it.' I hear my mother's voice again. *See? You can do pleasant small talk if you try.* But how do I know whether or not she'll like it? I've never met her husband so can have no idea at all as to whether he will. But I am learning to say what is expected of me when it is expected. God! It's hardly worth speaking at all sometimes, the rubbish people come out with.

Monday 9th November 2009

Today is dragging. I need to do something to liven it up a bit. I think I will move Strand 3 of my 'Annoy-Maureen' campaign on a bit if I get the opportunity. Strand 3 involves wiping the smug expression off her face regarding her work. The incident of the accidently-dropped twenty pound note has been forgotten so it is time that the powers that be are reminded that she is not quite as perfect as she seems. This needs to be a bit cleverer. We keep a roll of Sellotape in the cash office to stick together any notes that have been torn. They need to be identified in the bundles because they make them weigh too heavy on the scales. My plan is very simple but will need Maureen to be looking the other way. I have practiced slipping the paper bands on and off the bundles of notes. I can do it really quickly now so it should be OK. First I take one of the tattier ten pound notes that I am counting and tear it in half.

'Maureen,' I say, 'I've got a torn note here. Can I have the Sellotape please?' She is the keeper of the Sellotape. She throws it over to me.

'Give it me back as soon as you're done with it.'

'Will do,' I say pleasantly, and spend a long time perfectly mending the torn note. This meets with her approval as she likes things done properly. I also stick a piece onto a perfectly good note and include it in a bundle of notes which is one short of £500. The note with the unnecessary Sellotape will cause the bundle to weigh correctly when the duty manager comes in to check the banking. I sign the paper band to say that I have counted it and make another mark so that I can identify it later, and then hand the Sellotape back to be stored safely in her drawer.

'Make sure that torn note is on top,' she reminds me, 'so that Mary Morris can see it when she checks the banking. She's duty manager today.'

I look up slowly. 'I've already done that.'

'Yes of course. Sorry Judith. You've picked it up so quickly since you've been here. Are you sure you've never worked in a cash office before?'

'Quite sure.' Does she really think I wouldn't have remembered? 'I have worked with money though.' I stop there. Never forget Strand 1: don't tell her things. I might think of something to tell Anita next time we are together, like that I used to be treasurer of a society my dead husband belonged to. Yes, that sounds good. I'll give it a bit more thought.

'Any preference for which lunch break you want?' she asks when she realises I am not going to say any more.

I gauge how far we have got with the work and decide that we are far enough ahead for me to prepare the banking early.

'Late, if you don't mind,' I say.

She looks surprised that I have answered properly, but then she is so predictable.

'OK. We've got on really well this morning. Will you start to prepare the banking while I'm out?' See what I mean? The plan just simply falls into place.

'Yes, of course. No problem.'

We work in silence until Sal comes in at midday as usual and Maureen leaves for lunch. Sal goes about her normal routine of preparing the cash trolley to do what we call a note-lift. That means that one of us will accompany the duty manager and checkout supervisor along the bank of checkouts taking the notes, gift vouchers, coupons and card receipts to do an interim count. The money that we count in the morning is the final take from the day before that we balance against till readings. I start to collate the notes for banking and the other forms of tender to do a check of the cash office float. While Sal has her head in the cash trolley, making sure the little boxes are in till order, I slip off the paper band on my bundle that is ten pounds short and swap it with one of Maureen's. I continue to do the preparation necessary and start to count the change in the safe.

At precisely one o'clock Maureen returns and sends me for lunch. When I return at two o'clock there are three worried faces: Maureen, Sal and Mary Morris.

'Is something wrong?' I ask innocently.

'The cash office float is ten pounds over,' says Maureen. 'I've counted it twice. Will you do it, Judith?'

'What is the point of that, Maureen?' snaps Mary Morris, the general store manager. That is a stroke of luck that she is duty manager today. 'You've already counted it twice. We'll need to check every bundle of notes, and quickly before Securicor gets here.'

'I'll do that,' says Maureen, 'but Judith can check the float again, just to be sure.'

'I'll help you count the notes,' says Mary Morris, and as luck would have it, she picks Maureen's tray to count. It is just a matter of time now. I painstakingly take out all the bags of coins and count them back in, just to string it all out until

Mary Morris says, 'Maureen, this bundle is ten pounds short. And one of the notes has Sellotape on it.'

'Well, that explains the store float being over,' she says with relief, 'but who signed the band around that bundle?'

Mary Morris handed it to her. 'You, if I am not very much mistaken.'

My day is made. Even if it wasn't Spanish tonight, today would be the best day of the week.

Spanish class is quite hilarious. We learn to talk about hobbies so I mention my interest in art, just to continue a theme, and say I enjoy going to the cinema. Joanna says she enjoys keeping fit, cooking and going to the cinema. Something else in common; I'll store that one away for another day. I say that I have been to see *This Is It* and someone else says they have been to see *Men Who Stare at Goats*. Nobody knows the words for 'stare' or 'goats' so it turns into a bit of a charades game. I think it is the first time I have genuinely laughed out loud for months. When Ken asks the inevitable question tomorrow I will tell him that's what I want to go and see this week.

Thursday 12th November 2009

It really is getting a bit too cold to be hanging around in a park but I do it anyway just in case she is there with Ricky. I decide against taking a sandwich, and plan to suggest going to a cafe for lunch if I do see them. I wear my new boots so at least my feet will be warm. After a brisk walk around the bowling green and tennis court I spot two heads of red hair by the kiosk and turn to walk in that direction. Ricky sees me; really, children are so observant.

He shouts, 'Granny, Granny, look.'

At first I think he's calling me 'Granny'. Bloody cheek, I'm only about ten years older than his mother, then I realise that he is talking to a woman who is quite obviously his granny. The family likeness is so striking down the generations. She looks worried as Ricky runs off towards me and she tries to catch him up but he is too quick. As he reaches me, he stops, suddenly shy. I realise I have to act quickly.

'Hello Ricky,' I say casually, 'are you having a race with that girl?'

'What girl?' he asks.

'The one with the same colour hair as you. Is she your sister or something?'

That does the trick. He bursts into fits of giggles and catches his granny's hand as she draws level with us.

'Granny, Judith thinks you're my sister!' and he can't say anything else for laughing.

It breaks the ice with Joanna's mum and me. She introduces herself as Gaynor, and says she is Joanna's mum in case I didn't realise. I say that I do realise and Ricky takes one hand of each of us and drags us down to the fairly insignificant duck pond.

'We should go to the other park, Ricky,' says Gaynor, 'there are swans there and lots more ducks.'

'I know, Granny, but everyone feeds *them*. Nobody likes these ducks so they'll be hungry if we don't come and feed them.'

Bless!

I ask Gaynor which park she means and she tells me about Hammond's Pond at Upperby, off Blackwell Road. I have no idea where she means, but I show interest and chat for a while until it gets too cold for all of us.

As we part I ask whether Joanna is working today and she says no, and that she has gone down with the cold that's going round.

'I had it a few weeks ago,' I say. 'It knocked me out for a fortnight.'

She makes a face and says she hopes Joanna won't be ill for that long as she has to work on Friday evening and all day Saturday. I say that I have to work on Saturday too but if it would help I could sit with Ricky on Friday evening. She hesitates, not wanting to appear to mistrust me but clearly not able to let Ricky go to a stranger.

'That's really kind of you, Judith. I know Joanna likes you a lot; she's told me about Spanish class. But I couldn't ask you to…'

'To what, Gaynor? I'm not suggesting I take Ricky anywhere but if it would help I could come to Joanna's house and sit with him until his bedtime; just so that she wouldn't have to run around after him or entertain him.'

'Would you really? I'd prepare his tea and get him into his pyjamas early. It would really be just babysitting from about five-thirty until nine-thirty, and he will go to bed at seven.'

'It's no problem, honestly. I'm not doing anything tomorrow night. I'm on the early shift at work so will be finished by three. Just tell me where to be and I'll be there for five-thirty.'

'Oh thank you, Judith. I'll prepare you some dinner as well.'

Well, well, well, there's a turn up for the books. The thought of babysitting fills me with dread but we can read books or something, or whatever one does with four-year-olds in the evening.

Friday 13th November 2009

I make sure that work is uneventful today so that I can get away on time. Maureen disappeared for about an hour during the morning and we think Mary Morris was having a chat with her about the two mistakes with money in the last month. Her eyes look bloodshot when she comes back in so

I tactfully don't look at her. That's not difficult of course. There are no problems with banking or cash reconciliation today and there won't be for a few more weeks then her carelessness may take a more sinister turn. I haven't quite decided what to do yet so I concentrate on being the perfect cashier.

I get the No. 76 bus from the car park at Stanwix all the way to Cumrew Close. I follow Gaynor's directions and turn down the narrow lane past a small play area into the next close. Joanna lives at No. 8, a fairly small terraced house with a crazy paving path leading to a new white UPVC door. As I approach the front door Gaynor opens it and ushers me in. Ricky runs up to say hello then runs up the stairs to tell his mum (or 'mam' as he calls her) that I have arrived. We were never allowed to call our mother 'mam'.

'Come back here, Ricky,' Gaynor calls after him, 'leave your mam to sleep.'

He peeps in on her to confirm that she is actually sleeping then bumps back down the stairs on his backside.

'He's had his tea,' she tells me, 'but he can have some pudding and a drink of milk between now and seven. That's all though; Joanna is very strict about that.'

'Fine with me,' I agree pleasantly. Then to Ricky I say, 'What books do you like to read Ricky? If you haven't got any I can read you some of my book. I brought it with me.' This sets him off giggling as usual. Really, it's like feeding candy to a baby as the saying goes.

Gaynor is wearing her M&S uniform and seems happy that Ricky and I are getting along well. She gets ready to catch the next bus into town.

'I'll be back shortly after nine-thirty. I get a lift back so I don't need to wait for the bus.'

'OK,' I say, 'we'll be fine. I used to babysit for my niece when she was small. Please don't worry.'

As the evening goes on, Ricky plays me up a bit asking for sweets and more drinks but I stick to the rules. I wouldn't like to be caught out on a technicality. There are plenty more mistakes that I am likely to make, but not following instructions isn't one of them. We read books and play with his wooden train set then at seven I watch him clean his teeth, rather badly, then watch him sneak in to give Joanna a soft kiss goodnight so as not to wake her up. She is awake though, and gives him a weak hug.

'Judith,' she croaks, 'thank you so much for this.'

'No problem,' I reply quietly, 'but can I get you anything?'

'No, I'm OK. I'll go straight back to sleep now I know Ricky's in bed.' Her head sinks into her pillow.

'I'm going to eat the meal your mum left me then read my book. She'll be back in no time. See you Monday night.'

She nods and I shut the door quietly behind me.

'Judith,' whines a little voice, 'please may I have a drink of water?'

'No, Ricky, time to go to sleep.'

'But I need one.'

'If you still need one when Granny gets back you can ask her,' I say firmly to imply that is the end of the conversation and go downstairs.

Gaynor has paid for a taxi to take me home and it arrives at the same time as her so we have little time for small talk. I assure her that everything is fine, she thanks me again, and I thank her for the taxi.

Monday 16th November 2009
Joanna doesn't turn up at Spanish. I explain to Senor Rossi and he teaches us some Spanish words for common ailments. It is not as amusing as last week.

It's a busy day in the cash office. They reckon that people are starting to stock up for Christmas already. We have had Christmas goods in for a few weeks so I suppose it must be true. I think about Christmas; mother in the nursing home now, sister not speaking to me, niece embarrassed by me. It's going to be great. I was in two minds when Maureen discussed the Christmas rota. On the one hand, I feel like flying away somewhere hot like I did last year but on the other hand the other staff will want time off with their children and I can command favours later as payback. I can earn some extra money doing overtime too, and am less likely to spend it if I'm cooped up in here all day and every day.

'Are you listening, Judith?'

I realise that Maureen is looking at me and has probably just asked me whether I have finished balancing my cash, or asked what time I want to go for lunch, or one more of her daily questions.

'Yes,' I say vaguely, 'all done.'

'What?'

'Yes, I've balanced. Isn't that what you said?'

'No, it isn't! You weren't listening to a word.'

'I didn't hear you. Say again.'

'Didn't hear me? There's only us here.'

'I was miles away. Anyway, I'm listening now.' I turn and make deliberate eye contact, and hold it for longer than is necessary or polite. She looks flustered, as though she has to brace herself to start it all again.

'I see you've been to the pictures with Ken three times this month.'

I continue to stare at her but I am rather impressed; she has taken me completely by surprise.

'Pardon?' I say just to buy a few more seconds of thinking time.

'You heard. What's going on?'

'Yes, I heard, but I meant 'I beg your pardon' as in 'what has it got to do with you'?'

'It is to do with me, Judith, because it is frowned upon.'

'What is?'

'Going out with management.'

Wow, that's twice in the space of five minutes that she has taken me by surprise. I really am slipping.

'Frowned upon?' I sound incredulous. 'It's not the Middle Ages, Maureen, or the Industrial Revolution. In fact, it's the twenty-first century. Who frowns on it? You?'

'No, management frowns on it.'

'Oh, management frowns on management fraternising with the mere mortals. That makes sense.' I reach for the policies manual that gathers dust on the shelf above Maureen's desk. 'Has Ken asked you to speak to me about it?'

'No, of course not.'

'Oh, has Mary Morris asked you to speak to me about it?'

'No, she hasn't. Stop this, Judith, you know exactly what I'm saying.'

'Yes, I rather think I do know what you're saying, actually!' I start flicking through the pages of the weighty file.

'What are you doing?'

'I'm looking for where it says that in the policies manual. In fact, perhaps you would find it for me? I really wouldn't know which section to look in.'

'Of course it's not in the policies manual. Really Judith, I think you try to be difficult sometimes.'

Sometimes? 'Do you really think that, Maureen?' I turn on the eye contact treatment again but this time with a softer tone to my voice.

'No, of course not. Sorry. I shouldn't have said that, and I know you've had a difficult time over the last year or two.'

God, Witch-woman, you don't know the half of it! I look away to indicate that I may be feeling a little upset and luckily the buzzer goes and we see Sal on our CCTV monitor waiting to be let in.

Monday 23rd November 2009
Joanna returns to the fold that is the Spanish class tonight with a box of chocolates for me. It's a thank you present for babysitting and is a nice thought. She isn't to know that I don't much care for chocolates, but it gives me an excuse to appear nice so I share them with the whole group

'You must come for dinner one night, Judith, so that you can be a proper guest in my house instead of the babysitter.'

'Thank you, Joanna. I'd like that,' I say as we walk away from Trinity School to our respective homes.

'We'll arrange it really soon. Oh no, look at the time! I'll have to run or I'll miss the bus. Bye.' And with that, she literally runs all the way up the road towards the bust stop. *God, the energy,* I think as I turn towards the underpass and start the long ascent up the hill, over the bridge and into the estate that I call home.

Wednesday 25th November 2009
Ken and I go to see *Lesbian Vampire Killers*, which he tells me is supposed to be hilarious. I think it's pathetic but don't say so. I didn't really want to go out at all tonight as he is getting a bit too friendly, wanting to hold my hand and put his arm round me in the cinema. I thought he was going to try to kiss me last week but he didn't, thank God. The trouble is I need to keep this going for a while if I am going to irritate Maureen for a bit longer. I really need her to dislike me a bit more and put the other staff in a difficult position regarding loyalties. *That's the trouble with you, Judith, you don't know when to stop with your stupid*

pranks! My mother's voice again, but I'm on a roll and I can't stop quite yet. I don't mean any real harm; I really don't. Anita and Sal quite like me now and have told Maureen that they don't know what her problem is with me. Ken told me that. He overheard them in the canteen. Careless talk, Maureen, is something you will never accuse me of. I pretended to be a bit upset at that and say I don't know why she doesn't like me. I don't tell him about her little chat with me. If he finds out I can pretend I was too embarrassed by it to tell him.

Hexham, November 2008

Monday 3rd November 2008

Judith knew that she should have spent the weekend preparing to interview for Kate's replacement but she couldn't regret having spent the time driving around in her shiny new red sports car. She had driven across to Newcastle and then up to the Northumberland coast. It wasn't warm enough to have the top down, but still exhilarating. Now normal life kicked in as she re-read the CVs of the three people she had decided to interview. The interviews weren't until the next morning but she needed to have a good tidy up so they knew the standard expected and then she pursued the idea of having an in-tray sort of exercise for them to do with the mountain of filing that grew bigger every day. She left the telephone on voicemail so that she wouldn't need to answer it. As she unlocked the door at nine o'clock the postman came in with the usual bundle of mail.

'Morning. Someone waiting to see you,' and he stood aside to let in what could only be described as a little old lady. She looked vaguely familiar, and Judith racked her brain to remember who it was.

'Good morning, Mrs…' she started, hoping that the woman would identify herself. Instead she looked around then sat down in the chair used by clients waiting to see Judith. 'What can I do for you?'

'I am waiting for an answer, Miss Dillon,' she replied.

'I'm sorry, but what is your question, Mrs…'

'Henson. Audrey Henson. I wrote to you asking about the progress with my accounts but I haven't had a reply.'

'Audrey Henson.' Judith sat down at Kate's desk and tapped the name into the computer database; sure enough there was an Audrey Henson. The last entry that Kate had made was at the beginning of September to say that she had collated the papers and passed them to her. Why couldn't she remember?

'I'm sorry,' she said, 'but my administrator left three weeks ago and things are a little behind.'

'I brought my books in well over a month ago,' she said as she consulted her diary, 'on the 25th of August. Are you saying that you haven't looked at them at all?'

'What is your line of business, Mrs. Henson?' Judith asked thinking that the old woman was just one more nutcase in her life at the moment. Her mother had lost the plot completely, her sister was rapidly going the same way, Henry Lloyd lived in his own world most of the time, and now this one was sitting in her reception area and looked set for the day.

'It is a family business based just outside the town on Corbridge Road, Henson Electrical. My son runs it now, of course, I just see to the book-keeping. I was assured by Kate that you were still quick and efficient.'

'I am, Mrs. Henson, but I have had a lot going on lately with family and with the business.'

'I know all about your mother, of course, but it shouldn't affect your work. We have had family tragedy too but we haven't let it get in the way of customer service.'

God, everyone knows my business, thought Judith. 'Yes, you are quite right. I will apply myself to it today and call you back by the end of the week.'

She stood up as tall as her five foot frame would allow. 'Make sure you do,' she ordered, and left.

Judith did not have any recollection at all of seeing the Henson Electrical file so she left the tidying and went to look for it in her office. She thought it was probably amongst the filing, and if so, it could take all day to find. She sighed heavily to herself and decided that an organised and concerted effort was needed. She locked the door, made a cup of strong coffee and started to systematically go through every piece of paper in the office and put it in a pile of urgent, not urgent and wait to be filed by the new person.

At lunch time Judith felt the need to go out and speak to another human being, even if it was just the woman who makes up the sandwiches in the shop across the road. She picked up the phone and dialled Chloe's shop. It had been two weeks since she had been there.

'Hello Chloe, Judith. I'm popping out for a sandwich. Would you like one? I'll bring it round.'

'Er, no thanks. I brought mine with me today.'

'OK. Shall I bring mine round and we can eat together?'

'Well, I might be busy. It gets busy at lunch times now.'

'If you're busy I'll just sit in your office or admire the paintings. Don't worry about me. I'll be there in about twenty minutes.'

Chloe put the phone down and immediately picked it up again. She dialled a number.

'Louise, it's me. She's coming round for lunch again. Are you in town?'

'No, sorry. Tell her you're busy.'

'I did but she's still coming round.'

'You said you liked her.'

'I do, but…'

'I think she's OK if you keep on the right side. She seems to like you, so sell her something and make the most of it.'

'Ha ha very funny. Oh, customer, got to go.'

'Seriously, just keep her at arm's length, be professional and you'll be fine. Call me later when she's gone.'

Phoenix Antiques was quite busy and Chloe popped in and out of the office as she served her customers. She always said that Louise was the retailer but she could charm people too. She flitted like a little butterfly, never quite still but always attentive and listening for the buying signals. Judith looked around and noted the tidiness as always, and that everything on view was antique except for office equipment. She wondered whether she could slide open one of the drawers in the Victorian oak desk but decided that neat little Chloe would notice anything out of place. She jumped as the phone rang. Chloe was busy so it went to voicemail.

'Hi Chloe. Only me. Can you pick me up on your way to the theatre on Friday? About six? We can go to The Kings for a drink first. Cheers.'

As the afternoon wore on, Judith found Audrey Henson's file and set her mind to preparing the accounts for tax purposes. She reflected that the day had been rather good after the unpromising start. She heard someone try the door and decided to leave it locked. She could get so much more done when she didn't have to answer the phone or deal with people wondering in off the street. Perhaps tomorrow she would find the perfect administrator who would take that burden back off her. She completed Henson Electrical's file and cast it on the pile for action by someone else and spent half an hour deciding on questions to ask at the interviews and deciding how she could get these people to do some of the filing while they were here.

Judith bought a local paper on her way home and found an advertisement for the local operatic society; *South Pacific* at the Queen's Hall Arts Centre in Hexham every night that week. She phoned and reserved a ticket for Friday.

Tuesday 4th November 2008

Judith sat back and contemplated the day. She had found a suitable replacement for Kate but had had to work for it. The first two interviewees were impossible. The first one had various childcare responsibilities although she knew she couldn't give that as a reason for rejecting her, and the second had a concoction of health worries. That would be like living with her mother, or like having a child to look after. The third applicant, however, had recently moved to the area, was of middle age and her eyes had lit up at the prospect of having a good sort out. Judith had shown her the filing system and Helen had tutted sympathetically and suggested alternatives. She was able to start on Monday, not having to give notice, and handed over some references from previous employers 'down south' which Judith thought she should really follow up some time. Not today, though. There was an hour of daylight left so she went for a drive in her new car. On her way home, in a moment of family concern, she decided to go and visit her mother.

'Hello Mum,' she said, a bit more loudly than usual as she approached her in the large sitting room full of very upright armchairs.

'Why are you shouting, Fiona?' she said.

'I'm Judith, not Fiona.'

'Oh yes. Fiona never comes to see me.'

Judith knew that Fiona came out nearly every day but she didn't correct her mother. 'So how are you? Do you like it here?'

'I don't know. Where am I?'

'At Mill View. Remember? With Tina, Mrs. Walters I mean, and your new friends who live here as well.'

'Why doesn't Judith come and see me?'

'Mum, I am Judith and I am here to see you.'

'Oh.'

74

'How's Henry Lloyd?' Judith lowered her voice a little, not really wanting anyone to know that she was interested.

'He's dead.' Her mother looked out of the tall window towards the distant hills.

'He is not dead. Really, Mum, that is just ridiculous. Never mind, I'll ask Tina on my way out.'

'He's dead and Tina's gone to see him off.'

Judith suddenly felt exhausted and started to get ready to leave. She wished she hadn't come at all. There wasn't much point. Still, needs must and all that. It was dark when she left and she drove home slowly to her empty flat.

She called her sister. 'I've just been to visit Mum. She hadn't a clue which one of us I was and she didn't know where she was.'

'That's quite normal. You'd think after a month she would be used to it but she doesn't always know me or Rosie. Rosie seems to accept it but I can't.'

Judith heard her sister's voice breaking up and fought back her irritation.

'I went to see Mum's solicitor last month and he gave me some stuff to read about power of attorney. I'll dig it out; haven't had a chance to study it with Kate leaving and everything.'

'Do you want some help with it? I could do with concentrating on something.'

Her first instinct was to refuse, but she said, 'I'll find it and see what it says then bring it over for you.'

'Thanks.' Then silence.

'Right, well I'll do it in a few days. Still busy at work.' She realised that Fiona was sobbing and incapable of speech. 'I'll call soon.'

I wish Fiona would get a grip, thought Judith as she prepared

75

dinner. *It really isn't helpful her crying all the time and making herself ill. It will just put more bloody responsibility on me in the end.*

Friday 7th November 2008

Judith was pleased that the week was over. She had realised that she needed an administrator more and more the longer she didn't have one. The office looked like a bomb had hit it again but she didn't make any effort to tidy up as Helen was due to start at nine o'clock on Monday morning. It seemed like the sort of job she would relish. She decided to finish early as she was going out.

At six-fifteen, Judith bought herself a sparkling mineral water and sat down in the lounge bar of The Kings Arms just around the corner from the theatre. She had brought some information about gaining power of attorney to read should she not 'bump into' Chloe and her companion. She didn't appear to need it as five minutes later they arrived. She waited until they had bought drinks then looked up and waved.

'Chloe! Hello, we meet again.' Judith wasn't sure but she thought a flicker of irritation had passed over Chloe's face as she heard her call. It disappeared just as quickly; she must have been mistaken. She saw Chloe turn and say something quietly to her friend then walk towards her.

'Are you going to see the show?'

'Yes, are you?'

'Yes. We always support the local productions. Actually we used to help paint the scenery way back when we were teenagers. I didn't this time with opening the shop, but Pauline did.'

Judith looked up expectantly at where Pauline had been standing but she had gone to sit at the other side of the pub and was talking to a couple of older people.

'Anyway, I'd better go and join my friends. Enjoy the show.'

'Yes, you too,' said Judith to Chloe's back. She slumped back into her seat and pretended to read the papers that she had brought with her. She had half a mind to go back home. If challenged later she could say that she had felt unwell, but thought she might as well stay until the first interval and see what it was like. At a quarter to seven, she walked next door to the theatre and took her seat. She was in the stalls, about half-way up in the old fashioned, velour-covered seats, always dark red in these provincial theatres. She enjoyed the buzz of conversation around her but had no desire to join in. Several people she knew walked past and spoke briefly then moved further down and shuffled along their rows to their seats. The heavy curtain at the front of the stage was lit from below and the orchestra in the pit even lower down had warmed up and tuned up and were ready for the overture. Judith mentally ran through the medley of songs she could remember; 'Some Enchanted Evening', 'Happy Talk', 'I'm Gonna Wash That Man Right Outta My Hair'. A party of four people came and sat behind her. She turned and saw Chloe who seemed more relaxed. She smiled and introduced Judith to her friend Pauline and Pauline's parents who were in Hexham for a short holiday, and it was only natural that they invite her to join them for drinks at the interval. Judith chatted easily to Pauline's parents, discussing Norfolk, which is where they lived now, near their other daughter who had two small children. She asked whether they had been to Phoenix Antiques yet, and told them that Chloe was looking out for a seascape for her. It was all very pleasant.

Driving home, Pauline looked at her friend with concern.

'What's the matter, Chloe?'

'Nothing. Why?'

'Something is. Why didn't you want to sit with Judith in the pub? Why were you so quiet at the interval?'

'I don't know. I can't explain, but she makes me feel – I don't really know what. Uneasy I think. Louise doesn't trust her at all. It's only since she said anything that I've noticed that she's a bit strange. She's always on her own, for a start.'

'Lots of us are like that, Chloe. Being on your own doesn't make you strange.'

'I know. But she says things that other people say aren't true. Like her and her sister for instance, she told me that they were really close but from what I've heard since, they can't stand each other.'

'Lots of families don't like their dirty linen washed in public. I don't blame her for that. Actually I quite admire it.'

'Yes, I suppose so. Maybe I'm making too much of it.'

'Sounds like it to me. You're usually such a trusting soul, and friendly to everyone.'

'I know. I don't like myself for feeling like this. Maybe you're right and I've been too easily swayed. I'll call Judith next week and invite her over for a sandwich at lunch time. I can keep it all on a professional basis if I'm friendly in a work way.'

'She seems to have money. She might buy stuff from you. That's a brand new flashy car she's driving.'

'Yes. She offered me a ride but I said no. Maybe she's lonely and wants to show it off to someone.'

'That sounds more like it, and more like you.'

'Yeah. Thanks Pauline. I feel better about it all now.'

Sunday 9th November 2008

Fiona arrived at Judith's flat to pick her up to go to visit their mother at Mill View. She looked around enviously as always. She was a bit fed up with living in their mother's old house. Judith's flat was part of an old building conversion in Shaw's

Lane. It was very posh, standing back from the road and overlooking its own lawns and across to hills in the distance. Her sister must be doing well for herself living here and driving her new red BMW.

'I'll take my car, Fi.'

'Don't be silly. We may as well all go together. Rosie's in the car waiting for us.'

'I don't really want to go at all. She'll be fine with you and Rosie.'

'I know you don't want to go. That's why we're going in my car, so that you can't slope off.'

Judith sighed and put her coat on. 'What is the point of all of us going? She doesn't know who's who at the best of times. She'll just get confused.'

Fiona dragged herself away from everything she longed for in a dining kitchen; from the Belfast style sink, integrated oven, centre island with a Neff gas hob. She was still struggling on with their mother's oven that must be over twenty-five years old.

'Maybe she'll be less confused if she sees us together. It might help her sort it out in her head. Anyway, I want to broach the subject of power of attorney to make sure she knows what we're planning. Actually it's more that we are all agreed on what we want to do. You haven't involved me in it at all yet.'

'You've been off your head on tranquilisers for the last month!' Judith said this as she got into the car.

'Judith, don't talk to Mum like that. She's been really worried about Granny. That's all. And you haven't been much help.'

With a huge amount of self-control, Judith turned to her niece, smiled and said, 'Yes, Rosie, I know. Sorry. We are all dealing with this in our own ways.' She smiled to herself knowing that that would shut them up.

At Mill View they eventually got through the security doors and signed in at reception then made their way across the coarse, hard-wearing carpet into the day room. Judith wondered, not for the first time, how they managed to make the carpet smell of bleach. Still, better that than other things. They looked round.

'Ah, Judith, Fiona, and hello Rosie. Your mother's in her room. She didn't want to come downstairs after lunch.' One of the carers, about their mother's age, had known them all their lives and took a special interest in Mrs. Dillon.

'OK,' said Rosie and ran up the stairs to find her granny.

'How has she been?' asked Fiona.

'A little unsettled, actually, since Henry Lloyd died.'

'So Henry Lloyd *is* dead?' asked Judith, 'Mum said he was when I popped out here last week. I thought she'd got confused.'

'He died peacefully in his sleep. It's always sad when we lose a resident but it is the best way for them to go.'

'Yes, indeed,' agreed Judith as she recalled her last conversation with him. She remembered that Henry had a nephew somewhere who had once been sweet on her. She might need to use that to her advantage if people start snooping around looking at his finances. It was indeed the best way for him to go. Certainly if any foul play was suspected there would be investigations into his last payments.

'Mum, Ju, come up quick,' called Rosie, looking over her shoulder down the long corridor, which was the way to her granny's room.

Fiona ran up the stairs to join her daughter.

'It's Granny,' started Rosie, but before she finished the sentence, her granny appeared on the landing with her coat on and a case packed.

'Ah good. You've come to take me home at last.'

Judith instantly forgot Henry Lloyd and marched up the stairs to steer her mother back to her room and unpack her bag.

Later that evening, Fiona and Rosie sat at the big kitchen table eating supper and drinking tea.

'Mum, don't cry again, please.'

'It's not only Granny,' she sniffed, 'it's Judith as well. She's such a, a, a *cow* sometimes.'

'Oh Mum, she's just like that sometimes. It's just her way.'

'It's true though. All that rubbish about 'we are all dealing with it in our own way', that was to make you think she's suffering as well. She isn't. She and Granny always had this thing between them. It was never an easy relationship, well, not since...'

'I know, Mum, don't go through it again. It certainly isn't your fault.'

'No, and she knows that but she's always been bitter. I think she's glad Granny's at Mill View and out of the way. She seems to want Granny's money. That's why she won't let me go with her to the solicitor.'

'You can go to the solicitor. Just do it if you want to.'

'You can come if you want.'

'Not really,' said Rosie.

'She wants us out of this house as well, you know.'

'She does not. She wouldn't do that. We've lived here for years looking after Granny. Maybe you're over-reacting a bit because of the tablets you're taking. Judith wouldn't make us leave. She couldn't make us leave, could she?'

'Well, that's what she wants. She wants the house sold and the money shared out so she doesn't have to see us any more and we don't have to see her.'

'Mum, she doesn't, she wouldn't! I'm going to ring and ask her.'

'Calm down, Rosie. Don't ring when you're upset by it. You'll be off to university next year and the house will be too big for just me. It is sensible; it's just that Judith will try to force it through more quickly than I want.'

'I bet it takes ages to sort out all the legal stuff. OK, I will come with you to the solicitor but only to make sure that Judith doesn't bully you.'

'Thanks, love. I'll make an appointment for after school next week.'

Judith sat in her flat with her feet up and a large glass of Sauvignon Blanc. Her favourite place to sit was in a deep, comfortable armchair in an alcove with a window from floor to ceiling. Even in the dark she looked out with the curtains open. Really, she despaired of her sister. If she hadn't been there today, Fiona would probably have brought their mother home again and they would have been back at virtually square one. The sooner that house was sold, the better.

Wednesday 12th November 2008
Helen the Whirlwind was waiting at the door before Judith arrived at the office, and so was Audrey Henson. Judith cursed silently. She had been so delighted at Helen dealing with the backlog of filing that she had forgotten completely about Henson Electrical's accounts. She also made a mental note to get a key cut for Helen. The pressure of having to be at the office at the very beginning and very end of every working day was going to get tiresome.

Mrs. Henson blanked Helen completely. 'Ah, Miss Dillon. I thought you opened at nine in the morning.'

'Miss Dillon was delayed this morning,' said Helen, 'perhaps I can get you a cup of coffee while you wait.'

'Wait?' Mrs. Henson sounded incredulous. 'Wait for what?

I wish to speak with Miss Dillon immediately. My time is valuable, even if hers is not.'

Helen stood between Judith and Mrs. Henson until Judith had gone into her office. She quickly retrieved Henson's file and had it open on her desk when Mrs. Henson eventually got past the sturdy Helen and barged in.

'All done,' she smiled. 'I would have posted it to you. You really didn't need to come in to pick it up.'

'You said you would contact me by the end of last week.'

Ah! Good point, thought Judith. She had forgotten that. 'I did ring a couple of times,' she eventually lied, 'but there was no reply.' And by some miracle, Mrs. Henson did not contradict her. 'So, the accounts are here and the invoice will follow in the post.'

'Thank you,' she said, picked up her books and walked out.

Helen came into Judith's office.

'Thanks Helen. Good try, but you'll have to block the door completely to keep Mrs. Henson out.'

'Call me your gatekeeper,' she said cheerfully. 'I'm usually better than that.'

'I was thinking of getting a key cut for you,' said Judith. 'Kate didn't need one because she kept school hours and I was always here before and after her.'

'Good idea,' and she held her hand out for the key. 'If you give it to me now I'll get one cut at lunch time when I'm out.'

'Thanks,' said Judith as she handed it over. She couldn't believe her luck.

Friday 14th November 2008

It was a full week before Chloe rang Judith, and she felt bad about it. Louise was due in at two o'clock to take over from her so she felt on safe ground inviting Judith at about one.

'Thanks Chloe. Shall I pick up sandwiches on my way over?'

'No, it's OK, I've got plenty. Oh, as long as you're not veggie.'

'No, I'll eat anything. See you about one o'clock.'

'So, I expect you're working all weekend?' said Judith as they ate ham sandwiches.

'No actually. Louise is going to work this afternoon and all day tomorrow. I've got an auction to go to in Newcastle.'

'Really?' Judith took a guess, 'At Millward's Auction House?'

'Yes, actually. Do you know it?'

'Yes, I go there quite a lot. I was thinking of going myself tomorrow. It's always good for art.'

'So, you're cutting out the middle man, eh? I'm glad all my customers don't think the same way.'

'Chloe, I'm so sorry, I didn't mean that at all. I just like to go and watch. I like the atmosphere, you know.'

'Yes, I know. It's OK. I was only kidding. I like the atmosphere too.' Chloe suddenly realised that Judith was going to turn up there tomorrow. 'It's a good chance for me to meet up with old friends in the business. We spend all day talking business.'

'It sounds fascinating.'

They heard the door open in the shop and Chloe jumped up to greet her customer. It was Louise. She tried to keep a straight face as Chloe mouthed something to her in silence. Louise shook her head.

'You'd better get off or you'll catch all the rush hour traffic in Newcastle. Call me later.'

'I'll finish lunch first. Judith is here. Come and say hello.'

'Hello Judith,' called Louise as she hung her coat in the store room and went back to the shop to greet a new customer.

Back at the office, Judith looked up the auction house on the internet to see what was happening there the next day. Sure enough there were lots of paintings for sale. There seemed to be a lot of American artists that she hadn't heard of; Harold Altman looked interesting, and Wally Ames. She wouldn't buy anything of course, but it would be a day out.

Chloe got home and called Louise straight away.

'What did you tell her all that for? You know she has nothing to do with her time. What are you going to do tomorrow? Hang out with her all day?'

'No, I don't want to. I'm going there to work and to meet my old colleagues from the gallery. I don't want her there at all.'

'Too late, I think. Be more careful what you say next time.'

'I was going to keep it all professional. I've already had two nights out with her and now a jolly day out!'

'You're too chatty. Think next time, before you tell her *anything*.'

Saturday 15th November 2008

Judith sang along to the *Sounds of the Sixties* as she drove across to Newcastle. She didn't like any of the songs and certainly hadn't been around when they were hits, but somehow you just know them all. *'Build Me Up Buttercup'*? My God, what a stupid song! You couldn't imagine anyone agreeing to release that these days. And Herman's Hermits; what a stupid name for a pop group. Never mind, it passed the time and soon she arrived on the outskirts of the city and switched on the satnav. It was one of the wonderful gadgets that came with the car. She found the auction house and a nearby car park and made her way there to have a good look before it all started at eleven. She looked around for Chloe but didn't see her, so she picked up a catalogue and walked around making notes. The notes actually said things like 'Don't forget to invoice Henson's' and 'Find out what's happening with Henry's estate' but it looked as though she was serious.

Chloe was there already but when she saw Judith approaching she made her way to the dealers' coffee lounge and struck up a conversation with a few acquaintances. She knew she couldn't put it off for ever and when the people she was talking to went back out, she did too. She didn't know them well enough to ask them to shield her so she took a deep breath and decided she would avoid Judith as long as she could. It wasn't too difficult if she stayed alert as there were several rooms with several ways in and out, but it wasn't helping with her work. She couldn't concentrate if she carried on like this, so she decided to put her mind to the job in hand and to finish making notes on pictures she would bid on later.

If Judith saw her, she didn't approach, and at ten to eleven when Chloe sat down for the auction she saw Judith at the other side of the room. There were no spare seats near her but Judith didn't look as though she was going to move anyway. So far so good. There was a half-hour break at twelve-thirty and Chloe's anxiety rose again. Again it was unfounded. Judith came over, said hello then went outside for a breath of fresh air. Chloe felt that she had been worrying about nothing, and in the afternoon Judith didn't come back at all. She couldn't help looking over her shoulder every now and again just to be sure. She jumped a mile when someone came up behind her.

'You look guilty. What's going on?'

'Peter! If ever I needed a tall, dark, handsome stranger to come to my rescue, well actually it was four hours ago. Never mind, now is good as well.'

Peter looked around. 'Shall I find a tall, dark…?'

'Yes, OK, you're not a stranger so I'll settle for that. I'm avoiding someone, actually.'

'Intriguing. Who?'

'Someone from Hexham who has, thankfully, disappeared since lunch time. Where have you been all day, anyway?'

'My dear! I have staff these days who do this stuff for me. I'm still the van driver, though, and have come to carry the booty back to the shop. I hope they have bought well.'

'Well, I didn't get much. I bet they bought what I wanted at a higher price.'

'They better not have spent too much. What is it?' he asked as Chloe jumped.

'Nothing. Sorry. I thought I saw her at the window.'

'Who is this person?'

'Just a woman who has a business in the town. She makes me nervous. And I don't believe what she says. She said she was coming here today, but only after I said I was. I don't know. I…'

'Do you want me to walk you to your car? In case she's lurking outside.'

'No, it's OK thanks. I got a space out the back because I was here at the crack of dawn. Thanks anyway. I'll be fine.'

'OK, well it was good to see you. Keep in touch.' He kissed her cheek and went off to find his staff and their purchases.

Friday 21st November 2008

Judith rang her mother's solicitor.

'Look,' she said, 'I know you gave me some stuff to read but I haven't had the chance to look at it properly and wonder whether you could talk me through it.'

'Yes, of course,' he answered. 'Perhaps you would like to come on Tuesday afternoon as well.'

'As well as what?'

'As well as your sister and niece. I have arranged to see them at four o'clock.'

'Oh, yes, of course. That will be perfect. Thank you.'

She called Fiona straight away.

'Have you made an appointment at Greig's?'

'You obviously know I have. Do you want to come along as well?'

'Yes I do! Why did you do that without telling me? Are you going behind my back for some reason?'

'No, Judith. I've done it because I ring and leave messages for you and you don't ring me back so I can't discuss it with you.'

'I've been busy. I've got a new member of staff, you know?'

'Yes, you're busy when you haven't got anyone, and you're busy when you have got one. You're always too busy for us so we decided to do something for ourselves, well for all of us, you know what I mean.'

'What do you mean, all of us? Is Rosie going too?'

'Yes, and Mum.'

'Oh really, Fiona. Do you think that's wise?'

'It's going to be necessary at some point. I'd rather take her to Greig's than have John Greig go through it all at Mill View where everyone will know what's happening.'

Good point, thought Judith. Fiona was obviously capable of rational thought again. 'OK, I'll see you at Greig's at four; unless you want me to pick up Mum.'

'I'll do it. After all, you are so busy with your new member of staff.'

The sarcasm wasn't lost on Judith. She had just stopped before saying it was easier for her to get away now that the capable Helen was in place.

Judith drove to the supermarket after lunch then called round to her office. She was alarmed to see someone move across the first floor window. She was debating whether to call the police when Helen appeared at the door next to the wedding shop and turned to lock it behind her.

'Helen. You gave me a fright then. What are you doing here on a Saturday?'

'My husband's gone fishing,' she said as though that explained everything. When Judith continued to look at her expectantly she continued the sentence, 'and I was bored at home. I thought I would come in and finish the backlog of filing.'

'I thought you had finished it. It all looked up-to-date to me yesterday afternoon.'

'An administrator's work is never done,' she laughed as she turned to walk away. 'See you Monday.'

'Yes, see you Monday.'

Judith went upstairs and looked around the office. The reception area was clear of clutter just the way she liked it but now it had a new potted plant growing happily near the window. Her own office looked slightly re-arranged though she couldn't say what was different. She took out Henry Lloyd's file and went back through the last few years to make sure everything was in order. It was only a matter of time before the executor of his will would start to make enquiries. Judith loved this sort of work; precise and methodical and requiring her expert knowledge. The next three hours flew past and she considered it a good afternoon's work. She thanked the Lord for Helen. The last few weeks of having to open mail and answer the phone and flit from one part of the job to the other had seriously affected her motivation to work. Now she could concentrate on getting the business back on track. She had barely thought about Alison for the last week. She would spend Sunday looking at her cash flow and onward business plan, and then everything would be fine.

It was just about five-thirty when she left. She picked up her car from Gilesgate, drove back along Market Street and followed the one-way system around the Market Square. Glancing to her left, she saw Chloe leaving Phoenix Antiques. She wondered where she lived. She always seemed to be driving so she couldn't live in town. Actually, she thought she had heard her say she was going to try catching the train sometimes now that winter was coming and the roads would be getting worse. She watched Chloe walk down Hallgate. She could be going to the station or Wentworth car park. Either way, if Judith drove down towards Station Road she would see her leaving the car park or walking into the station. Sure enough a little red Seat Ibiza pulled out of the car park and headed down past the station towards the roundabout. Judith followed, not getting too close. Chloe turned right down Rotary Way and over the River Tyne. At the A69 she turned left onto the dual carriageway. Judith continued to follow until Chloe turned off at Haltwhistle, then she turned at the next junction and made her way back to Hexham.

Chloe turned off the main road and followed the old B-road through the centre of Haltwhistle and past the railway station then turned right into Bridge Street. She parked outside a traditional stone-built terraced house with modern white front door and windows. Inside she dumped her bags on a chair in the sitting room and went to get wine from the fridge in the narrow galley-style kitchen. Her hands shook slightly as she poured, and only stopped as the cool liquid hit her stomach. She jumped at the sound of the telephone.

'Only me. Are you still coming over for lunch tomorrow? Geoff says he hasn't seen you for ages. He also says that I see more of you than I do of him these days!'

'Poor Geoff. Is he fed up with me? Should I not come over?'

'Joke, Chloe. Don't be daft. What's wrong?'

'Nothing, sorry. Temporary loss of sense of humour. Remembering other times. Nothing, really. See you at lunch time.'

Chloe thought, not for the first time, that she must be really easy to read. Everyone noticed as soon as she wasn't alright; well, everyone except Judith. She wished she could get that woman out of her mind; she had thought for a while that Judith was following her home tonight. Other people have red sports cars and it was quite a way behind. It might have even been a different make of car. Lots of people have red cars.

She sat down and thought about a red car that she once followed home. She should have relegated Tim to history by now but nearly everything reminded her of him: red cars, strong coffee, John Martyn, country pubs, the list was endless. He should have been here with her now but in the end he couldn't do it. The children were too young, they were at a difficult age, they were taking exams and now they were preparing for university and all the expense that entailed. Chloe realised now that however long she waited, he would never leave his family. She went into the room at the back of the house and switched on her computer. Against her better judgement she logged onto Facebook under a false name and caught up with what he had been doing in the last two months.

As an afterthought she entered Judith's name. There was no account. What was she thinking? She was becoming obsessed with the woman.

Sunday 23rd November 2008

Judith spent the day going through her own accounts. She loved doing it and always wondered why she didn't keep them up-to-date. They painted rather a sorry picture. She had lost a few clients lately, some because she had been unreliable over the last month, and some like Henry Lloyd had simply dropped dead. She decided that she needed a concerted effort to get more clients now that Helen was dealing with all the boring stuff.

It was nearly four months since Alison had disappeared to London all of a sudden. No goodbyes; no explanation; just a note saying she had to get away. Well, Judith didn't need her any more. She worked through until dusk.

Tuesday 25th November 2008

Judith arrived at Greig's Solicitors at three-forty-five hoping to gain an advantage on Fiona and the others but they were already there.

'Ah, here's Judith now,' said her mother rather more lucidly than she would have liked. At the same time John Greig came out of his office and viewed them all over the top of his half-moon spectacles.

'Good, good. Now we have Mrs. Dillon and the three Misses Dillon,' he said, clearly enjoying his own little joke. 'Come through, come through.'

Judith wondered whether he was going to say everything twice. She thought that if he persisted with it, she would do it too and see how irritating he found it. They got settled around the table in the meeting room and his secretary brought in tea and biscuits. She thought, as she always did when she was there, that John Greig's meeting room was a bleak and unwelcoming place; just the table and chairs, no pictures on the wall even.

'How can I help you ladies today?'

'My daughters believe that I need one of them to manage my financial affairs.'

'And what do you believe, Mrs. Dillon? What do *you* believe?'

He's doing it again, thought Judith. *It is so off-putting.* She wondered whether it was a deliberate ploy, and one she should use with her clients.

'Frankly, John, I don't know what to believe.'

'Perhaps one of the Misses Dillon would enlighten me.'

Judith decided it was time to take things in hand, especially as they would probably be charged by the minute. 'My mother has been diagnosed with dementia,' she began, 'and is currently living at Mill View.'

'Many people live at Mill View for many years with some form of dementia and don't need anyone to take over their affairs.'

'Yes, I know that,' continued Judith. She refused to be intimidated by this man. She was a professional business person too, after all. 'However, there are times when my mother is very confused indeed, to the point of not recognising us, or not knowing which one of us is which. She forgets where she is or what she is doing there. In short, she is simply not able to look after herself or her finances and property anymore.'

'I see,' said John Greig.

Don't say it again!, screamed Judith silently.

'I see.' He started to make some notes.

'I'm not confused today, Judith. I can see what you're trying to do. You want to get Fiona out of my house so that you can sell it. Why do you always have to take everything too far?'

'Mother! I do not!'

Rosie and Fiona continued to stare straight ahead.

'What?' said Judith and looked over towards them.

'You think so too, Fiona? Well, it's not going to happen,' said Mrs. Dillon firmly, 'not while I'm still alive.'

'According to the Mental Capacity Act 2005,' said John Greig, 'an adult has the right to make their own decisions and must be assumed to have capacity to do so unless it is proved otherwise, and until there is evidence to the contrary.'

'There is evidence,' said Judith, 'nearly every time we go to visit.'

'Maybe your mother simply needs help to make her decisions on days like today when she is clearly very aware of what's going on?'

'Maybe she needs help to decide to hand the management of her assets to us. Now. While she is able to do so.'

'Maybe so, maybe so. How do you feel about that, Mrs. Dillon?'

'Feel about what?'

'Handing over the management of your assets to your daughters.'

'I don't know what you mean, Mr…'

Judith looked across at Fiona who looked horrified at the sudden change in their mother. Judith thought it was the best thing that could have happened.

Their mother looked at Rosie and said, 'Fiona, dear, are you going to take me home?'

'I'm Rosie, Granny, and we really have to try to sort out your things while we're here.'

'Where are we?'

John Greig had caught on to what was happening at 'Feel about what?' and was quick to change his point of view. He suggested that they should complete the forms for Lasting Power of Attorney in respect of property and affairs, and in respect of personal welfare. He said he was qualified to provide a certificate of capacity but would prefer it to be a doctor then he could act completely independently. He said that ideally their mother should have drawn this arrangement up when she was still capable of making the decision for herself. He saw that Judith was about to challenge the practicality of this and pre-empted her comments by saying that it was not always possible to anticipate. He provided them with the forms and they left. Judith took the forms and Fiona and Rosie took Mrs. Dillon back to Mill View in time for the evening meal.

CHAPTER 7

Carlisle, December 2009

Wednesday 2ⁿᵈ December 2009

My God, it's cold in Carlisle in winter. I have decided to start the bridge-building process with my family and to make Christmas a way of doing it. In one way, I'm not bothered. I haven't really missed them as people but they are family and they're all I've got. I don't want to spend Christmas with them but it's weird not having them around. A visit to Marks and Spencer should do for present-buying then I'll go round to Cafe Bar Sierra for lunch. Joanna should be there on a Wednesday and I'll catch up with her properly in the park tomorrow.

She's too busy to talk when I get there. The whole town is busy but I take my time eating the home made lasagne and reading my book, and we manage to exchange a few words in Spanish. Ken's working late this evening, thank goodness, so I can break our regular Wednesday night outing.

Thursday 3ʳᵈ December 2009

I meet Joanna and Ricky in the park as usual, by the duck pond. She says she is getting busier at work and finding it difficult to get time off. While Ricky is feeding the ducks she says that she simply doesn't know when she's going to get the chance to go shopping for Ricky's presents.

'Judith, I'm going to see Santa in a minute.' Ricky is bursting with excitement about Christmas. 'I'm going to tell him what I want.'

'We're going for lunch first,' Joanna says firmly.

He can barely contain himself over lunch but she makes

him sit and eat his pizza properly or else 'No Santa'. My God, that boy can fidget and she has the patience of a saint. I realise that I will have to buy a present for Ricky as well, so walk up to Santa's Grotto with them after lunch before going back to the shops. While Ricky is talking to Santa she turns to me so he can't hear what she's saying.

'I don't know when I'm going to get time to buy this stuff that he wants,' she says again, 'I'm having to work more and more hours and so is Mum. I wish Santa really would deliver.'

'I could babysit one morning or afternoon if you want, so you can shop for a couple of hours in peace.'

'Judith, would you really do that?'

'Of course, he was no bother at all when you were ill in bed.'

'He's quite a handful when we're out, but at home he can watch a DVD or read books. Only if you don't mind, though.'

'I don't mind at all. Is a week today leaving it too late?'

'No, the later the better, really. Less time for him to snoop around and find things. Actually I can leave them at my mam's. That would be safer.'

'OK a week today. I'm going to Hexham next Wednesday to visit my family. I haven't seen them for a while.'

'That sounds good. Anyway, Ricky's coming back. We can sort out the details at Spanish on Monday night. And thanks, Judith.'

Saturday 5th December
The first Saturday in December. Maureen has been gearing us up for this day; the real start of the Christmas rush in the store. She says we will be amazed at how much more cash there will be to count, and how it will continue to get busier now up to the day before Christmas Eve. She has planned the rotas meticulously and I have offered to work the days either side of

Christmas so that the others can have an extra day with their families. We'll be closed on Christmas Day and Boxing Day. Notice I say 'we' now. I truly belong here (sigh). I would like to say it won't be forever, but I simply cannot see any other option at the moment. We are all working more hours than normal but we still need extra help, which we will get in the form of Kirsty from checkouts. She is a relief cashier, trained up ready for occasions such as this but I get the impression that Maureen would rather do without her. She is in for two half-days this weekend to get her up to speed. She's chattier than Maureen likes, and doesn't necessarily talk about things that please Maureen either.

'Judith,' she greets me like an old friend, 'we meet properly at last. I've seen you out with Ken. Did you enjoy *Lesbian Vampire Killers*?'

My natural reaction to such intrusion would be to say no and carry on counting cash but the opportunity to further Strand 1 and Strand 2 of 'Annoy-Maureen' at the same time is too much even for me.

'Actually, I didn't enjoy it much. We went for a lovely drink afterwards though. That made the evening worthwhile.'

'Yes, I saw you go into Cafe Bar Sierra.'

'Yes, the manager and I are friends. I go there a lot. Anyway, must get on, there's money to be counted.'

I get that in then because I can see Maureen reaching the point where she would feel the need to tell us off. Better that I take the initiative. She goes back to counting and balancing till receipts. I keep an eye on Kirsty. She's quick but careless, seeming to be happy to do something twice rather than get it right first time. How annoying, but it may be useful for me in Strand 3 in terms of setting Maureen up as being less than perfect after all.

Maureen clearly doesn't like the idea of my getting too

friendly with Kirsty so she sends us on different tea breaks and lunch breaks. That suits me fine. The last thing I want is the nosey little thing becoming my friend. It makes Maureen feel more in control. That's fine. I can wait.

I go on my break with Anita and tell her about my plans to go back to Hexham next week. She does the big-eyed sympathy look and asks whether I will be OK to go back. For one dreadful moment I think she has found out about the incident at the beginning of the year. I am about to defend myself when I realise she is referring to the dead husband. God, it's hard remembering all this.

'Yes, I'll be OK,' I say. 'I have an elderly mother in a nursing home. I really need to go and visit to gauge how she is likely to be at Christmas. The last time I spoke to my sister and the manager there, she wasn't recognising anyone.'

'Oh Judith, you have had a difficult time. Are you and your sister close?'

'We're OK you know. Just grown apart a little over the years. I have a niece that I'm very fond of so that keeps us closer than we might naturally be.'

I really must stop this. I need to drip-feed this information otherwise I won't have anything left to confide to Anita and I'll have to make more things up. I do my usual response to Anita's sympathy and go a bit quiet. She knows how to play this now and changes the subject. Bless her.

Sunday 6th December 2009
Well, Maureen was right and there is more money to count than usual. The checkouts seem to need change more often and we need to fit in an extra note-lift as the tills become full more quickly. All this is good. It disrupts the routine of the cash office and, along with the careless Kirsty, gives more opportunities for me to set Maureen up. As Maureen is

showing Kirsty how to prepare the trolley for the note-lift (this actually involves the intellectually demanding job of making sure the numbered till drawers are in numerical order) I slip a ten pound note out of one of the bundles that Maureen has counted. No-one saw me do it as Anita was answering the buzzer from one of the checkout supervisors at the same time. I'm quick anyway; I've practiced it so many times that I bet I could do it in front of Maureen's eyes. No need for that; I have plenty of opportunities. I just need to be ready to take advantage of the situations as they occur. I've been giving some thought as to what to do with the money this time and decide it's time to execute the next stage of my cunning plan. For a fleeting second, probably because I've been thinking about her, my mother's voice says, *What are you doing this for, Judith? You've made your point. Leave it now.*

I will, I answer silently, *just this one last time; just because I can.*

'Maureen, I've got a torn note. I need the Sellotape. I'm getting it from your drawer, OK?'

She looks at me suspiciously, probably remembering the last time I asked for Sellotape. She looks at the trays of notes that she has already counted and double checked that are on her desk.

'OK. I'll move my cash out of your way so you can sit there and mend it.' She moves the money well out my reach and where she can see it as she tests Kirsty on the job that is to be hers whenever she is in the cash office.

As usual, I take great care in the repair job. You could barely see where I had torn it a few minutes ago. While Maureen and Kirsty have their heads in the trolley and Anita is concentrating on what she is doing, I fold the note I had taken from Maureen's tray earlier, tear off another piece of Sellotape, and stick the ten pound note from Maureen's bundle on the underside of her desk but inside the drawer where the Sellotape lives. It would fall down eventually, of course, but that's OK. I hope I'm not at work that day, although I would love to be the proverbial fly on the wall.

When Ken comes in to check-weigh the notes before sealing them in bags for banking, the now familiar scenario is played out. Click, sign, click, sign, click, sign, click, silence, click, click. This time it ends with a sigh and a sideways glance at me. Maureen picks up on it straight away.

'What is it Ken?'

'One of the bundles is weighing light.'

'It'll be one of Kirsty's I expect. She's quite careless. Give it here and I'll check it.'

'It's not Kirsty's. It's yours again.' Ken looks a bit guilty when he says 'again' and actually it isn't necessary. She already knows it's again.

'It can't be. I double checked every one.'

Ken has already taken off the paper band and is counting each note. Then he counts them again. Then he hands them to Maureen who counts them. She looks at me.

'I'll start counting the store float while Ken weighs the rest,' I say, for all the world the helpful employee.

'Thanks, Judith,' says Ken.

'Don't weigh the bundles, Ken,' Maureen says, 'every one of them will need to be counted by hand. Judith, where's the bundle with the torn note in?'

Ooh, the implication that it's my mistake! I like it. 'It's not in a bundle. It's in the safe. I didn't have enough notes to make up another £500.'

Afternoon tea breaks are cancelled while we all count frantically. It's actually a good system that can pick up one banknote missing amongst hundreds of thousands of pounds. After two hours Ken regretfully, his word, tells us that he is going to have to inform Security and we will all have to be searched. He also informs Mary Morris and I realise that she has left him alone all afternoon. That makes a change. Maybe she's too busy with all the extra business.

Kirsty has already left the cash office as she was only working the morning so she escaped the searching. Maureen starts to question the wisdom of having her in the cash office to help us. She's doing the afternoon shift on the checkouts so she is questioned. She says she doesn't want to work in the cash office for the next four weeks if this is what happens.

A good day's work, I think.

Wednesday 9th December 2009

It's ten months since I've driven a car so I order an automatic for the day. I go to pick it up and decide I will keep it for two days so I don't need to catch the bus to Joanna's tomorrow. Public transport really is tiresome. I get a silver Ka. I hate Fords and hate silver cars but on my budget I can't afford anything else at the moment, or to be fussy. As I turn onto the A69 and head for Hexham I remember the joy of the open road, even though it takes about ten minutes to get up to sixty miles an hour. Mill View is this side of Hexham so I don't need to go into the town. I don't think I could stand that yet. It was bad enough going through the station on the train. On reflection I should have caught the bus, but on even further reflection, I remember that the bus stops at the station so that wouldn't have helped.

I pull into Mill View and park where I used to park my beautiful BMW Z4 on my visits here. *Oh well. Here goes.* I ring the bell and wait for the interminable security procedure to start. Tina Walters comes to the door. She has obviously seen me on the CCTV screen as she doesn't look surprised.

'Judith,' she says.

'Tina,' I reply.

She sighs as though deciding what to say next. Breeding will out, however. 'So, how are you?'

'Fine thanks. A bit cold standing out here.'

'Yes, of course. Um, come through to my office.' She looks over her shoulder as she says this and sees an empty reception area. 'Yes, come through now.'

'I've come to see my mother,' I say rather unnecessarily. 'How is she?'

'She's stable. She's made a friend, actually, and they spend most of their time together in the day room.'

'Anyone I know?'

'I don't think so. He hasn't lived up here very long. He was diagnosed with dementia shortly after moving.'

'He?' I wasn't expecting that.

'Yes, Mr. Leith. He's a lovely old gentleman.'

'Well, can I drag her away for a chat?'

'It may not be a good idea. It can be disruptive.'

'I've brought my mother a Christmas present and I would like to give it to her.'

'I could give it to her for you.'

'I would prefer to give it to her myself, Tina, if you don't mind.' She knows she can't stop me but, my God, she's trying to.

'Are you in Hexham for long?'

'No, I've only come to see my mother and to give her a Christmas present. Then I'm going back to...'

'Where do you live now?'

'I'd rather not say.'

'You are one of three next-of-kin listed on your mother's notes. I haven't even got a mobile number for you.' She looks at me expectantly.

'No. Please take me off the next-of-kin list. My sister can deal with any emergencies.'

'Yes, she can,' said Tina. I know what she means but I'm not playing.

'So, please take me through to see my mother now.'

Tina scans the rota as we are leaving her office, then glances at her watch. 'How long do you think you will be here?'

'Does it matter?'

'No, I just wondered.'

'Well, I don't know yet. I'll see how it goes.'

She leads me down the corridor and into the day room where my mother and Mr. Leith are sitting by the picture window looking out at the garden, glorious in the winter sunshine. As I approach I notice they are holding hands. I turn to Tina and she nods.

'It's quite normal, this hand-holding. A lot of our residents find comfort in it.'

'What else do they get up to?'

She didn't grace me with an answer.

'Mrs. Dillon. Look who's come to see you,' she says gently.

My mother turns and looks at me. For a moment I think I see a flicker of recognition.

'Who is it?'

'It's your daughter, Judith, remember? She went away at the beginning of the year.'

'Where's she been?'

'I don't know. Maybe you can have a talk to her and ask her.'

That dig isn't lost on me. She is determined to find out. I decide it's time that I take control of this situation.

'Hello Mum,' I say quietly and bend down to kiss her cheek.

'Hello…'

'Judith,' I say, 'Fiona's sister. Your daughter. Remember me?'

'Yes, of course, Judith. Come and sit here with Jack and me.'

'I would like to talk to you by myself, if you don't mind.'

'Well, I do mind. Jack is my friend.'

'OK.' I reach into my bag and bring out the present I bought in Marks and Spencer last week. 'I brought this for you, Mum.'

She seems a little unsure and looks to Mr. Leith for support. He nods.

'Thank you Judith,' she says making a huge effort with my name. 'Why have you brought me a present?'

'Because it's nearly Christmas. Look at the decorations and the tree. It's only two weeks until Christmas. Are you having a concert here?'

'I don't know.' She looks at Mr. Leith again. He nods again. 'Yes, we are,' she says after a few seconds.

'Good,' I say, 'good. That will be really nice.'

'Will it?'

'Yes, Mum, it will.' My God, this is hard work. I glance at my watch. I have been here over half an hour and it seems like half a day. Already I've run out of things to say.

'What time is it?' she asks.

'Twelve-fifteen. What time is lunch?'

She looks at Mr. Leith who nods. I'm getting the hang of this now. 'I don't know,' she says.

There is a flurry of activity in the day room. Two jolly care assistants appear to have just come on duty. They are going round speaking to all the residents, asking how they are today, telling them it will be lunch time soon.

'Soon,' says my mother. 'It will be lunch time soon.'

'So I gather,' I say wearily as one of the hearty women approaches us.

'Oh Mrs. Dillon, have you got a visitor?' she asks.

'It's you!' she croaks at first, then gets louder, 'It's her!' She backs away and continues shouting, 'What's she doing here? She's come back!' then rushes from the room and bumps into Tina who has come to see what all the noise it about.

'Shelly, you're early, go and wait in my office.'

Shelly continues to stand in the doorway staring at me. Her face has gone a worrying shade of red and tears start to jerk from her eyes as she goes back to choking. 'She's come back.'

'She's only here for a visit, and she's going now. Shelly, I said go and wait in my office.'

Shelly does as she is told, although we can hear her sobbing to her colleague that I am here. I stand up to leave. My mother goes back to holding hands with Mr. Leith who looks at her and nods. Tina escorts me to the door.

'I don't think it's a good idea, just turning up like that. Some of my staff are still very upset about the, well, you know, the incident.'

'So I see. Don't worry, I won't be visiting again.'

'That's not what I said, Judith.' But Tina is talking to my back as I walk towards the door and my hire car, and I don't respond.

Thursday 10th December 2009

I drive to Joanna's house for the appointed time of ten o'clock so that she can go shopping for Ricky's Christmas presents. She's all ready to go and catch the bus, and Ricky is ready with books to read and DVDs to watch. He has our morning's entertainment planned out. That's good. It saves me thinking of ideas to keep a four-year-old occupied.

She sighs, and says, 'Go and sit down Ricky,' and to me, 'I'm sorry Judith but he wasn't feeling well in the night. He's had a bit of a fever and I think he might be going down with what I had. I don't know why, a month later; maybe it's something he picked up from my friend's little boy at the weekend. He'll either be a complete pain or very quiet and sleepy.'

'I'll cope,' I say more confidently than I feel. I hope it's the sleepy option. 'You go and do your shopping. We'll be fine.'

'OK, thanks. I'll be back at lunch time. I'll get some lunch for us on my way back. Better go. The bus will be here any minute.' She kisses Ricky and dashes down the lane into Cumrew Close where the bus loops round to go back to Carlisle city centre.

Ricky is under the weather and seems happy to sit next to me on the settee while I read one book after another. When we get to the end of all he had brought out, he hands me the first one again. I start to read it and vary some of the words and rhymes.

He looks up sharply. 'Judith, that isn't what the bear says,' he corrects me. I wish children wouldn't do that. If they know the stories, why can't they just read to themselves?

'I thought it would be funny if he said something different this time,' I say.

He slumps against me, shakes his head and closes his eyes. 'Do you want to go for a little sleep?'

He shakes his head again and tries to keep his eyes open.

'How about if you lay on your bed and I'll read to you?'

He nods and I carry him upstairs. For a little thing, he seems to weigh about a ton. He's quite hot too. He kicks his slippers off, lays his head on the pillow and before I finish the book he is asleep. Well, he appears to be asleep. I read to the end, just in case, then creep back downstairs.

I make a coffee. I know where all that stuff is from last time I was here babysitting. I tidy up the books and realise that I didn't bring my book. I didn't think I'd get a chance to read it, not getting the bus, and thinking Ricky would keep me busy.

I look around the room. I study the pictures on the wall; nothing original but quite nice. I wouldn't have picked them myself. I prefer the sea to mountains, and I prefer real paintings to prints. I look at what books she's got and I'm surprised to see some textbooks on marketing among the usual suspects of best sellers. I wonder why she has marketing books. I look in the top drawer of the dresser and see letters to and from the Open University; offers of a place on the course, dates of summer school, invoices. I knew Open University courses weren't cheap but I am very surprised at what she's paying. That cafe job must pay more than I thought. I flick through some assignments and read the feedback from her tutor. I think it is a bit harsh in places but overall quite fair.

I look down through the files and papers to see what else the tutor says about her. Nothing else, but there are some photographs tucked into an envelope. I pull them out and have a look through. It's her and Ricky, I would say about a year ago; ah yes there's a date on the back: August 2008. I can't help thinking that August 2008 was the last time my life was anything like normal but even by then Alison had gone down to London to live. I continue looking through then see a picture of her and a man. It's not a good picture in that it's sideways a bit, and most of Joanna is chopped off, but I guess that Ricky took it and that's why they're both laughing. There's another one of the three of them which looks for all the world like a happy family holiday snap. I wonder whether Gaynor took it or whether Joanna asked a passing stranger in the way that people do these days. I wonder where he is now. He could be Ricky's dad; he wouldn't need to have red hair and freckles as well. I suppose if he were around she would have mentioned him. Well, we certainly don't need him so good riddance. I think about hiding the two pictures with him in them but instead I jump as the door opens. I try to slide everything back into place but I'm not quick enough. Bugger! This is why I am always prepared; I hate anything happening unexpectedly.

'Judith, what are you doing?' Gaynor is clearly not happy. She stands and waits for an answer. That's my trick, being silent until the other person speaks. I remain silent while I try to think of something plausible to say.

'I was looking for where Ricky's books are stored so that I could tidy up before Joanna gets back.' I know it sounds pathetic but I'm not good at thinking on my feet.

'Oh, really?' She's put her bags down and is standing with her hands on her hips. God, she isn't *my* mother.

'Yes, really.'

'It didn't look like that to me.'

'Well, that's how it was. Where do they live? I'll put them away now.'

She suddenly realises that Ricky isn't in the room and that he is very quiet. She looks around.

'Don't worry, Gaynor,' I say in my best soothing voice, 'he wasn't feeling too well so I carried him up to his bed. He was asleep within a few minutes.'

'Oh, poor Ricky,' she said, seemingly forgetting me for a moment. She ran upstairs to see if he was alright.

Joanna arrives home at that moment. It was probably the best time, with Gaynor being distracted. She comes back down the stairs and Joanna asks if she can take Ricky's presents round to her house to hide until Christmas. She offers to take them with her now and leaves us, casting me a 'look' as she leaves.

I decide to pre-empt the conversation Joanna will have

with her mother later. 'I was looking for where Ricky's books live. I'm afraid Gaynor found me opening drawers in the dresser.'

'Oh, you were close; we keep them in a box in the cupboard underneath. That way he can get them out and put them away himself.'

'That is actually quite logical now that you point it out,' I laugh. 'You can tell I haven't had children of my own.'

'You soon rearrange everything,' she says, clearly not bothered that I had seen in the drawer. 'I've got soup and bread for lunch. Is that OK? The bread was hot from the bakery. I'll just pop up and see Ricky before I prepare it.'

'I'll put the soup on,' I say as she goes upstairs to see her poorly son. It seems that he has woken up and she carries him down as though he weighs nothing at all. He joins us for lunch, a subdued little boy for a change. I think I like him better like this.

'Did you have a nice time with Judith?' she asks him.

He nods.

'Did you watch a DVD?'

He shakes his head. 'Read books,' he says quietly.

After something to eat, he perks up a bit. 'Judith didn't read the Mr. Bear book properly,' he says with a cheeky look in my direction. 'She made him say the wrong things.'

'No wonder you went to sleep then,' Joanna says, 'if Judith can't read properly.'

He starts to giggle at my silliness and all is back to normal. I stay for coffee then leave mother and son together. That was enough childcare for me for one day even though he was asleep for most of the time.

As I drive back to the car hire place, I remember that I didn't ask her about the marketing course.

Monday 14th December 2009

The atmosphere in the cash office has just about got back to normal although the ten pound note hasn't been found yet. Well, I say it's back to normal, but Maureen has a bit of a haunted look about her as though she's lost the plot. It's not surprising I suppose as she hasn't actually made any mistakes. The other staff are being jolly and arranging a night out before Christmas. The evenings are so busy now that I wonder how anyone will have the energy to go for a drink after work, especially as the store is now staying open until ten every night. Ah, my mistake, we close earlier on Sundays. There I go again, saying 'we'. They all agree that this coming Sunday will be the only time we can all go. I can't think of much worse than spending the evening with Maureen socially. It's bad enough in here where we don't need to talk much. Anita and Sal are trying to persuade me when Ken comes in to sign the banking. Oh, that terrible time of day when Maureen dreads her cash being short. She doesn't need to worry, at least until after Christmas. It will all be fine until January. I'll decide then what to do.

'Go on, Judith, say you'll come with us,' says Anita.

'Where are you all going?' asks Ken, 'Christmas drinks?'

'Yes. Le Gall probably. It's quite central for everyone getting home.'

'We've been there, haven't we Judith?' Ken twinkles.

OK, any excuse to wind Maureen up. 'Yes, it was good wasn't it?' I smile back at him as I continue working.

'You should go out with them. I usually call in for a quick one when this lot are out. They're quite different when under the influence.'

'You cheeky thing!' Anita pretends to be shocked, but everyone knows she loves to get away from her family from time to time, and really lets her hair down. 'What about you, anyway?'

'What about me? I'm always the perfect gentleman, aren't I, Judith?'

'Judith hasn't seen you after six pints then!'

'No she has not, and neither have you, actually. I just pretend to be merry to save you any embarrassment.'

'Any chance we can get on?' says Maureen, clearly not happy about being left out of the conversation with Ken.

'Sorry Maureen,' we all say at about the same time, then burst out laughing. It is just one of those moments.

When he's finished checking and signing the banking, Ken turns to me and says, 'Are you going to Spanish class tonight?'

That raises a few eyebrows.

'Yes,' I say, 'it's the last one of this term.'

'Have fun,' he says as he leaves the cash office. The smell of his aftershave stays with us for a little while longer.

Maureen decides to join in the conversation at this point, presumably now the stress of the banking is over. 'Do you go to Spanish classes, Judith?'

'Yes,' I say, and leave it at that.

Spanish is fun tonight. Senor Rossi brings in some Spanish wine and some tapas. We are not allowed to have any until we ask for it correctly. Then we ask each other what we are doing for Christmas. I have been dreading this bit and consider lying and saying I am going to see my mother in Hexham but I have enough lies to cope with already so I tell the truth and say I am staying in Carlisle on my own. I am actually talking to someone else at the time but I get the feeling that Joanna overhears.

After the class, which finishes a bit earlier than usual, we all go to the pub for a quick drink. She sits next to me and looks at me very seriously.

'Are you really spending Christmas on your own?'

'Yes. My mother isn't well enough for visitors. I would like to see her, of course, but the manager of the care home says it's quite difficult when I go.'

'That is so sad. What about your sister?'

'She and my niece are going away for a few days. The stress of my mum is getting too much for Fiona again and Rosie has insisted.' Nobody's going to find out that lie. I just need to remember it to tell the people at work if they ask. Ken's bound to ask, and Anita. I suddenly realise that Joanna has asked me something. It's OK because she'll think I am thinking longingly about family Christmases. 'Sorry, Joanna. I was sort of miles away there.'

'Yes I could see that. Look, I know it's no substitute but would you like to come and have Christmas lunch with us?'

'Oh, Joanna, I couldn't. But thank you for asking.'

'Of course you can. Why not?'

'Because it's your family time. I wouldn't want to intrude.'

'It will be just like every Sunday. My mum will come round, Ricky will be hyper, she'll get tired of him and come and take over the cooking from me then we'll sit down and eat. Please come. It will be so good for us; and Ricky really likes you.'

'Does he?'

'Yes, of course, why wouldn't he?'

'I never think I'm particularly good with children.'

'Oh stop it. You make him giggle all the time. That's a brilliant gift to have with children. Please say you'll come. Please.'

'You'd better check with your mum first.'

'Nonsense. Now, will you come for Christmas dinner?'

'Yes, thank you, Joanna. I will.'

Someone says they will have to go for their bus soon and could we have one chorus of 'Viva Espana'. I personally think this is ghastly, but I'm learning to join in. Soon everyone in the pub is singing along with us, and it's actually quite funny, and fun. There is fun to be had in Carlisle after all.

Sunday 20ᵗʰ December 2009

This was such a bad idea, leaving cash office Christmas drinks until now, and especially as the weather is so bad. Le Gall is packed and probably has been for hours. Nearly everyone is drunk and will be slipping and sliding around when they leave. Well, we're not drunk, the ones who have come straight from work. Sal is already here because she worked the morning shift, and she's bought two bottles of wine to get us started and has managed to wedge herself into the corner of the upstairs area and capture a couple of chairs between what will be eight of us, and half the table which she has filled with the wine glasses.

'I got these in while I could get to the bar,' she says. 'Come on, get stuck in. Red or white, Judith?'

I'm very fussy about which white wine I drink so decide to stick with red. It's more forgiving, especially as it's quite hot in here and the white will soon reach room temperature. Actually, the way the others are knocking it back, maybe it won't get the chance. I pick up the white to read the label. Chardonnay; yuk.

'Are you an expert, Judith?'

'No, not at all,' I say, then remember Anita's favourite phrase, 'but I know what I like.'

'Yes,' she says, not realising that I am taking the mick. 'That's the main thing, knowing what you like.'

Maureen is getting into the spirit. She's on late shift tomorrow so she can have a lie in. 'Are we getting more wine? A tenner each in the kitty should do it.'

Everyone reaches for their purses to put a ten pound note into the pot.

'How much have you spent already, Sal?' she asks. God,

she always has to be in charge, and she makes sure Sal is reimbursed for the first two bottles before anyone is allowed to fight their way to the bar to buy another two.

'I'll go for them again,' says Sal. 'I know the barman and I'll get served quicker than you lot.' Tall and slim with her long dark hair loose around her shoulders instead of being tied back, she weaves her way through the crowd to the top of the stairs and bumps into Ken who is on his way up with a bottle of each. He waves them in her direction, which she acknowledges but goes to get some more anyway. My God, the early shift is looking difficult for tomorrow.

Ken eases his way round to where I'm standing. Maureen intercepts him.

'Hi Ken,' she sort of shouts over the sound of the music, her hair glowing eerily under the one bright light.

He's a nice guy and stops for a while to speak to her. She half watches me to see whether it's making me cross, which it isn't because he's half watching me as well as he tries to escape. I do like him but he just isn't grown-up enough for me. He's two years younger which isn't much when you reach middle thirties, but he just hasn't been very far or done much. I think he's worked for Cost-Save since he left school; actually I think he started there while he was at school. He's been offered several promotions but that means moving away from Carlisle, which he won't do. He's back living with his parents as well. I think that's weird but he says it's while he does up a house. It's easier for me; at least he never invites me back to his place after we've been to the pictures and I never invite him back to mine. I think he is too much of a gentleman to ask. Eventually he squeezes past her and sidles round our tiny table to where I'm leaning.

'You don't look like you're enjoying yourself much, Judith,' he says.

How observant of the dear man; I hate these mad, bingey,

115

girly, noisy, hot nights out. 'I'm feeling a bit woozy,' I say back.

'Shall we go outside for some air? It's pretty damned cold outside though.'

'Yes, please. I think I'd prefer the cold.'

I tell Anita that I'm feeling a bit faint and going outside for a while. Apart from that we don't say anything to anyone. I don't mind what they think or say because it will make Maureen crosser than ever. I have no intention of going back in there, and don't. Ken and I buy take-away coffees in cardboard cups and go for a little walk. He offers to see me home but I insist that I can catch the bus so he walks me down to West Tower Street instead and it is only a few minutes before the bus comes. I leap on before he can try to kiss me goodnight. I have no idea whether he will go back to the party but I suspect not. I don't really care one way or the other. The bus makes it up the hill alright, thank God, despite the icy road.

Monday 21st December 2009

Well, it's lucky one of us left the bar at a reasonable hour and reasonably sober. I think the others put my smug look down to whatever Ken and I got up to after we left. I know it's because I'm not tired and I haven't got a headache. Maureen looks terrible when she comes in at two. For once she doesn't interfere when I take control in the cash office and I make sure everything's done in my last hour before I finish at three.

I am twiddling my thumbs in the ten minutes before I finish and start to think about Christmas Day. I was planning to do my shopping before leaving the store today but I have realised that I haven't checked with Joanna to see what food I can contribute to the lunch at her house. I know she's working today so think I will walk into town and ask her in person.

That means I'll have to come back here tomorrow to do my shopping on my only day off. That's OK. Not much else to do. I suppose I will have to buy something for her and Gaynor as well so perhaps a trip to town today is a better plan.

Sal and Kirsty arrive for the late shift. Sal is looking a bit worse for wear but enjoying it.

'Oh I feel terrible! Where did you get to last night, Judith?'

'Wouldn't you like to know?' I say as I leave.

I walk home for a quick shower and change before heading into town. I order a latte at Cafe Bar Sierra and wait until Joanna has a few minutes respite from the queue of shoppers needing to sit down before they drop. After about twenty minutes she joins me at my table.

'So, what can I contribute to lunch on Friday?' I ask.

'Nothing, really. It's all sorted.'

'You must let me bring something. A starter? A sweet? Wine? Brandy?'

'Well, my mum's partial to a drop of brandy after dinner,' she laughs. 'OK, a starter then if you really want to. You don't have to.'

We agree on avocado and Palma ham although Ricky won't like it, but there'll be plenty for him. I decide on some sparkling wine to celebrate Christmas and brandy as a present for Gaynor. I can get all that at work and as I walk back towards the underpass I see Waterstones and remember the marketing assignment I read in her drawer about iconic designs. It came across as a passion of hers and although we haven't discussed it, I decide to look for a book about design for her present. I find one, buy a book for Ricky, a couple for myself then walk down Castle Street to the wonderful, huge second-hand book shop, which I know will keep me occupied until it closes. As I approach, it closes. I cannot believe how the time has flown today. Never mind, I can come back. Time is something I'm not short of.

Friday 25th December 2009

I don't know why people go on about waking up alone on Christmas morning. I think it's alright. I stay in bed reading one of the books I bought in Waterstones, *The Girl with the Dragon Tattoo*. I like it; it's complicated with the huge family tree to work through but it keeps me interested. I am much more intrigued by the girl with the tattoo than with the family. I've ordered a taxi for twelve o'clock so I have loads of time to lie in then to shower and get ready. I think about calling my sister to say Happy Christmas but chicken out, and there is no point at all in ringing Mill View.

The taxi is on time and drops me off at about ten past twelve. Carlisle is rather nice without any traffic. Joanna had asked me to stay for tea as well as lunch but I don't want to outstay my welcome so I confirm with the driver to pick me up at four-thirty. I am sure that will be enough for all of us. They say Christmas Day is one of the most stressful of the year. We'll see; hopefully not this one.

I feel like a sort of Santa walking up the path with presents for Joanna and her family, and Ricky opens the door for me before I get close enough to ring the bell.

'Happy Christmas, Judith,' he shouts then runs outside and pushes me in through the door from behind. Good God! I think I preferred the shy little boy who wouldn't speak for ages. Well, maybe not. It's quite sweet really, and welcoming in a weird sort of way. He shuts the door behind us and shouts, 'Maaaaaam! Judith's here.'

I hate that northern thing of calling mothers 'mam'; we always said 'mum' but then my mother was always trying to rip us from our northern roots. It's no wonder I don't know who I am.

'So I see. Happy Christmas, Judith. Come in and sit down. Gaynor will be here in a minute and I'll do us all a drink then.

She's on her way now. Ricky, please will you put Joanna's coat in my bedroom.'

I take off my coat and hand it to Ricky, then take the wine and the ingredients for the starters through to the kitchen. Joanna insists that I don't need to prepare them so I go and sit down in the sitting room with the presents. Gaynor arrives at the same time. Ricky is bursting to know what is in the presents but he has to take his Nana's coat up to the bedroom first. She greets me pleasantly enough. Perhaps she has forgotten about catching me rifling through the drawers of the dresser. She goes through to the kitchen and Joanna gives her the job of pouring drinks. We all get wine and Ricky gets Coke in a wine glass. We chink glasses. I sip the wine. It's lovely but then I chose ones I like. Gaynor seems to down hers in one which surprises me a bit. I never had her down as a drinker.

'What's in your presents?' asks Ricky.

'They're not my presents,' I tell him.

'They are. You bought them.'

'Brought them,' Gaynor corrects him automatically.

'Bought and brought, actually,' I say, 'but they're still not mine.'

'Whose are they then?'

'Well, that one's for you,' I say as I hand over the largest box.

He grabs it, but before he can unwrap it Joanna looks at him sternly.

'Thank you, Judith,' he says seriously.

'You're very welcome. I hope you like it,' I say back, and he sets to tearing off the paper. Inside is a train set which needs to be put together then the train can go round in figures of eight. It is a great success, thank God.

He looks up, beaming. 'I do like it,' he says and starts to work out what to do with it.

So far, so good. I hand Gaynor an envelope. I decided against the brandy and went for something more imaginative. She is always well-groomed but never seems to have any time for herself so I bought her a manicure at the new nail bar that has opened down near Debenhams. She is clearly touched and delighted, and I think she is softening a bit. She tops up our glasses although I have hardly touched mine.

'Drink up, Judith.'

'I will. We've got a bit to get through. I brought some to have with lunch as well.'

'Did you get Mam a present?' asks Ricky suddenly not wanting his mother to feel left out.

'Of course. It's here. Do you want to pass it over to her?'

He takes it off me. He can see it's a book, as we all can. Joanna opens it and her eyes open in delight.

'Judith, that is a perfect present for me,' she says, 'but how did you know to get this?'

Ah, a sticky moment I hadn't anticipated. Gaynor misses the connection between the drawer incident and the book of iconic designs of the twentieth century and I feel I have got away with it. 'I noticed the marketing books on the shelf when I was here babysitting. I thought you must have an interest in it.'

'You are so clever. That is perfect. Thank you. Here's mine to you.' She hands me what is also clearly a book. It is a book about Spain.

'That's perfect too, thank you so much,' I say and actually mean it. So far this is much better than the Christmas charade of pretending you like what people give. 'The photos are stunning.'

Gaynor tops us up again, and once again urges me to drink up. I'm going to have to find a convenient plant to pour it into if she keeps pressurising me like this. I like a drink as much as the next person, and indeed I have a couple of bottles back at my half-house for later today and for tomorrow. I just don't like drinking too much with people I don't know very well. Joanna goes through to the kitchen to check on lunch and Gaynor goes to find another bottle so I look around. The big cheese plant by the window is my only hope. It's big enough to withstand a couple of glasses in with the Baby Bio so I wander over to the window and surreptitiously pour most of my glass of wine into it. When Gaynor comes back in with the new bottle, she seems pleased that I am joining in and drinking up. She refills my glass.

'There's one present left, Judith,' says Ricky without looking up from the train set which he has laid out right next to the door to the kitchen.

'Yes, I know.'

'Who is it for?'

'Wait and see.'

'How long do I have to wait?'

'I don't know yet.'

Who does know? My mam?'

'No. Nobody knows yet.'

'Who will know when it's time?'

'I will.'

'You will, but you don't know yet?'

'No. Not yet.'

He gives me one of his funny sideways looks that precede a fit of giggles. I laugh with him. He really is quite a funny little chap.

'Lunch is nearly ready,' his mother's voice floats in from the kitchen.

'I'll come and give you a hand,' says Gaynor and leaves Ricky and me giggling on the floor by the new train.

Lunch is lovely. The avocados and Palma ham that I bought are cool and refreshing and ideal before the full roast turkey meal with all the trimmings. We all eat happily with Gaynor continuing to top up glasses. Joanna doesn't seem to notice; perhaps she always drinks a lot. I continue to sip and she tops me up with a thimble-full each round while pouring herself a full glass each time. Joanna's somewhere in between. We decide to have a break before moving on to the sweet, and she allows Ricky to go and play for a while. She potters around the kitchen tidying up ready for the big dish-washing later on.

'So,' says Gaynor to me apropos nothing at all, 'you're a widow, are you, Judith?'

How does she know my cover story? I can't remember telling anyone here but I suppose I must have. I have rehearsed it now so I feel quite comfortable talking about the basics then looking a bit sad so people don't press for more details. 'Yes,' I say.

'How long ago did he die?'

'It'll be two years in March,' I lie easily.

'How did he die?'

'Mother! Stop this at once,' Joanna orders from the kitchen sink.

'Well?' She doesn't give up.

'A heart attack,' I sort of sigh. That usually works to stop Anita asking any more.

'Did you live round here?'

'No, I've only been here since April last year. I travelled around a bit when I left Hexham then didn't want to go back there to live.'

'I can understand that,' Joanna joins in, 'there must have been so many associations.'

'Yes, exactly,' I say.

'What's wrong with that? I'm a widow and I still live here.'

'Well I didn't want to. I tried but I had to get away.' I do my sad faraway look. Really, this is becoming intrusive. I glance across to Joanna for support.

'Everyone's different, Mam,' she says. 'You know that. Let's leave it for now.'

I smile at her gratefully, and excuse myself to go to the bathroom so that she can give her mother a good telling-off. Ricky hijacks me on the way back so hopefully that is the dead husband conversation finished with. I sit on the floor with him for a while and play with the new train until we hear Joanna call.

'Anyone ready for pud?'

'Yeah, yeah, yeah,' shouts Ricky and abandons our game as he runs through to sit down for the sweet. When she sets fire to the Christmas pudding, his eyes grow wide in part-excitement and part-alarm but as soon as the flames go out he claps his hands and demands that she does it again.

'Oh, no. You'll have to wait until next Christmas. Now, do you want cream on that or ice cream?'

'Both,' he says then realises his mistake as nothing happens. 'Please,' he adds.

I rather think that Gaynor is looking the worse for drinking over a bottle of wine. Her face is red and her words are starting to slur. Joanna takes the bottle off the table and won't give it back when she protests.

'Later, Mam. We'll have some coffee then start again after a walk.'

'So,' she looks at me again, 'you used to live in Hexham, did you?'

'Yes I did.'

'Do you miss it?'

'Sometimes, but I'm starting to settle here.'

'So you work in the cash office at Cost-Save, do you?'

123

'Yes, I do.' God, this is getting tedious.

'Is that the sort of work you did in Hexham?'

'Similar.'

'What then?'

'Mam,' Joanna attempts to come to my rescue again, 'I said stop it now.'

'Well what did you do? Was it top secret?'

'No, of course not. I worked in an accountancy practice.'

'Oh, doing what?'

'Mother!' Joanna uses her Sunday voice again.

'It's ok,' I say, 'all sorts really.' Well that is true considering I didn't have any staff for a lot of the time after Kate left. 'I even did some book keeping.'

'Have you got family there?'

'Yes, a mother, a sister and a niece.'

'Why aren't you there now then?'

'Mother, that really is enough. If you can't stop being so inquisitive, you can go home now.'

I sense a big family argument brewing and about to boil over. God knows I've known enough of them with my own family. I thought I was going to avoid it this year. I decide I have given Gaynor more than enough information, pissed old bat that she is. Ricky starts wriggling about in his chair.

'Did you mention a walk before, Joanna?' I ask. 'Maybe we should go now while it's still light and have coffee when we get back.'

'Good idea,' she says. 'Ricky, there's a job you can do. Go and get everybody's coats, please.'

He's glad of something to do and does as he is told. Gaynor refuses to come with us so Joanna, Ricky and I walk to the small play area and sit on the bench while Ricky wears himself out.

'Sorry about my mam,' she says. 'She's suspicious of people.'

'Is that all it is?' I test the water a bit.

'Yes, really. I was quite friendly with someone last year and he went away to work. I was upset so now she wants it to be just the three of us for family occasions.'

Right on cue, Ricky falls over and starts sobbing. The excitement of the day has suddenly overwhelmed him. We hold one hand each and swing him home.

'I think this is time for you to open my last present, Ricky,' I say as we get into the house.

Joanna looks at me as if to say, *oh no, not more, not right now*.

'It'll be fine,' I say, 'I'll read to him until my taxi comes. It won't be long.'

'OK, that'll settle him down, actually. I'll make us all a coffee.'

Gaynor has gone home leaving a note to say that she feels rough. I should jolly well think she does.

Back at the bijou half-house, I open a bottle of Pinot Grigio, my treat for myself, pour a huge glassful and settle down with my book. I struggle to concentrate, though, and have to keep reading the same pages over and over again. Gaynor is really bothering me. What was all that questioning about? It can't be just because she saw me looking in the drawer of the dresser.

I pick up the phone to ring Fiona. I do that thing that means the other person can't find out where you're calling from and dial her number. It rings and rings, and eventually switches to the answering machine. I hesitate then say, 'Hi Fi, hi Rosie. It's me. I've just called to say Happy Christmas. I hope you've had a good day.'

I imagine them in my mother's house listening to my voice as I leave the message. I don't blame them for not picking up. I don't even want to speak to them; I just wanted to have some contact for a brief moment.

CHAPTER 8

Hexham, December 2008

Monday 1ˢᵗ December 2008

Mrs. Henson settled herself in the cafe at Robb's Department Store and waited for her companion to finish looking at the menu.

'Tea and scones, I think,' he said, 'same for you?'

'Yes please,' she replied and waited for him to order their tea then to ask about the purpose of this meeting. He was far too polite to get straight to the point.

'How is your family, Mrs. Henson? I hear your son runs the business now.'

'Yes, he's doing well but I fear his heart isn't in it. Since his brother decided that his interests lie elsewhere, you know.'

'Yes. I heard he'd moved to London.'

'Yes, better all round I think. I don't think he ever really fitted in Hexham. He is able to lead a much more colourful life away from here.'

He had no idea what she was talking about, so as the waitress brought the tea and scones, he broached the subject of what he was doing here.

'So, can I help you in some way, Mrs. Henson?'

'No, young man, it is I who can help you.'

Martin Lloyd was not aware that he needed any help but his upbringing prevented him telling this to a perfectly nice elderly lady. He waited.

'Your uncle and I were friends for many years.'

'Yes, you played bridge together, didn't you?'

'Yes, and he did some work with my husband many years ago. I would say that I knew him for about fifty years, off and on. It is very sad that he is no longer with us.'

'Indeed. Yes, you knew him for a long time.'

'Yes, and I can tell you that he was behaving a little strangely towards the end, and having meetings with his accountant; secret meetings.'

'He liked to keep his business and financial affairs to himself. None of us knew the extent of his wealth until last week.'

'I still think you should, um, how can I put this delicately?'

'Check her out? Judith Dillon? Why?'

'I can't put my finger on it, not in any definite way, but she is not the person she was. Confidentially,' she leaned forward at this point, 'I have had to chase her for some very basic work for our business. Normally she would have done it in an afternoon, but she was evasive and difficult, and even bordering on rude. I have a bad feeling about her.'

'Our solicitor is the executor of my Uncle Henry's will and he has asked for all the paperwork. I'm sure if anything is amiss then he will find it.'

'I'm sure he will. I am just alerting you to my fears. I shall be taking our business elsewhere.'

'Really? Are things that bad?'

'Really! Well, young man, thank you for the tea,' she said and stood up. Martin Lloyd stood with her and helped her on with her coat, then sat back down to consider what she had said. She may be as mad as his uncle had been but she seemed very sharp, and it took a lot in this town for people to 'take their business elsewhere'. He decided not to do anything about it other than to be alert.

Tuesday 2nd December 2009

'Miss Dillon, please.' Mrs. Henson stood at Helen's desk. 'I'll wait.'

Helen disappeared into Judith's office. Judith was deep

in information about The Mental Capacity Act, guardianship and enduring powers of attorney.

'Who?'

'Mrs. Henson; from Henson Electrical.'

'What does she want? Can't you deal with it?'

'She won't talk to me. She won't even sit down. She says she's going to stand at my desk until you see her.'

Mrs. Henson marched in.

'Yes,' she said, 'but I had no intention of standing there for long.' She sat down on the chair at Judith's desk and faced her squarely.

Judith nodded at Helen.

'Would you like some tea or coffee, Mrs. Henson?'

'No thank you. I won't be staying long.' She waited until Helen had left and shut the door before she continued. 'It is only fair that I tell you that I had tea yesterday afternoon with Henry Lloyd's nephew, Martin.'

Judith returned Mrs. Henson's level gaze. 'Oh how lovely. He is a charming man, just like his uncle, well just like all the family really. How is he?'

'You are not at all concerned that I spoke to him?'

'No, of course not. Why would I have any feelings about it at all?'

'You were Henry's accountant, were you not?'

'Yes.' It was taking all of Judith's self-control not to tell this old bag that none of this was her business, but she was on a mission to keep clients at the moment rather than lose them. 'And so he will remain until I hand over his books to his solicitor.'

'I see. Well, I have told you. I thought it was only fair.'

'Thank you, Mrs. Henson. Is there anything else I can help you with today?'

'No thank you. Not today.' With that she stood up and walked out.

Helen came straight through.

'Everything alright? What did she want?'

'I have no idea what she was on about. She told me she had been out for tea yesterday. Thanks for trying to head her off, by the way, but it will take more than that to stop her getting through my door.'

'I do my best. I try to filter what gets through to you so you can concentrate on the clever stuff.'

'Oh, great, thanks. Anyway, do you want to come through with the diary and we can sort out what's happening this week?'

Judith reflected that life had become so much easier since Helen had arrived.

Thursday 4th December 2008

Chloe had reluctantly agreed to decorate her shop for Christmas. Louise, as she kept telling her, was the retailer and she knew best. Chloe had, however, insisted on fresh holly and ivy and berries, which meant that it all had to be replaced and refreshed every few days. They were working together snipping and tastefully tying ribbons as they planned their Christmas do.

'I agree that we should have something like the opening event,' said Louise, 'but champagne cocktails aren't necessary. People will always expect that if you do it twice running.'

'What then?'

'Wine and cheese. That will be enough. A little snack and a little drink on people's way home from work will be perfect. It's enough to get them here but they won't stay half the night.'

'Hm, OK, wine and cheese it is. Are we still on for a week Friday; I haven't left it too late to invite people, have I?'

'Not at all. If we do it from four o'clock onwards, people can come here and still go out later.'

'OK, I'll finish the invitations and take them round to local businesses personally today. The ones for out of town I'll post while I'm out so they'll get them in the morning.'

'Are you going to invite Judith Dillon?'

'Of course.'

'She spooked you at the auction in Newcastle.'

'She didn't at all. I spooked myself. It's you keeping on about her anyway. She's done nothing, actually, to upset me at all. As I said, I quite like the woman. And I've been feeling bad about not seeing her since that day. I will deliver hers first. In fact, I'll call now to make sure she'll be in later.'

'If you must. I still don't trust her though.'

'Because of? Town gossip about her family that doesn't seem to match what happens with her family? What else? Tash says some of the kids at school think she's weird? She lives on her own and treats herself to a new car?'

'Well, there was her friend Alison who moved here from London about three years ago. She was an accountant too, in a big practice. There was talk about why she suddenly moved back down south; gave up her job and everything.'

'Maybe she just didn't settle here. Hexham is not London by any stretch of the imagination. Maybe it didn't live up to the rural dream.'

'OK, OK. La la la. I heard you. You invite her and I will be charming. You can trust *me*.'

After work Judith drove out to Mill View to visit her mother. She felt that, on the whole, the visits did more harm than good. Her mother either didn't recognise her, or called her Fiona, or moaned about her and Fiona either being there all the time or not visiting at all. On the odd occasions when she did know her, she thought she was going to be taken home. It seemed to annoy Fiona when she went, and she had started saying that she went to see their mother more at Mill View than when she had lived at home. There was no pleasing anyone. If she didn't go, they'd all complain about that as well. Judith was in a good mood this afternoon following Chloe's visit so thought she could take on everyone, whatever they threw at her.

Tina asked to see her when she arrived. She wanted to talk about Henry Lloyd. Judith was wary, and thought she was going to ask about the last meeting she'd had with him. It wasn't that.

'Your mother keeps asking about Henry,' she said. 'I've told her that he isn't coming back but she seems to think he will.'

'I don't know why,' Judith replied, 'because on the day of the funeral it was her who had told me that he'd died. Actually I didn't believe her, but she insisted that you had gone to see him off.'

'Yes, I used that phrase. I think now I should have made it clearer, that it was his funeral, I mean.'

'Well, she'd known him for a long time. I suppose he was her only real friend here. I know some of the staff have known our family for ages, but Henry was always about town, a member of everything, and a charmer.'

'Yes, maybe it's that. Well, if your mum's a bit unsettled, I think that's why.'

'OK, thanks for the warning.'

Judith's mother was very quiet. Judith broached the subject of the solicitor and the power of attorney, and she simply nodded and said yes, whatever Fiona felt was right.

'I'm Judith, Mum.'

'Yes, I know. But I said we will do whatever Fiona feels is right.'

'Yes, of course, but it would be better if we all agree.'

'I agree with you, dear.'

'You agree that we all have to agree, or that you still think I'm Fiona? Oh never mind, I'll talk to her about it anyway.'

'I saw Henry the other day. I thought he was dead.'

'He is dead, Mum. You told me that, remember?'

'Yes, but I saw him.'

'Ah, maybe you saw Martin. He's here visiting and sorting out Henry's things. You remember Martin, his nephew.'

'Martin's only small. This man was grown up, older than you I would say.'

'He's grown up now, Mum, and he looks like Henry; tall with white hair. That was Martin.' She hoped that that would put her mother's mind at rest and settle her down again. 'I'll tell Tina about the mix-up when I go. It's an easy mistake to make.'

Fiona and Rosie arrived.

'All the family together; that's nice isn't it Granny?' said Rosie, planting a kiss on her grandmother's cheek.

'Fiona, how lovely to see you,' beamed Granny.

'I'm Rosie,' said Rosie, completely at ease with the usual conversation.

'If you're me, and Rosie's me, who does she think I am?' Fiona muttered to Judith, then as she kissed her mother's other cheek, 'Hello Mum, it's me, Fiona.'

'Hello Fiona. I am so glad you're here. Judith's explained everything to me about Henry so there's no need to worry.

The three younger women stared at her.

'It seems that I have been seeing Martin, not a ghost.'

'Good, just try to remember it, Mum. Do you think you can do that?'

'Yes of course.'

Sunday 7th December 2008

Rosie was laying the table for lunch.

'Shall I set a place for Auntie Ju, Mum?'

132

'Yes but I don't suppose she'll stay.'

'Why is she so, so, so *funny* with us all the time? She's always been like it. I know she likes us really.'

'It goes back a long way, back when your granddad was alive. She and Granny fell out and it was never mended properly. You could try asking her about it, but not today please. I can't stand any arguments today.'

'Here she is anyway,' said Rosie, peering out of the window and waving.

Judith arrived with copies of The Mental Capacity Act 2005 and a printout from the Alzheimers website about Enduring and Lasting Power of Attorney. She also had paper to make notes.

'That all looks very official, Ju. Do you want a drink?'

'Just coffee please,' said Judith, 'I need to be able to concentrate on this.' She sat at the end of the dining table and distributed papers for each of them to look at.

'This isn't a business meeting, Ju.'

'Yes it is, Fiona. We have to treat it as a serious business decision.'

'But it's our mum we're discussing here.'

'Oh, don't start crying, please. It's better if we keep to the facts and decide what's best for her objectively; not through your tears and what's going to make you feel less guilty.'

'Auntie Ju, don't be mean to Mum,' Rosie said, ever the peacemaker.

'Well, let's just get on then.'

After sifting through and discussing each document they were in agreement that they would apply for Lasting Power of Attorney in relation to their mother's Property and Affairs and also her Personal Welfare. They agreed that if possible they would get her agreement but also agreed that it may be difficult to find a day when she had sufficient understanding to join in with a decision. The difficulty came when discussing who would hold the power.

'I'm the eldest,' said Judith, 'and I am an accountant so it would seem obvious that I am the best person to do it.'

'I've lived with her for the last few years, and looked after her,' countered Fiona, 'so I know what is best for her welfare.'

'You can do it jointly,' said Rosie who was reading on, 'so I suggest you do that.'

'We'll just argue over every decision if we do that,' said Judith.

'You'll walk all over us if it's just you,' countered Fiona.

'I'll be it then,' offered Rosie, 'or at least be one as well.'

'You're not eighteen,' they both said.

'Let's take advice from someone else then, and go with what they suggest,' said Rosie.

'I'm not trusting anyone else to make that decision for me,' said Judith and sighed.

'No, me neither, so we'll have to share the responsibility. I'll ask Tina to arrange for a doctor to do a certificate of capacity then we can ask John Greig to help us with the forms.'

Judith sighed again, but knew she wasn't going to get any better than that. 'OK, you win.'

The dinner had started to smell delicious and decidedly cooked. Rosie got up and said, 'I'll put the veg on, Mum. Are you staying, Auntie Ju? Roast chicken.'

Judith was going to say no, but changed her mind. 'Yes please. I'd like that.'

'Good,' said Rosie and disappeared into the kitchen to finish cooking.

'Shall we go out to Mill View later, then, and ask Tina to make a start on all this?'

'She won't be there today,' said Fiona, 'she told me she had a family christening to go to this afternoon. Come with us to see Mum, though.'

Monday 8th December 2008
Judith was awake early and had got to the office before Helen. The place was so tidy and she was up-to-date with her work so she opened the mail as she waited for the kettle to boil. There was the usual stuff, then a letter from Mrs. Henson advising her that she would no longer be needing her services due to the 'disproportionate amount of work' involved in dealing with her. *Good riddance*, she thought, then changed her mind. She was fed up with losing clients; she needed to keep them. She decided that a charm offensive was needed. As she considered how to win Mrs. Henson round she opened another envelope from a very small business advising her that he would be doing his own book-keeping from now on and requesting that all of his documents be returned to him as soon as possible. Two people on one day; not good. Judith left the open mail and took her coffee through to her office to work on a plan to keep them.

Helen came through.

'Morning Judith. Is everything alright?'

'Yes, thanks, well no actually. Mrs. Henson is taking her business away and so is Lennie May. He's a small builder and hates doing his own accounts. I don't understand that. I'll work on Mrs. Henson and get her to change her mind but I don't know how I've upset Lennie.'

'I'm sure I don't know,' said Helen.

'I'm sure you don't,' replied Judith, 'and I don't expect you to. I need to get to the bottom of it though. Anything urgent for me to do today?'

'I'll ring Lennie,' said Helen, 'it might be easier for him to talk to someone he doesn't know.'

Judith considered this for a moment. 'OK, you ring

Lennie and I'll do Mrs. Henson. Let me know what he says. And make sure he knows he can talk to me if he wants to.'

Judith called Henson Electricals and spoke to Mrs. Henson's son Jason. She arranged to call round later. He sounded quite friendly, she thought. She spent the rest of the morning writing an advertisement to go in the local paper to attract more business.

Jason called his mother.

'Do you know why Judith Dillon wants to come and see me?' he asked.

'Probably because I am taking our business elsewhere. I don't trust her any more.'

'I think you could have consulted me on this. We've always used her ever since she set up. I'm not sacking her; you'll have to come down and see her.'

'It isn't convenient today.'

'It isn't convenient for me either. If you don't come down I'll tell her to carry on.'

'Really Jason, you are difficult sometimes.'

'Mother it is you that is difficult sometimes, not me. If you insist on staying a part of our business, you must come and see your decisions through. She's coming at two.'

Judith was ready to leave.

'Did you get hold of Lennie?' she asked Helen.

'Yes, I did. He's trying to save money, that's all. Nothing to worry about.'

'It is to worry about. Small businesses like his are hard work in the beginning but now I know how he works, it's easy money. We can't afford to lose him, or any others.'

'Well, he's lost. I offered him to talk to you but he said he'd decided.'

'OK, well, thanks for trying. I'll go and try to save the Hensons.'

Judith had a feeling that she could win Jason round. He was a soft touch and just wanted an easy life. She was dismayed to see his mother waiting and knew from the outset that it was a wasted journey. On her way back to the office after an uncomfortable twenty minutes drinking horrible coffee she patted her new car and wondered whether she had been just a little bit reckless buying it.

Back at the office Helen was going through a client's file.

'Looking for something in particular?' asked Judith.

'No, thinking I would put together some sort of cover sheet for each one so we can keep track of what needs to be in there, what is in there, anything we're waiting for and any key dates we should be aware of. That sort of thing. I'm trying to remember what we used in my last place. Here, look.'

'Hmm, good idea. You're so efficient, you need to watch out that I don't reduce your hours. There won't be much more for you to do soon.'

'I thought you were working on getting more business,' Helen laughed, clearly not worried at this hint of a threat, 'we need to be ready for the rush of new clients.'

'You really are most impressive, Helen. Well done.'

Judith thought that Helen smiled the smile of someone who knew that already but she didn't let it bother her. There was work waiting for her today and she could get on with it knowing that the capable Helen would deal with everything else.

'By the way, before you start on that tax return,' she said, 'Martin Lloyd rang. I've made an appointment for him to see you on Wednesday.'

'Right, thanks,' said Judith. She went into her office and was tempted to get Henry's books out again to check that they

137

were in order. She knew they were. She checked the date. His bank statement was due next week. She received them directly every three months. There was plenty of money in his accounts, but this quarter it would show rather a large payment into the H.M Revenue and Customs. She would deny all knowledge of it, of course. The executor may even have all of Henry's books by then.

Wednesday 10th December 2008

'Martin Lloyd's here, Judith.'

'Thanks. Show him straight through please.' She stood up to greet Martin.

'Hello Judith,' he said, shaking hands then giving her a tentative air kiss. 'It's good to see you. I've been meaning to call in but there's been so much to sort out with Henry's stuff.'

'Yes, I'm sure. It was hard enough for us moving Mum from home to Mill View. I can't remember doing anything when my dad died but can imagine how much sorting out there will be when Mum's time comes.'

'I've seen her a few times. I understand I've caused her a bit of distress, quite unintentionally, though.'

'Yes. It's all sorted out now, at least for as long as she remembers our conversation about it. It was nice for her to have Henry at Mill View. They go, went I mean, back a long way.'

'They played bridge together when his wife and your father were alive. Remember?'

'Yes, I remember.'

'I don't think they had so much to do with each other in recent years though.'

Silence for a few seconds. 'So, have you come about Henry's accounts?'

'No,' said Martin, 'I came to see you.'

God, thought Judith, *he can't still fancy me. He's almost as fossil-like as his uncle was, and he's not even ten years older than me.* She hovered for a moment thinking about what he was likely to inherit, but she couldn't entertain the thought at all. 'I see. I, um, I…'

'Don't worry, Judith. I have long since realised that you aren't interested in me, nor ever will be. I do care for you, though, and think you should know that Mrs. Henson tried to warn me about you. I wouldn't listen to her, but she's not doing you or your business reputation any good at all.'

'She was upset that I was late doing their accounts round about the time Mum was getting bad and Fiona and I were having to make difficult decisions about her. I know it's no excuse, but, well, you know, we're all human.'

'I know and understand. I simply wanted to let you know so that you can plan your counter attack, as it were.'

'You're a good man, Martin, thank you. And I haven't even offered you a cup of coffee.'

Helen came in. 'Would you like some coffee? I'm so sorry I forgot to ask.'

'Yes please,' said Martin and stayed to talk for a while about their school days and what other people were doing now.

Friday 12th December 2008

Chloe and Louise were putting the finishing touches to the shop in preparation for the cheese and wine Christmas celebration. Chloe was considerably less worried than when they had been preparing for the opening.

'How many replies did you get in the end?' asked Louise.

'Thirty-five. I bet they don't all come, though.'

'I bet we get some who haven't replied as well. I think we'll have enough. We can take home anything that's left.'

'Mmmm, cheese all weekend. Cheese sandwiches, cheese on toast, quiche, cauli-cheese. Can't wait.'

'There won't be much left, trust me.'

'You will be nice to Judith, won't you? You promised.'

'If I promised, then I will.'

'I still feel mean about keeping my distance.'

'Be careful, Chloe, you only need to be friendly-professional.'

'Yeah yeah. I'll be fine. Oh look, people, customers, I mean guests, approaching.'

People came and went, and several of them were casual shoppers who appeared delighted to be offered wine and cheese and several bought things.

'We must give our customers wine every day,' Chloe whispered to Louise as she went to the store room to get a vase to replace one that she had just very carefully wrapped. She turned as she heard the door open again. 'It's Judith.' Chloe nearly dropped the vase she had in her hand.

'Careful with that! You OK?'

'Yes. I'll go and say hello. Just make sure you come and say something to her as well.'

'Will do.'

'Judith! What can I get you to drink?'

'Just orange juice please. I'm driving. Those cheeses look lovely, though.'

'They are. Help yourself. Here's a plate.' Again Chloe fumbled with the china, but at that moment someone asked her about silver cutlery and she excused herself and made another sale. After a long flurry of activity she came back to Judith.

'Sorry to have been neglecting you.'

'Don't be sorry. Were you expecting to sell that much tonight?'

'No, not at all. It's a real bonus. So many people still

buying Christmas presents, and there's less than two weeks to go. I can't believe it.'

'I can,' said Judith.

Chloe looked surprised.

'I mean because I know how late people leave it to do their tax returns every year.'

'I see what you mean.' Chloe glanced at her watch. 'It's nearly seven,' she said, 'and time I had a drink myself.'

'Is Louise driving you home tonight?'

'No, I'm on the train. Since it's got colder I've decided to catch the train when I can. It's just as easy really as long as I haven't got any stock to move around.'

'Where do you live? Haltwhistle did you say?'

Chloe paused; she didn't remember telling Judith where she lived but decided not to pursue it now.

'You mentioned it one day when we were having lunch here.'

'Oh, OK.' Chloe's hands started to shake. She snatched them away from the antique glass vase on the pedestal and took a deep breath. 'Anyway, it's just as easy to walk to the station as it is the car park from here.'

Chloe broke off with relief to say goodnight to a group of people from one of the cafes in town who were starting to display the effects of early wine after a busy day. Judith went to find her coat as well.

'I'll be off too. Bye Louise, bye Chloe.'

'Bye Judith. Take care,' Louise called from the store room.

'Will do. I'll call in the next couple of days.'

The last two couples followed her lead and left shortly afterwards.

'Woo hoo! That was fab-u-lous,' said Louise pouring herself another drink. 'What a lovely evening. It was fun and we sold loads.'

'I wish I could give you the day off tomorrow, oh wondrous retailer, but I need you here for the next couple of weeks,' Chloe replied as she refilled her own glass.

'Try and keep me away,' said Louise, 'I love it when it's busy. Cheers. You alright?'

'Me? Yes.'

'Something. What is it?'

'Have you ever told Judith where I live?'

'No, of course not. Why?'

'She said, 'You live in Haltwhistle, don't you?' kind of thing. I don't remember ever mentioning it. I thought she was following me home one day; decided I was getting paranoid so I never told you.'

'Well, everyone does know everyone's business around here, but … '

'What?'

'Nothing. Just a gut feeling. Don't trust the gut, that's what Geoff says.'

Sunday 14th December 2008
Judith decided to call into the office on her way to Mill View to visit her mother. She had left all her stuff about power of attorney on her desk and wanted to discuss it with Tina. She parked around the corner in the Market Place and was lucky to find a space as it was busier than usual. *Bloody Christmas shoppers,* she thought, then remembered that she still hadn't got anything for Fiona, Rosie and her mother. She hurried along the road but had to wait for traffic to sort itself out before she could cross. She automatically looked up to the first floor windows and was surprised to see Helen there again, this time leaning against the window with the telephone to her ear. 'Bloody cheek. What's she doing here again?' Judith muttered to herself as she opened the door and crept up the stairs to catch her out.

She peered through the door at the top of the stairs and found Helen sitting filing, for all the world as though it was a week day. Damn, she'd heard her come in.

'Morning Judith. What brings you in on a Sunday?'

'I could ask you the same question actually.'

'My husband's gone fishing.'

'Again?'

'Yes and I don't know many people so I thought I might as well come in and tidy up.'

Judith looked round. 'It is tidy. It was tidy before you left on Friday. You don't need to come and tidy up on a Sunday.'

'I know, but I was bored.'

'Who was that on the phone?'

'I was checking for messages. Here they are.' She pushed a couple of notes across to Judith. 'OK?'

'Yes, of course. Sorry. I'm not used to people coming on Sundays voluntarily. I've come to get some papers I left on my desk.' Judith moved into her own office and looked around. It all looked the same as it had on Friday, so why did she feel so unnerved?

She jumped as Helen said 'You found them?' right behind her.

'Yes. Thank you. Are you staying?' She hovered about wishing she could think of a good reason to force her to leave.

'I think I will, for a while. Then I'll go home and start cooking.'

'Right, well, I need to go now. See you tomorrow.'

Tuesday 16th December 2008

Helen came through to Judith's office with cheques and letters to sign. She looked a bit worried.

'Is something wrong, Helen?' Judith asked.

'I don't know how to tell you,' she started.

'You're not leaving, are you?' Judith couldn't think what else it might be.

'No, I'm not, but Sparkles is. You know, the window cleaning company.'

'Yes, I know them. Why are they leaving?'

'Same as Lennie May, cutting back on costs. They all seem to be finding it difficult to make ends meet these days. Mr. Spark says his wife will do the books.'

'She's hopeless! It was because of her book-keeping that they got into such a muddle a few years ago. It's a false economy, for them anyway. I'll ring them and talk them round.'

'I thought you'd say that so I've already done it. I didn't tell you yesterday because I was hoping I wouldn't have to.'

Judith sighed. 'I've put an advert in the paper in the hope of pulling in more clients but I don't know how effective that will be just before Christmas. I'll book another one for January; in fact will you do that today please. I made some good contacts at Phoenix Antiques on Friday night too so we may get more business to compensate for the recent losses. I don't like it though.'

'No,' agreed Helen. 'It's not good to lose so many clients so quickly.'

Judith looked at Helen as she said this. What was it about this woman? To all intents and purposes she was perfect; but there was just something about her. Judith resolved to follow up the references she had given her and reflected that maybe she should have done that before now.

The phone rang. It was Fiona wanting to sort out a time for them to go back to Grieg's to get the form filled in to take over their mother's affairs. Judith nodded to Helen who left to go and do whatever it was that she did in a fully up-to-date and immaculate office.

Chloe was locking up at five-thirty as Judith was walking back from the solicitors. She stood on the pavement and looked back into her shop. It was perfect. Just enough carefully placed antiques to look welcoming but never cluttered. The words 'Phoenix Antiques' etched into the glass looked so classy. She noticed Judith stop when she saw her and wait as she crossed the busy road.

'Off home?' asked Judith.

'Yes. It's been busy today and I have to go and pick up some stock in the morning. I'm shattered.'

'Have you got your car, or are you getting the train?'

'Train. Doing my bit to save the planet and all that. Saves paying for parking as well.'

'Do you want a lift home?'

'No thanks, I'm fine on the train.'

'It's no bother.'

'No, really, thanks. I have to dash or I'll miss it. See you soon for lunch.' Chloe had to stop herself from running down Hallgate and past the Old Gaol to get out of sight.

Judith glanced at her watch. Chloe really would have to hurry to catch the train and in fact probably wouldn't make it. She decided to drive down to the station to see.

Chloe was sitting in the waiting room looking cold and practically hugging the black marble fireplace when Judith walked in. She jumped when she saw her.

'I said I'd get the train, Judith, I'm fine,' she said.

'You missed it. I thought you would. You've got over half an hour to wait until the next one. I'll drive you. Come on.'

'No, no thanks, really. I'm happy waiting.'

'But, why?'

'Because,' she hesitated a little too long to be convincing, 'because it's my thinking time. I've got my notebook and I need to do some thinking and make notes about what I need tomorrow. Stuff like that, you know?'

She wished Judith would go. It looked as though she was going to stand there until the next train came along. She wished she could put her finger on what made her nervous. She reached into her bag and brought out the notebook as if to say *See? Here it is.*

'OK, if you're sure.'

'I'm sure, but thanks for the offer.'

Thursday 18ᵗʰ December 2008

Rosie came downstairs to make a cup of tea just after eleven. She looked at her mother's red eyes and her blotchy face.

'What's wrong? Is it Granny?' she asked her mother.

'No. Judith.'

'What's she said now? I wish she would be a bit nicer. Well, she is nice sometimes but you never know how she's going to be. What is it?'

'I asked her to come with us to have Christmas lunch with Granny at Mill View and she said 'not bloody likely' along with a load of nasty things about the other residents. I said if she can't be bothered to make the effort for Granny then I can't be bothered to make any effort for her and she shouldn't think she's coming round here later.' Tears started to roll down her face again.

'It's just you two sisters squabbling,' said Rosie although she didn't mean it. She tried to keep things light between the two of them. The family had enough problems without Judith upsetting her mum all the time. 'Forget it. She'll change her mind.'

'She won't. And she wants to get this house ready to sell. Just before Christmas; I ask you! I told her to forget that.'

'Does she really want us to move out?' Rosie stopped trying to placate her mother and looked serious.

'I think she wants the money. I never thought of her as being short of cash but maybe she's struggling.'

'That's her fault for buying such a flashy flat and car. She could easily economise. We have to.'

'I know. But she is right. You'll be away soon and this place is too big for just me.'

'Next October isn't soon. It's nearly a year. She can't force us to sell. And she can't use the power of attorney for her own gain; I've read all the stuff.' She squeezed her mother's hand. 'We'll have fun with Granny. Forget Judith.'

'Yes, but that means that Judith will be on her own at Christmas.'

'That's her bad luck. Anyway she'll make friends with you before then.'

Judith was fed up with arguing with Fiona but their conversations always seemed to end badly. She decided to call Chloe about their lunch date.

'Hi Chloe. You busy today?'

'Yes, very.'

'I'll pick up a sandwich for you when I go out to get one. Anything in particular you fancy? Is Louise there? Does she want one as well?'

'Thanks Judith, anything for me. I don't think I'll have long to stop, though. Louise is popping out later so she's already had hers.'

'She'll be starving by four o'clock, then.'

'Yes, but she'll just eat again then. She never puts on a scrap of weight. It's really not fair.'

'OK, see you about half twelve.'

Whatever was wrong with Chloe on Tuesday, she seemed

to have got over it. Who knew what was going on in her life? She seemed friendly but didn't give much away. Judith decided to finish off the self-assessment tax return she was part-way through before going out. It was quite complex with different income streams and just the sort of job she loved doing. It worked wonders for her mood and she forgot about the argument with Fiona.

Louise looked across at Chloe. Her friend so seldom sat still.

'What?'

'Judith's bringing me a sandwich later. I feel so stupid about the other night. I don't know what to say.'

'She wasn't put off that you didn't take up her offer of a lift?'

'No, it doesn't look like it.'

'She's thick-skinned. Don't say anything then. You don't have to explain your choices to her. Just behave normally.'

'OK, and hopefully she will have got the message and won't ask me again.'

'Yes, better to keep business and pleasure separate.'

'Good advice from the woman who married her best customer some years ago!'

Louise laughed. 'Exactly! Take it from one who knows about these things.'

'Fair point and well made. I will do as you say.'

'Do you think she fancies you? Is that why you feel uncomfortable?'

'I never know when a guy fancies me so I probably wouldn't notice if a woman did.'

'I notice these things, and I would say not, actually. I'll take more notice when she's here. I am assuming you want me to hang around until she goes?'

'If you can, yes please. What time do you need to go out?'

'I've got an appointment with the dreaded bank manager, but I can call and make it later than two if you need me here. Wait and see. She probably won't stay that long.'

Lunch was quite jolly. Between customers Chloe and Louise were looking through some of what they called 'new' stock but which was clearly rather old. Chloe had bought quite a lot of antique jewellery and Judith decided to buy all the family Christmas presents there and then; a brooch for her mother and earrings for Fiona and Rosie. She told Chloe and Louise that these were extra presents for them after the difficult time they'd all had recently.

'Something for you as well then, Judith,' said Louise looking at the colour of Judith's eyes. 'Green, I think, will suit your colouring.' She held up some jade earrings to her face as she directed her to look in a mirror with an ornate gold surround she brought over from the selling area. They dangled just below the sharp cut of her hair.

'They look fabulous, Judith. Gosh Louise, you are clever to pick out something just like that,' said Chloe.

'Ah ha, I don't have many talents, but that is one of them. They've got your name written all over them, haven't they? Chloe, couldn't we do Judith a really good deal as she's buying the other pieces?'

'Yes, of course. It's nice to be able to offer a bargain to our friends. What do you think Judith? Do you like them?'

'I love them,' she said. 'Yes, you are clever Louise. I would never have picked them out for myself.'

Louise started a complicated charade of pricing and discounting that left even Judith's accountancy head reeling, but eventually she settled on £186. She noticed Judith twitch slightly at the amount and quickly said, 'OK, make it £175, because it's you. Not a word, Chloe, it's only fair to look after one of our favourite customers.'

Judith realised that this might be Louise's way of telling her that it hadn't gone unnoticed that so far she wasn't a customer of any sort. She had taken far more than she had ever given to Chloe's enterprise. She didn't feel as though she could refuse.

'Perfect,' she said, 'just perfect. I'll need to go to the bank. I don't carry that sort of cash around with me.'

'We take credit cards,' said Louise as she lifted the machine from the neat desk drawer and placed it in front of Judith.

Chloe smiled and cooed over the purchases as she covered them carefully in tissue paper then gift-wrapped each one. There was no turning back. Judith handed over her credit card.

'£175!' said Chloe as Louise put on her coat to go to the bank later. 'You know I wouldn't have put any one of those pieces at over thirty pounds each?'

'I know. See you later.'

At five-thirty Judith crossed the road to walk down the lane to the car park and saw Chloe talking to someone. She turned to move on as Judith approached and jumped as she heard her call out.

'Chloe, we really must stop meeting like this!'

'Yes, we must,' she replied, meaning it. 'I must get on or I'll miss my train, again.'

'I'll give you a lift. My car's right here.'

'No, really Judith, I want to catch the train,' she said and marched off down the hill. 'See you soon.'

Oh really, thought Judith, *what is wrong with that woman? What's wrong with my sister? What's wrong with my secretary? I am fed up with all of them.* Then the posters in the travel agent caught her eye and she decided there and then that she would go away for Christmas. Bugger the lot of them.

Friday 19th December 2008

Helen had asked for the day off to go Christmas shopping in Newcastle so Judith pottered around the office. She had booked a holiday on-line the night before and spent the day finishing off bits and pieces. There wasn't too much to do so she started to look through the filing cabinet that Helen kept so neatly. Everything was in alphabetical order as before, but she had devised some sort of colour code that Judith was determined to crack. It appeared quite simple; the coloured stickers denoted the level of turnover of each business. No, it couldn't be that, thought Judith as she examined a couple with blue spots. No, it was more to do with the complexity of the business. James's, for example, had a high turnover but relatively few transactions and they were all very simple to account for. That had a blue spot. A small, private training company with a mixture of income streams, some of which incurred VAT and some which didn't, had a red sticker. They were trying to keep below the VAT threshold because they had a lot of individual clients and charity clients who wouldn't be able to claim it back. Yes, it must be to do with complexity. She wondered why Helen needed that sort of information on a day-to-day basis. She would keep an eye on it. Not today, though. She needed to leave a note for Helen then go home and pack ready for her early flight the next day.

'Helen. I have decided to book a last-minute holiday. Fly tomorrow. See you on 29th.' She added as an afterthought, 'Have a good Christmas.' Then she thought she ought to buy her something so dashed out and bought a bottle of wine and a card and left them with the note.

Monday 22nd December 2008

Helen read the note and put her present and card into her bag. It was a large bag, easily big enough for a bottle of wine, some

151

grocery shopping at lunch time and a couple of files with blue dots on.

The postman arrived.

'Morning Helen. On your own today?' he asked, looking through the open door into Judith's office.

'Yes. She's gone off on holiday. Last minute thing, but I don't know where.'

'Oh well, alright for some.' He handed over a bundle of letters and turned to leave immediately. 'It's my busiest week.'

Helen opened each one and dealt with it as she went. She subscribed to the 'only handle a piece of paper once' theory, if possible anyway. Several were from HMRC, that being the nature of their business, but one in particular looked more personal. It was concerning Judith's own account asking whether she wanted her overpayment to be refunded. *Curious*, she thought. The next letter was a query from the executor of Henry Lloyd's will asking about a large cheque that was paid shortly before he died. *Curiouser and curiouser*, she thought. She put both of them to one side. Those two were worthy of being handled more than once.

She switched on the computer while the kettle boiled then checked and dealt with the emails in the same way that she did letters. Read, respond and file away. Job done. Time now to go back to the new filing system and identify the clients whose books were easy to deal with.

The phone rang. It was Rosie wanting to speak to Judith. She was fed up with her relations arguing all the time and she was determined to smooth everything over before Christmas.

'Judith's not here, Rosie, sorry.'

'OK, what time will she be back?'

'29th December apparently. She's got a last minute holiday bargain and just gone.'

'When? Where?'

'Saturday but I don't know where. I found a note when I came in this morning.'

'Thanks, Helen. I'll tell Mum. I don't suppose she knows. See you soon.'

Helen put down the phone and reflected on Judith and her family. She didn't understand their relationships and truly believed that they didn't either. Oh well, none of her business anyway. She pulled out the file marked S.L. James Business Consultancy. She had already marked it with blue as a possibility, and she spent the rest of the morning fielding phone calls for Judith and studying the accounts in James's file. By coincidence, S.L. James phoned just before Helen went out to buy a sandwich for lunch.

'Hello,' he said, 'I was expecting Judith to call me back this morning. Is she there?'

'No, I'm sorry, she isn't available until after Christmas now.'

He sighed.

'Anything I can help with?'

'It's about my accounts. Can you help? I'm not sure.'

'I'll do my best. I have been looking at your accounts, actually, while Judith is busy with more, um, more complex cases.'

'I see. I'm not big and important enough, is that is?'

'I wouldn't say that, exactly, Mr. James, but I am able to deal with less complex ones.'

'Are you? Well maybe I should just pay you rather than her exorbitant fees. Or do you charge exorbitant fees as well?'

'I do a little bit of book-keeping for my own small set of clients. Mostly friends, of course, but I don't charge much, no.' *Don't push it*, Helen thought, *don't be too obvious*.

He sort of laughed as though pretending he had been joking. 'OK, I'll tell you what I have in mind and see what you think.'

Really, thought Helen afterwards, these people with so many skills have such limited knowledge when it comes to dealing with their own business finances. His query had been easy. She wondered how he managed to advise other people about their business affairs. He seemed happy with her advice. She would leave it now and come back to it later. S.L. James would be a good client to get for herself. She would make sure he got fed up with dealing with Judith in the New Year.

Friday 26th December 2008

Fiona and Rosie had eaten their lunch and were settling down in front the television to watch and old film together.

'You're a good girl, Rosie, spending yesterday with me and your granny, and staying in with me today. You deserve your night out tonight.'

'Yesterday was OK, wasn't it? I'm glad Auntie Ju wasn't there. She would have been tutting and sighing. I wonder where she is?'

'I wonder but I'm trying not to think about it. Where are you off to later?'

'I'm going round to Laura's first then we're going into town to meet the others.'

'Do you need a lift?'

'No, it's alright. I'll get the bus back, or walk. I don't mind. You get a bottle of wine open and take it easy.'

The phone rang and Fiona answered it. She listened intently then said that she would leave immediately.

'What is it, Mum? Judith?'

'No. It's Granny. She's had a bad fall and the ambulance is on its way. I need to go and meet it at the hospital.'

'I'll come too.'

'Rosie, you really don't have to. Relax now then enjoy your night out. I'll go.'

'No, Mum, I'm coming too.'

The hospital was only a few minutes away by car and they arrived just ahead of the ambulance. Fiona pulled into a parking space and Rosie jumped out and rushed over. Mrs. Dillon tried to sit up and look round but the pain in her shoulder was too much and she lay back down, clearly agitated.

'Granny,' called Rosie as she ran across the car park to her grandmother whose stretcher was already being transferred to a trolley. 'Granny, are you OK?'

'Fiona, what's happening?'

'It's Rosie, Granny, here's Mum now, I mean Fiona.'

'Who's here? What's happening? My arm hurts.'

'I know, Mum,' said Fiona as she walked along beside the trolley. 'We're at hospital. They'll sort you out and stop it hurting.'

The staff rushed Mrs. Dillon through and Fiona and Rosie were soon informed that she would need an operation to realign the bone in her arm. They were advised to go home. The nurse assured Fiona that she would get a call as soon as her mother was out of theatre.

'How long is it likely to be?' asked Fiona.

'A few hours, probably sometime this evening.'

'OK, thanks. Come on then Rosie, let's go.'

By seven o'clock Fiona had persuaded Rosie to have a sandwich and to get ready to go out.

'I don't want to go now,' she protested. 'I'll wait here and go back to the hospital with you later.'

'No, Rosie. I want you to go out. There'll be nothing for us to do at the hospital anyway.'

'OK, but ring me if anything happens, or even if you just want some company.'

'Thank you. I will. Off you go now.'

Rosie kissed her mother on the cheek and said, 'Have you tried ringing Auntie Ju? She should be here as well.'

'Yes, I've tried. Her phone goes straight to voicemail. I wouldn't be surprised if she didn't even take it with her.'

'She wouldn't have gone without it,' said Rosie with the conviction of a seventeen-year-old who couldn't imagine being parted from her mobile for longer than it took to have a shower.

'Never mind. We're here. It doesn't need all of us. Go on out. I'll call you if I need you, promise.'

By ten o'clock Fiona was back at the hospital sitting at her mother's bedside. She wasn't fully conscious yet and looked very frail. Fiona held her lifeless, but surprisingly warm hand, and wondered where all the years had gone. Her own mother, looking like this, needing to be looked after and protected. She had never imagined it would have come to this. She had always been so strong. Judith was the same, whereas Fiona herself was more like her father. She knew why Judith and their mother hadn't got along but it was all such a long time ago. She wondered whether to talk to her about it when she came round from the anaesthetic; maybe in that half-consciousness she would agree to make it up to Judith. On the other hand, maybe it would be better not to go over it again. A hand on her shoulder gave her a start.

'Hi Mum. How's Granny?'

'I didn't mean you to come here, Rosie. I only texted to let you know.'

'It's OK. People were starting to drift away home or on to the club. I didn't want to go to either. I'll go and find us a coffee, shall I?'

Sunday 28th December 2008
Judith got home as the sun was setting. She pressed the message button on her telephone to be told that she had three messages.

'First new message. Hello Judith, Tina here. I need to speak to you urgently. Your mother has had a fall and I've called the ambulance. Contact me when you get this message please.'

'Second new message. Hello Ju, it's me. Mum's being taken to hospital. Oh, you're away aren't you? I forgot. Force of habit. I'll call your mobile.'

'Third new message. Hello Judith, Tina again. I've got hold of Fiona. Would still appreciate a call but everything is in hand regarding your mother.'

Judith sighed and switched on her mobile. That will be what the four messages on there would be about as well. She really wanted a shower before doing anything else but called Fiona first.

'Hi, it's me. How's Mum?'

'Where have you been? We've been trying to get hold of you for days.'

'Away. And it was only two days. How's Mum?'

'You've been away all week. You could have said where you were going. I've been worried about you and worried about Mum. I can't cope with it all. You must keep in touch.'

Judith fought back the instinct to tell Fiona to mind her own business. She appeared close to tears again, and sounded tired. 'Sorry. I was so fed up last week that I thought I would disappear for a week. I took an apartment in Tenerife and just read books in the sun.'

'Well, that's alright for you then! Mum had a fall and ended up having an operation. Rosie and I sat in the hospital half the night. She's so weak and old. It's heart-breaking.'

'I know,' soothed Judith. 'Where is she now? Shall I go and see her?'

'Yes, do. She's still in hospital but they want her to go back to Mill View as soon as possible, probably tomorrow or the day after. I think she should stay for a few more days but they won't take any notice of me. Try to persuade them, Ju, you're better at that sort of thing.'

157

'I'll try, but I don't really think I can fight the medical profession.'

'Are you going straight away? I'll meet you there.'

'Yes. See you there.'

She put the Christmas presents she had bought for them in her bag, and applied a squirt of duty free Chanel to make up for the lack of a post-travel shower. Even she could see that she had some making-up to do. It turned out to be the best thing she could have done. Her mother was sitting up and was chatting happily to Fiona and Rosie when she got there. She recognised everyone and had no idea that Judith had been away. Judith handed out her gifts and they were all delighted. Rosie especially said that the antique earrings were exactly what she would have chosen for herself.

I've managed to do something right, Judith thought to herself.

'Where did you get them, Auntie Ju?'

'From that new antique shop, you know Phoenix Antiques, just round the corner from me.'

'Oh yes, you're quite friendly with Chloe, aren't you?' said Fiona.

Judith tensed as she remembered her last conversation with Chloe. 'Yes,' she said, 'I am.'

Monday 29th December 2008

Judith got to the office before Helen especially to look in the filing cabinet. She noticed that the blue sticker on S.L. James's file had been replaced by a green one. Interesting. In her office she found a beautiful plant in a painted pot on her desk along with a Christmas card from Helen.

At lunch time Judith walked around the town and noticed Phoenix Antiques had a sign in the window telling customers that it would reopen on Saturday 3rd January.

Friday 1st January 2010

Oh my God, there's a man in my bed. How on earth did I allow that to happen? It's Ken, of course. We had a really good New Year's Eve. He came round with steaks and oven chips, loads of wine and champagne for midnight. Oh yes, and a box set of *Not Going Out*. I love the humour in that; it's so dry. I didn't intend for him to stay the night but it was so icy and cold outside that I couldn't have sent him home. He'll have to go soon. A night of booze and passion is lovely but I don't want him hanging around here all day. The worst thing is that he'll think we've moved to a 'new level in our relationship'. Actually I think he might have said that sometime during the evening. He's so nice; I really wish he didn't like me so much. I lie still, pretending to be asleep and plotting how I am going to get out of bed, to the bathroom then get showered and dressed without waking him up. I decide speed is of the essence so I look around for my jeans and a jumper so I can grab them along with undies and leg it to the bathroom. There's a towel in there already so I wait for the moment then slide out of bed and execute my plan. As I leave the room, he turns towards where I had been lying, his arm feeling around for me. I disappear before he realises I've gone.

I emerge from the bathroom to the smell of coffee and toast. Really, he is simply too good to be true. I offer him a towel to go and shower after breakfast and sit down at the table which is in the kitchen. His dark curly hair is all over the place and I can't help smiling at him.

'How's your head?' he asks in a whisper.

'Better than I dared hope,' I say, 'but I'll have another sleep when you've gone.'

He looks slightly disappointed at the notion of going so soon, but he probably remembers my dead husband at that point, and the fact that I haven't had sex for a long time or been close to another man for nearly two years. He is always gentlemanly and I know that he'll take the hint. We're both too tired for conversation so he dutifully goes for a shower and asks if I would prefer that he leave straight away.

'I think I would, Ken, if you don't mind. I have got a shocking hangover.'

'What about a walk in the cold fresh air before I go. It might help.'

'Yes, OK. I'd like that.'

We get dressed up in coats and scarves and walk along past the art college. I don't want to walk down the hill into town in case it's too slippery to walk back up.

Saturday 2nd January 2010

Maureen appears to be back with a vengeance. I look at the dark roots growing out into the blonde bob and wonder what's happened to her over the holiday. It would appear that she needs to assert her control and her position as supervisor. Really! Now that Kirsty has gone back to the checkouts, there is no need to supervise anyone in here. It makes me mad when she tells me to do things that are part of my job anyway.

'Judith, will you prepare the trolley for a change run, please,' she says at ten forty-five. We do the change run at eleven o'clock and it takes about three minutes to put the change into the trolley. It was going to be the next thing I did anyway.

'Judith, ring through to reception, please, and ask them to send Security down to do the change run with us.'

'Judith, don't forget to double-check every bundle of notes before you sign them. We don't want any more mistakes like before Christmas.'

Shut up, Witch-woman, you sound like my mother! 'Yes, OK Maureen, no problem.' She smirks. She can see that she's getting on my nerves.

'You can go on early lunch today, Judith.'

'Yes, OK Maureen, no problem.' She won't make me answer her back. I play a longer game than that, and the longer she keeps this up, the sooner it will be when the next mistake does occur.

Tuesday 5th January 2010

Maureen's monthly team briefing is the worst hour of the working week. There are only ever a handful of us in at any time, normally three now that it is so quiet in the store, but she insists on standing up and squeaking in a lower tone of voice to normal. She reads out the statement from Head Office about what a good Christmas it has been despite the difficult trading conditions generally, and how every member of staff is to be congratulated and thanked for their contribution. How nice!

She moves onto local issues; the duty manager rota for the month. She makes a point of handing it to me first, presumably so I can see when Ken is going to be working the late shift until store closing, then asks whether anyone has any particular requests for days off or shifts to be worked. Anita and I shake our heads. She asks whether anyone wants to book any holidays. Anita and I shake our heads, and Anita reminds her that she has requested all her remaining holiday days for the year.

'Yes, I know you have, Anita,' snaps Maureen. 'Judith? You'll have to use yours up by the end of March or lose them.'

'OK,' I say, 'I'll think about it and let you know.'

She handed me a couple of holiday forms. 'You'll need to complete one of these for each.'

'Yes, I know,' I say as I take them off her.

'Steady on, Maureen,' says Anita. 'Judith's worked practically every day these last two weeks so we could have time with our kids.'

'I know that, Anita,' she says in a softer voice. 'I was coming to that next, to say thank you to Judith for that. That's why I need to make sure she has a break soon.'

'Oh I see. Sorry Maureen. Good point you know, Judith, you should have a break soon.'

'I know. I will. It's just that, well, I was happier keeping busy over the holiday. You know…'

Anita gives Maureen a look that says 'back off and leave the poor widow alone', and Maureen does just that.

'Right, moving on then,' she says. *Oh my God! Isn't this briefing finished yet?* 'We are to be refurbished next month.'

'Oh, how exciting,' says Anita, 'I love getting new stuff. These desks are a bit past it. I snagged the arm of my new jumper on the corner of mine last week. It was a Christmas present, as well.'

I would dispute the wisdom of wearing a new Christmas jumper to work in the cash office, but I need to keep Anita on side so I look sympathetic and say, 'Oh no! What a shame.'

'My mam mended it. It's OK, but it could have been worse.'

'Yes, indeed,' I agree.

'Ladies, can we keep to the briefing, please.'

'Sorry Maureen,' we murmur in unison. That strikes me as funny and I glance at Anita who is smirking, clearly trying not to laugh.

'We haven't got a date yet but when we do, we'll have to pack everything up during the day and move it out overnight. The equipment people from head office will replace desks, chairs, shelves and filing cabinets, and then Security will get everything back in here for us ready for the next day.'

'We'll have to be very organised,' I say.

'Yes, Judith, thank you. I will be organising everything, and will issue a plan of what is to happen when. We'll need more staff in on that day so there may be some changes needed to the rotas. I'll let you know as soon as I have a date.'

She asks whether we have any questions or any other business. Anita and I shake our heads.

'Right, back to work then, please.'

It is such a pleasure to get back to work just to have her stop talking.

Wednesday 6th January 2010

Ken and I have been to see *Avatar*. After all the hype I was prepared to be disappointed but enjoyed it in a strange sort of way. I like the tall blue people. Ken hesitates before asking whether I want to go for a drink or a coffee. I realise that he wants me to invite him back.

'Yes, let's go to Cafe Bar Sierra,' I say and turn to walk in that direction.

'OK,' he says and catches me up to put his arm around my shoulder.

Oh, what the hell, it's so long since I've had a proper relationship, I might as well enjoy this one while it lasts. I know he has to be at work early tomorrow so he won't stay all night, or if he does, he'll be gone early. 'Actually, do you want to come back to mine instead? I have wine and coffee.'

'Only if you're sure, Judith,' he says with concern. 'I don't want to be pushy.'

'Yes, I'm sure. I'm certainly not ready to live with anyone yet, but staying over sometimes is nice.'

'No pressure, honestly. You only have to say.'

'Well, I do like my own space. I've just got used to it, I suppose.'

'I'll be gone early. I'm working tomorrow.'

He's got the message. We walk to the bus stop and huddle in the meagre shelter out of the wind. It's still too icy to walk up the hill and the bus stop at the top is just around the corner from where I live.

Inside my warm bijou half-house Ken opens some wine and I put the coffee on.

'You worked a lot of hours over Christmas. You must be ready for a break,' he says, keeping the conversation light.

'Yes. I'll need to go and visit my mum again soon, and my sister.' We move through to the small sitting room and I flick on some music while we settle down on the sofa to enjoy our drinks. 'Actually I think it's Maureen who needs the time off more than me.'

'Really? How come? She had quite a few days together over New Year. That's a luxury in the wonderful world of retail.'

'I know but she seems really stressed; more than when we were busy in December.'

'In what way?'

'Are you sure you want to talk about this?'

'Of course, if it's worrying you. What do you think it is?'

'Not sure, really. She's really snappy and bossy, and she was moaning about how much money she'd spent over Christmas. She doesn't go on about it, but I felt that she needed to say it. Oh, forget it; I'm not making much sense, even to myself.'

'No, you might be right to be concerned,' he seemed thoughtful, 'we'll need to keep an eye on her; to make sure she's OK, I mean.'

'Yes, I know what you mean.' I do know what he means, and it's exactly what he is supposed to mean. I feel quite mean, actually. I don't know why I'm continuing with this when everything is quite nice here. She just winds me up so much. We'll see.

Thursday 7th January 2010

I walk down to Bitts Park to feed the ducks with Joanna and Ricky. Now that the first rush of January sales is over with, she is back to her normal rota. We throw bread and the ducks seem more grateful, or greedy, than normal. Perhaps the slivers of ice on top of the pond hinder the food available. Anyway, it's soon gone and we walk into town to get some lunch. We choose a cafe that we haven't been to before, order soup, bread rolls and drinks and sit at a quiet table. She looks a bit uneasy.

'Judith…,' she hesitates.

'What is it?'

'Christmas Day – my mam – her shocking behaviour. I am so embarrassed.'

'Don't be. We've all had too much to drink in our time. It was Christmas Day after all.'

'I know, but when I thought about it later, I though she seemed quite rude. I didn't see it quite that way at the time, probably because I'd had a few as well.'

'We all had. I can hardly remember what she said. Forget it.'

'Really?'

'Really!'

'Thank you. I didn't want any bad feeling. You and Ricky get on so well. I just don't know what Mam's problem is.'

'Maybe it's what you said; that she's afraid of anyone getting close to the family after your friend disappeared.'

'Yes, I expect that's what it is. It's no excuse to be rude, though.'

'Maaam, can I have another Coke? Please, I mean.'

'No, but you can get some milk or juice.'

'I want Coke.'

'Ricky, Ricky, Ricky,' I say, 'Christmas is over for everybody, you know.'

He stops to work this one out. 'I know.'

'So...'

'So what?'

'So, none of us can have what we want all the time any more. Your mum, your nana and me, we all have to go back to work. You can't have Coke all the time. It's the same thing.'

'Is it, Mam?'

'Yes it is. Thank you Judith, for explaining that so clearly.'

'Pleasure. I will explain to Ricky any time why working is the same as not drinking Coke.' He realises that I'm teasing again and gives me that funny sideways look. Joanna is laughing before he and I are, and he decides he doesn't want anything else to drink after all.

'It's not all bad,' I continue my conversation with Joanna, 'Spanish starts again on Monday. Have you got your Monday evenings off sorted yet?'

'Oh yes, I mean *si. No puedo esperar para el lunes.*'

'*Yo también,*' I reply as Senor Rossi has taught us.

'What did you say?' Ricky asks.

'Well, your mum said, *No puedo esperar para el lunes,* and I said, *Yo también.* What did you think we said?'

He stares at me hard for a few seconds, clearly deciding how to reply. '*Uno, dos, tres.* Spanish,' he says eventually.

'Correct. Well done.'

Saturday 9th January 2010

Well, she's made my mind up for me today. She hasn't stopped from the moment we started work at seven-thirty. There was only she and I here until Sal came in at midday. The store is so quiet that the rotas have gone the other way and we are practically a skeleton staff. We were wheeling the trolley down the line of checkouts inserting the till drawers with their cash floats neatly arranged when she suddenly started on about Ken again.

'I hear he spent the night with you,' she said sort of conversationally, but with an edge to her voice. She didn't look at me when she said it; she just carried on unlocking the tills, slotting in the drawer, then snapping them shut again.

I didn't answer. I cannot believe the cheek of the woman. I'll be thirty-five this year; I think I can decide who I sleep with. This is going to take all my self-control.

'So?'

'So what?'

'So did he? Stay the night with you?'

'It's none of your business, Maureen. If you have a problem with my work in the cash office, please speak to me about it. If you have a problem with accommodating my requests on the rota, please speak to me about it. My personal life, however, is my own.'

'It's a possible security risk; a member of the cash office staff going out with one of the managers.'

'Well, rest assured, we are not planning the next great heist.'

'But there is potential, you must be able to see that.'

Thankfully the checkout supervisor arrived and confirmed times for the change run and the note-lift. She told Maureen how many operators she planned to have on so we can gauge the amount of change that will be needed at twelve-thirty. I waited patiently by the door to the cash office. I couldn't go on in as there must be at least two people in there at all times.

For the last hour and a half we have sat in silence, counting and balancing the takings in each till drawer from yesterday. I would like to say it was companionable, or at least professional silence but I can tell she hasn't finished her line of questioning yet. I know what it's all about: she fancies him. Tough.

'Can't you see that it is a potential risk?' she tries that one more time.

'Maureen, feel free to check my work at any stage during the day. Spot check me at any time at all. In fact, I think you should do that to all of us bearing in mind the missing money before Christmas.'

'Don't tell me how to do my job, Judith.'

'Just a suggestion. Anyway, while you are watching me, Ken is probably right under the beady eye of the lovely Mary Morris, so I really don't think you need to worry.'

'I'm not worried. I'm telling you.'

'Consider me told,' I agree as the buzzer sounds to indicate that Sal has arrived to start her shift. She is always early. 'Shall I go for lunch first?'

'No, I'll go first.' She and Sal swop places in the little chamber between the cash office and the back of checkouts and when the inner door is shut, she lets herself out into the store.

'What's up with Maureen?' asks Sal.

I am unsure as to how much to say. 'I think she's cross with me,' I venture.

'About Ken? She's furious. Don't worry about it. How are you getting on? Do you need me to count money or shall I get the trolley ready for the change run.'

'Trolley I should think. We're almost done here.'

'OK.'

Sal starts to pull bags of coins from the safe to count into the trolley and I slip a twenty pound note from one of Maureen's bundles. She has left her desk drawer open so I grab the Sellotape and stick the note to the underside of her desk like I did last time. It doesn't seem to take any time at all. By the time Sal turns back to me to say that the trolley is ready to go I am back at my normal desk counting the money from the last till. It balances as do all the bundles of notes, bags of coins, vouchers and credit card slips.

'What did you go to see on Wednesday?'

My life really is an open book. I feel the slight intrusion annoy me, as always, but need to build my powerbase in here. '*Avatar*. Have you seen it yet?'

'No, we're going tonight. I haven't done 3-D before at the pictures. We have at Disney World but not in little old Carlisle. Did you like it?'

'I did actually. The 3-D effects are really good. I won't tell you anything else about it in case it spoils it.'

'I think everyone's heard everything about it already. A good old-fashioned love story; that's what I'm expecting.'

'You won't be disappointed then.'

The buzzer sounds and this time Maureen and I change places in the little chamber so that I can go for my lunch break. She looks slightly more relaxed and I wonder whether she has had a swig of vodka to steady her nerves. She'll need it later. Ken's in the canteen and he comes over to join me. I don't notice that the other managers have a problem with it.

I don't need to recount the events of early afternoon. It is a repeat of the last two times that money was found to be missing. Suffice to say that after we are searched by Security, again, that Maureen is summoned to the personnel office for a meeting with Mary Morris. I finish my shift before she gets back and go into the store to do a bit of shopping. Ken stops to talk to me at the fish counter. I do my best worried look.

'Judith, I'm going to have to tell Mary Morris what you told me on Wednesday night.'

I know I'm naughty but I couldn't resist it. 'What? How much I like having sex again?'

He bursts out laughing as Maureen walks past us. She has seen us, and heard Ken laughing but she doesn't look at us or say anything. She stares straight ahead and her eyes look a little bloodshot.

'No, of course not; about her worrying about money.'

'Do you really have to? I'm sure it's just a mistake. The cash will probably turn up later.'

'The last one didn't. And you did the full search again, didn't you?'

'Oh yes.'

'Anyway, you mean 'another' mistake. Even if it is a mistake, it's not good enough.'

I sigh and nod. 'I suppose so. She likes to be seen as so efficient. This won't be doing her any good at all.'

'It's not for you to worry about her,' he said kindly, and if we hadn't been at work I think he would have kissed me on the forehead.

'Hmmm. I suppose, but we're all under the microscope. I don't like it. Still, better get on. I want to go into town before everywhere shuts.'

He spots Mary Morris and continues on to wherever he was going before he saw me.

Monday 11th January 2010

Maureen was unbearable yesterday. It's the stress of being in' trouble about the money but thankfully she is off today. Anita and I work happily together until Sal comes in, then the three of us work happily together until I finish my shift. It's Spanish tonight so I get away smartly to go home, change and eat ready to be there at six. I like routine; it's good to be starting the classes again.

Wednesday 13th January 2010
There are still a few shops having sales after Christmas. My God, they string these things out. I hate the shops when they are half full of last season's old tat squashed up together smelling vaguely musty and half full of new stuff for the coming spring. I have saved some money at last and am thinking about a short break somewhere a bit warmer than here. A Nile cruise would suit me, I think. You get taken everywhere and fed endlessly. I go into a couple of travel agents then call in at Cafe Bar Sierra for a coffee and to read the brochures. Joanna isn't there which, on reflection, is a good thing as I am supposed to be considering a holiday in Spain. Never mind, I'll go back to one of the travel agents and pick up a brochure for there as well.

I meander down the pedestrian shopping area and stop to look in the window of Marks and Spencer and who should I see in the reflection but Gaynor. I see her see me, and see that I have seen her, see her hesitate and half-turn to walk away then she turns back to approach me. I turn round to face her properly. I resist the urge to ask whether she still has a hangover from Christmas Day.

'Hello Gaynor,' I say evenly with a smile that deliberately doesn't reach my eyes. 'How are you?'

'Hello Judith. I'm fine thanks. You?'

'Yes, fine.' I play my normal waiting game. I maintain eye contact like I do with Maureen at work, not exactly staring but not flinching, until she says something.

'Um, about lunch time, on Christmas Day, you know?'

171

I nod.

'Well, I wanted to say that I'm really sorry for what I said.'

I wait a bit longer.

'Well, for my whole attitude really.'

I continue to wait.

'I don't know why I was so funny with you. I thought you were snooping that day when you were babysitting. Anyway, Joanna explained everything, and I am really sorry. I know you've been a good friend to her for the last few months. She was feeling really down when, well anyway, she was, and she's cheered up a lot.'

I think I've made her squirm enough. 'That's OK, Gaynor. No problem. I can't remember what you said anyway.'

'Neither can I really. Friends again?'

As Rosie used to say when she was about fourteen, keep your friends close and your enemies closer. I am still not sure which one Gaynor is. 'Yes, of course.'

She starts to ask me what I have been shopping for when suddenly there's a hysterical woman being held back by her companion.

'Let me go, Tommy,' she shrieks and tries to wriggle free of his hold. 'It's her! It's her and I'm going to tell her exactly what I think of her.'

'What's going on there?' asks Gaynor as she turns round to see what all the fuss is about. I turn in the same direction and find myself looking straight at Ivy Shipton. She used to be bigger than she is now; she seems to have shrunk to half her normal size. Tommy looks bigger by comparison although he always did look after himself. You'd see him jogging around the leafy suburbs of Hexham with his faithful Collie running along beside him.

'I've no idea,' I say and turn away.

'Judith Dillon! Do not turn away from me!' Ivy shrieks.

'Judith, do you know her?' asks Gaynor edging away.

'I used to. You go. I'm fine.'

'I'm not going anywhere. She might attack you, or something.'

'She won't. Let's both go.'

At that moment Ivy breaks away from Tommy and rushes right at me. I drop my bags and catch hold of her wrists. My God, she really does feel quite frail. I hold on firmly until Tommy comes over to regain possession. Gaynor picks up my bags and moves a few paces back. A few people have gathered around us, openly awaiting the next move. Ivy stares at me wide-eyed and red in the face.

'You ruined my boy's life,' she shouts. 'He's never worked again because of you. I've never worked again because of the way he is. You don't even care. You just walk away from it all like it never happened. I hate you and I will never forgive you.' Her voice quietens as the tears start to roll down her bony face, then she starts sobbing. Tommy is holding her more gently now and with a sad but unforgiving look at me, he turns and leads her away. He always was a man of few words. Some things never change.

'Thank God they've gone,' I say and take my bags back from Gaynor. 'Right, I'd better get going. I'm going out tonight.'

'What was all that about?'

'Nothing. Well, something that happened a long time ago. A sort of misunderstanding.'

'Well, they clearly blame you.'

'Yes, they do, but it wasn't my fault.'

'What wasn't?'

'The misunderstanding; the incident. It wasn't anything to do with me at all. They have always blamed me and it is quite unfair. However, I refuse to lose any sleep over it. They are simply wrong.'

'You must tell me what it is,' she insists.

'Gaynor, I must not!'

'You babysit for my grandson. I need to be able to trust you.'

'Joanna needs to be able to trust me. He's her son, which is surely more important.'

'It's important for me too. I'm waiting for an answer.'

Now she starts to play the waiting game. Really, we can't have two of us doing this. A few people are still staring and I dare say at least one of them works at Cost-Save. This could well be all around the store by tomorrow. I can't risk a row with Gaynor in the street, and I also don't want to risk her turning Joanna against me. I lower my voice so she has to lean in to hear what I am saying. That makes the crowds think we are friends and that there won't be any more action.

'It was a long time ago. It wasn't round here. It wasn't my fault. And I am not going to discuss it any more. Goodbye, Gaynor.'

My knees feel unsteady as I turn away, and I clutch my bags close to stop my hands from shaking. So much for a relaxing day looking for a holiday and maybe something new to wear in Egypt. Bugger Ivy Shipton. Bugger Gaynor being there. Bugger it all. Won't it ever go away?

Ken has suggested going out for a meal tonight instead of the cinema. I think we are comfortable enough with each other now to have a whole evening of conversation, easy though it is to sit and watch a film for most of the time. I get the feeling he wants to talk to me about something. I dread to think what it is so I catch the bus home and as I stand under the shower I try to think of what it might be so that I can be prepared. I decide it might be us going away for a holiday together, which would be a precursor to living together so I don't want that. He may want to ask me more about Maureen which would be OK but

I somehow don't think so. I can't think what else it might be so I'll have to play it by ear and think on my feet; not something I like but that's how it will have to be. I consider my mix of metaphors and decide they work together. He's even going to come to the bijou half-house to pick me up rather than meeting me in town so it's like a proper date. I dry my hair and wonder how long it will be before he hears about the incident in town today. He's bound to sometime soon but I hope not yet.

We walk into town. It's cold but not raining and the river looks lovely with the moon shimmering in its flow. Ken has booked a table at an Italian restaurant and the food, the wine and the service is just right. He's been chatting away and I had forgotten that I should be expecting a question of some sort.

'Judith, I wanted to ask you something. I'm a bit nervous, actually, but I'm getting a bit of pressure put on me.'

'That sounds ominous,' I say, trying to keep my voice light. 'I don't like surprises, you know.'

'I know but there's no roundabout way of asking you.'

'God, Ken, what on earth is it?'

'Well...'

'You're making me worried now. If you don't say, whatever it is, the answer is no.'

'You might say no anyway.'

'Any more of this and the answer *is* no.'

'OK. Will you come and have dinner with my family one evening. At home, I mean. They want to meet you.'

I am taken completely by surprise. I had definitely not anticipated that and definitely do not have a suitable answer prepared. 'Yes, of course, I'd love to,' I hear myself say. I am clearly going mad, but after the day I've had I suppose it's not surprising.

'That's brilliant. I'm so pleased. My mum and dad are really OK, you know. My sister will want to be there as well, probably with her boyfriend.' He is positively glowing and I realise that there is no way out of this one. All I can do is avoid agreeing to an actual date.

'How old is your sister?'

'She's twenty-three; a bit of an after-thought I reckon, or an accident. She's OK. I didn't like her much when I was a teenager and had to look after a toddler but since she went away to uni and came back we've got on really well.'

'What does she do?'

'She studied accountancy and has got a job with a local firm. She's doing well so far. Her boyfriend works there as well.'

'Nice.' My God, that's all I need, to mix with young accountants. Still, it'll only be for a couple of hours.

'She's the brainy one in the family. I'm a bit of a disappointment career-wise I think.'

'What ambitions have you got, Ken?'

'Nothing earth-shattering. Cost-Save ask me to apply for more senior jobs from time to time, but they involve moving away.'

'What's wrong with that? You could move away for a while, get some experience then move back.'

'I could do. I thought seriously about it every time the opportunity came along. I know people at the stores in the North East, and in Lancaster. I probably would have done it if I'd had anyone to move away with me. Just didn't fancy it on my own.'

I sense the conversation is moving in a direction I don't want to follow, but wine has been consumed and Ken is in full flow. I decide to let him keep talking; it gives me thinking time.

'I had a girlfriend for a lot of years. She wouldn't move with me. She's Carlisle born and bred and had no intention of going anywhere. She's married with kids now. I stayed because of her then when she fell for someone else, I moved back with my parents temporarily and never moved out again; frightened of commitment I suppose.'

'I understand that,' I say, fully understanding that.

'I know you do Judith. That's why I would never put any pressure on you to live with me or even go on holiday.'

'Thank you, Ken,' I say and really mean it. Suddenly a few hours at chez Wilson doesn't seem so onerous. I invite him back to stay the night.

Thursday 14th January 2010

Ken brings me a cup of tea before he leaves. It's not too early as he is working late this evening and doesn't need to go in until midday. Before going home to change he sits on the bed and says how about next Wednesday evening to meet his family. I can't think of a reason to say no. My phone beeps with a message. It's a cheap pay-as-you-go thing that only three people have the number of. It isn't Ken; I doubt that it is Gaynor so it must be Joanna. I read her message.

'Hi J. Can't make the park today. Unexpected other plans. J.'

With a rush I remember the events of yesterday afternoon and guess that Gaynor has warned her off me.

'Everything alright?' Ken asks.

'Yes. Change of plan for today. I think I'll stay in bed and read.'

He passes my book over to me before kissing me on the head and getting ready to go. I think I can hear him humming to himself as he puts his coat on. For God's sake, Ken, don't fall in love with me. It really is not a great plan.

Saturday 16th January 2010

I'm working the late shift today. It's still icy underfoot so I set off for work in good time then find I have arrived too early.

I go into the ladies' locker room to change my boots into comfortable shoes and to get the book I keep for occasions such as this. I plan to go and sit in the canteen for half an hour in peace. I am concealed from the door by a bank of lockers in the middle of the room, but I hear the door open. Two familiar voices are in the middle of a conversation.

'I can't believe what she said this morning, either. Fancy blaming Judith for her own silly mistakes.' Sal's voice.

'I know. Well, if it is a silly mistake,' Anita's voice replies.

'What do you mean?'

'Well the first mistake was just that. She'd dropped a note under her desk and not seen it. The last two were never found.'

'Anita, it's not like you to talk like that.'

I am in a quandary now. Do I reveal myself, albeit a bit late, or keep quiet and hope they never know I'm here? I hear the door open again and their voices disappear out into the corridor. Well, well, well! She's openly blaming me now. That's a turn up for the books. I didn't think she was that bright. I wait for a couple of minutes to give them time to get away then go to the canteen for a coffee. When I go to start my shift I give Maureen my best smile and ask if there is anything in particular she would like me to do.

'Just count money, please,' she says, and doesn't smile back.

Monday 18th January 2010

Maureen has been off today but I saw her come into the store at ten o'clock. She met the shop steward outside and they had a brief conversation before going to the offices upstairs. I wonder what that can be about. She won't like it, of course, but they can't prove anything against her because she hasn't actually done anything wrong. I don't know how long they keep her in the Personnel office.

At Spanish class tonight Joanna sits with me as usual but I think she is a bit quiet. I hesitate before mentioning it, but at coffee break I ask if she's OK. She gives me a forced smile and says yes. I don't want to enquire too closely in case Gaynor hasn't said anything about last Wednesday. I will be very surprised if I find she hasn't but you never know.

'Did you have a nice day off last Thursday?' I ask.

'Yes. Actually it was Ricky that was asked out but I had to accompany him. We got taken to the coast. It was freezing but good fun. Nice to be picked up and dropped off in a warm car for a change.'

She obviously doesn't want to discuss it anymore and looks relieved when Senor Rossi comes to bring us back into the classroom. We are doing transport tonight so she is able to tell us all in Spanish that she went to the coast with her son in a car. I say that I was taken home in a taxi last Wednesday after a meal in town. We are all making such good progress.

At nine o'clock she says goodbye (*ciao* actually) and disappears without any further conversation. I'll just have to play a waiting game on this. I can do that. It's my strong point.

Wednesday 20th January 2010

Dinner at Ken's tonight. Why did I agree to this? I text him early in the day to say that I'm going to order a taxi to bring me home, and to ask him what time he thinks would be right. I hope he picks up on the fact that it is to bring *me* home, and not *us*.

He texts back, 'I can drive u back.'

I text him back, 'No, it's fine. Just say what time.'

There is a delay before I get my answer. I expect he is consulting with family. I hope he isn't going to be grumpy about it.

'10. OK?'

'OK. Thanks.' I refuse to do text-y stuff like 'thnx' or

'cul8er'. I know it's quicker to do 'u' like Ken just did but really, for the sake of two more letters? I go out for a walk, just for something to do. No point in dwelling on the Ivy Shipton thing. I thought some people were giving me funny looks at work yesterday but that could be for several reasons. Maureen is obviously accusing me of setting her up, I am going out with one of the managers, I was nearly in a fight in town last week, I am allegedly a widow; they can take their pick if they want a gossip. Oh yes, it might be because I took a BMW for a test drive last Thursday afternoon. Someone's bound to know about that, after all, there is nothing I can do in Carlisle that is private. I only did it for something to do. I was a bit worried once I was there that they might have my name on a database and refuse to let me take a car out. If I'd thought of that before I would have gone to the Mercedes garage instead. That's a bit of a trek by public transport from here; maybe an Alpha which is next door to the BMW garage. It doesn't matter now. I test drove a 1 Series; Sports version, of course. It was lovely. I will have money again one day; I have to.

At six-thirty Ken comes to pick me up. I considered having a drink for Dutch courage before he arrived but I have learned over the last few months that it is better to stay sober and keep my wits about me. I dare say there will be wine with dinner. I ate some toast so I don't need to drink on an empty stomach, not that I'll have much. I'll make up for it when I get back here on my own. I haven't arranged to meet Joanna tomorrow so I'll probably stay in bed for half the day anyway.

Ken drives through town and out towards his parents' house off London Road. He pulls into a lay-by and I think he is going to kiss me. It's like being a teenager. He doesn't, though.

'Judith,' he says, 'I wanted to drive you home later to talk about Maureen, off the record, you know.'

'About her accusing me of setting her up?'

'How did you know that? Has she said something to you?'

'No. I overheard Anita and Sal talking about it in the locker room. They didn't know I was there, and I was too embarrassed and upset to tell them. I just heard a snatch of their conversation then I had to go and work with Maureen for an hour before her shift finished. I should have told you, Ken, but I was so upset. I didn't know what to do.'

'You should have told me, silly.' He puts his arm around my shoulders.

'I didn't want to get her into any more trouble. I saw her outside with the shop steward on Monday and guessed what was going on.'

'Yes, well, that was inevitable after the last episode. There was no excuse then; it wasn't busy and there were no relief staff in. It was just the experienced people.'

'What's going to happen to her?'

'Well, nothing's been proved so nothing except that she's being watched. She's a bundle of nerves, and blaming you is just making everyone think worse of her.'

I do my best shocked look. 'Everyone? Who's everyone?'

'Well, Mary M and the personnel manager.'

'Oh my God!'

'No, it's OK. Nobody at all is blaming you. Nobody; well, except Maureen herself. I promise you that, Judith. I just thought you should know about it, and know that *nobody* believes anything she's saying.'

'Oh my God,' I say again a bit more faintly. 'Poor Maureen.'

'Poor Maureen, nothing,' Ken says firmly. 'Come on, let's go and meet my family. I could smell dinner cooking before I left.'

Friday 22nd January 2010

Today is the first day that Maureen and I have been alone together in the cash office for ages; certainly the first time since I heard about the outrageous allegations she has been making. I think it's time for a little confrontation.

'Maureen, can I have a word about something?'

'I'd rather not right now. I'm busy.'

'Well, we're nearly done and Sal will be here soon. I wanted to ask you something in private.'

She avoids my eyes. 'Well? What is it?'

'I have heard a little rumour that you are blaming me for the missing money.'

'Not exactly.'

'I've told you before; if you have a problem with my work I want you to tell me. I like to do a good job. Actually I *need* to do a good job. I thought I was doing a good job in here.'

'Your work is fine, Judith, you know that.'

'What is it then? How is the missing money my fault if my work is OK?'

'I don't know,' she says, and then suddenly finds some of her old fighting spirit, 'but be sure that I *will* find out.'

Oh, this is more like it. I prefer a fight to the sulks. There is nothing more annoying than someone having a nervous breakdown before your eyes. Bring it on!

The buzzer cuts through our moment of silence and Maureen jumps a mile. My, my, we are on edge, aren't we? I get up to let Sal in but Maureen gets to the door release button before me.

'I'll do it. You finish your work.'

Monday 25th January 2010

The store really is very quiet. Maureen and I work silently. She is still edgy but there have been no more mistakes, and she has taken my advice and started spot-checking everyone's work. I ask whether I should do hers, just so that we have covered everything. The look she gives me!

'No thanks, Judith,' she says, 'I have already asked Anita to check mine.'

'She's not in today,' I pick away.

'Oh, I forgot about that. Sal can do it then.'

'That's a good idea,' I say, mainly because she dislikes it as much when I agree with her as when she perceives criticism. 'Better really, because she hasn't been here all morning.' It's all for nothing, of course. I'm not going to do anything else. I know when to stop, and I am if not happy, at least fairly content with my lot at the moment. Now that I have firmly shifted the power-base in here, we can all find our rightful places.

Joanna seems a bit brighter at Spanish tonight. We move onto deeper subjects than eating, travelling and public holidays and find ourselves talking about the recession. To be fair, we don't know a lot about it in English, but we discuss the jobs situation in Cumbria and the price of houses. Senor Rossi tells us about the price of houses in Spain, and how it might be a good time to buy as a lot of English people are selling up. I look interested but know the state of my bank balance. When my mother dies I will inherit half her house and savings, if there are any left after Mill View has taken their fees. I know I should think about doing something more lucrative than working in the cash office, but don't seem to have the motivation. Contentment is a strange feeling, and not one I am used to.

At tea break Joanna asks me, in Spanish, whether I am still thinking about buying somewhere in Spain. I say no, but am thinking about buying somewhere in Carlisle. I say it because it seems an easier story to maintain but actually feel as though

I mean it. What on earth is happening to me?

Alison asks whether anyone is going for a drink after the class, and Joanna says no because she is being picked up straight afterwards. I look at her but she doesn't offer any further explanation. A few people say yes, and I do too.

Friday 29th January 2010

Maureen tells us that our refurbishment will take place on Tuesday night next week. Tuesday is a quiet day and she has arranged for two of the part time staff to come in earlier to help with packing files and paperwork, and moving everything that we can do without in the afternoon and evening to a storeroom. One of the security staff will come in during the evening shift to unscrew table legs and remove chairs, those being the last things to go. The new furniture and shelves will be put up overnight and someone will be in all night to move our things back in as the furniture men finish. She has it all organised and I simply offer my help if any should be required.

'Thank you, Judith,' she says, 'but I think I have covered everything.'

'OK,' I nod, 'but just say if you change your mind.'

Thursday 1ˢᵗ January 2009

Judith drove up to Mill View after lunch. Her mother had been moved back in as the hospitals always try to empty beds before the New Year's Eve onslaught. Fiona and Rosie had gone for lunch but Judith felt she couldn't bear it. It was a nice enough afternoon for them all to have a walk around the grounds as long as they wrapped up warmly. There would be afternoon tea and biscuits then she could leave with a clear conscience. She braced herself for the ordeal that was getting through the security doors.

'Hi Judith. Tina wants to see you before you go through.' It was one of the staff; one who knew everybody's business and Judith smiled through gritted teeth as she thanked him.

'Come in Judith,' said Tina, 'I need to make you aware of something.'

Judith had the feeling that she had been summoned to an interview with her head teacher. She sat down and waited for the telling-off.

'If you are to be a named person on your mother's contact list, and especially the first next of kin, we need to be kept informed of your whereabouts and availability,' she launched straight in.

'Tina, I merely took off for a week's holiday,' she said trying to keep her voice light and even.

'Yes, so I believe. Your mother had a nasty fall. It could have been a lot worse. I have decided that I am going to change our records and have Fiona as the first point of contact for us.'

Bloody cheek, Judith thought, but took time to consider

185

before answering. She decided to be nice. 'I think you're right actually, Tina. Please do so.' Ha! Now it would seem as though she was ordering Tina to do it.

'I already have. I just wanted you to know.'

'Oh, OK, thank you. I'll go and see my mother now, if you don't mind.'

'No, of course I don't mind. This is her home. Please feel free to see her whenever you both wish.'

'Thank you,' Judith said again, wondering why she still felt that she was in trouble and not completely in control of the situation.

'They're all in the lounge.'

'Thank you.' *God, I must stop thanking that woman.*

Monday 5th January 2009

Judith and Helen were back at work, their first day working together since Judith's holiday. They exchanged pleasantries about holidays and thanked each other for the gifts. Judith asked Helen to make some coffee before they started work on the business of the forthcoming week.

'I've put the advert in the paper to try to drum up more clients,' Helen said, 'I did the same one that you did before Christmas.'

'Yes, good. I'll ring round the people I met at Chloe's Christmas drinks as well. And there's a new course for business start-ups at the Enterprise Centre next week; I'll see if I can go and give a talk to them.'

'Good idea. Shall I make up a leaflet for you to hand out?'

God, this woman thinks of everything, thought Judith, *but then again I suppose I have left her with nothing to do for a few days.* 'Yes please, that would be really useful. I must see who I should have rung the week I went away; some of them are bound to be upset.'

'Some rang here and I dealt with them so you don't need

to.' Helen went through the list and ticked the ones Judith didn't need to contact. Judith noticed that James's was one of them. She took the list from her, along with the files that needed to be worked on during the week and queries that needed her attention. There was nothing of any note to worry about.

'That's great, thanks Helen. You are truly efficient.'

Helen smiled. 'I'm glad you think so,' she said and left to draft some leaflets for Judith's talk.

Judith worked on two clients' accounts during the morning and made some placatory phone calls. She waited until Helen had gone out for lunch before looking at the ones she said she had already dealt with. She watched out of the window until Helen had walked around the corner to the town centre then went through to the filing cabinet. Along with James's, another one of the people ticked had a green sticker and the last one had a red one. She called Stuart James first.

'Hello Stuart. It's Judith Dillon here. I owe you an apology for not calling you the week before Christmas.'

'No problem in the end,' he said, 'your assistant helped me out with a query.'

'OK good. Nothing I need to get involved in?'

'No, she was fine. Very knowledgeable, actually. You've got a good one there.'

'Yes, she is a treasure. Well, as long as you're OK now.'

'Fine, thanks. See you soon.'

So, thought Judith, *knowledgeable about accounts is she? And there was me thinking I'd employed her for her secretarial skills.* She dialled the next number on her list. It was the other green-sticker company which was a bed and breakfast business just outside of town.

'Bluebells B and B,' came Sally Fisher's sing-song voice down the phone. Judith had known Sally for many years.

'Sally, it's Judith. How are you? I owe you an apology for not getting back to you before Christmas.'

'It's fine, Ju, it would have waited. I just wanted some advice about something.'

'It must have been more than that if you rang to chase me up; or were you bored and wanted someone to talk to?'

Judith was joking. She knew that Sally had three daughters who had all had babies in the last couple of years and who all took advantage of her. 'You are joking! When do I have time to get bored? Anyway I didn't chase you up; your assistant phoned to see whether she could help.'

'And could she?'

'Yes, thanks. All sorted.'

'Excellent. I'll let you get on, then. How many are you looking after today?'

'Just one this morning, but expecting another to be dropped off at any minute. Bye.'

So, Helen had rung her; even more interesting. She called the last one, the one with the red sticker. When Judith finally got to speak to the Managing Director, he didn't know anything about a phone call before Christmas. Very strange.

Thursday 8th January 2009

Judith hated supermarket shopping, and especially on a Thursday evening. Usually she did it earlier in the week or earlier in the day but it seemed sensible to call in on her way back from Mill View. She was deciding whether to buy a steak or stick with chicken when a familiar face pointed to a marbled sirloin steak.

'We had that last weekend. It was delicious.'

'Hello Lennie,' said Judith, then deciding to get straight to the point, 'I am so sorry to have lost you as a client.'

'What do you mean? It was your idea.'

'What was?'

'To focus on your larger clients and subcontract the small-fry like me to your assistant.'

'Subcontract? Small-fry? What do you mean? The small businesses of Hexham have been my preferred market ever since I set up. I know what you're about and how you work.'

'Well, I thought it was strange but Helen said it was your idea, and that you'd still be there to help her if she needed your background knowledge and your expertise, of course.'

Judith stared at him.

Lennie's wife Sue joined them. 'What have you said to Judith?' she asked him.

'He has just explained a lot. Thanks Lennie. Come back to me any time. Helen won't be working for me after tomorrow.'

'It's not often you get to wrong-foot Little Miss Perfect,' he said to Sue as they watched Judith march purposefully towards the checkouts. 'I wouldn't want to be in Helen's shoes tomorrow morning, that's for sure. Quite like to be a fly on the wall though.'

'Should we take the accounts back to Judith, do you think?'

'Helen is so much cheaper. I feel mean, but let's see how we get on with her for a while. Judith is obviously doing well. That flat she bought last year is stunning, and have you seen her new car? I don't think she needs little old us.'

Judith drove straight to her office and looked up the number of Sparkles Window Cleaners.

'Mr. Sparks,' she said, 'I will get straight to the point, if you don't mind.' She knew him of old and knew that it may take a long time to get to the point.

'How's that new assistant coming along? I hear she's going to be doing our books from now on.'

'Not if I can help it. Do you mind me asking how she approached you?'

The story more or less matched Lennie's version.

'It is good of you to reduce the prices by such a lot. I don't think I could have afforded to keep paying you the old rate. Times are hard, you know. People have started washing their own windows again – or not. You should see the state of some of them. I feel like putting up a sign saying I'm not responsible in case anyone thinks I left them like that.'

Here we go, thought Judith, and cut into his flow. 'I know how you feel. Anyway, Helen won't be working for me any more so please come back to me any time you wish. You know where I am.'

'Times hard for you as well, eh?'

She knew he wouldn't understand what she was saying. Hints were lost on him. 'Yes,' she sighed. 'Got to go.'

By eight-thirty Judith had phoned the six businesses that were marked with green and blue stickers. She knew several of them quite well, but still felt a little desperate asking whether Helen had contacted them with a view to taking them over. She had contacted three of them and two were very interested in the proposal to move to a second tier accountant for a reduced price. She collated all her information ready to confront Helen in the morning and suddenly felt overwhelmingly tired. She couldn't go yet; she needed to go through the filing cabinet to see which files were missing. She was good at thorough and methodical work and soon identified two others by comparing paper files with computer records. Having completed her evidence she went home but couldn't face cooking the steak she had bought hours earlier.

Friday 9th January 2009

Judith sat at the reception desk with her head in her hands. *Deja-fucking-vu*, she thought. *Here we go again*. She cursed herself for being taken in by Helen so readily and, on impulse, she rang one of the companies that Helen had given as a reference. The number was unobtainable so she Googled it. No matches. She didn't bother with the second reference and put it down to experience.

She called Phoenix Antiques. Louise answered.

'Chloe's out buying,' she said, 'and I've got a customer.'

She called the local paper and asked them to run the same advertisement as last time. She called the temping agency and they said she would have to pay upfront for a temp for the next two weeks. She looked at the neat and tidy office and decided that she could cope with it herself this time without getting into such a muddle. She was up-to-date with all the work and even had time to spend the afternoon and weekend looking at her own accounts. That was the only area that she hadn't allowed Helen to deal with and she sighed with relief at that one small mercy. At least she didn't know anything about her private affairs.

Sunday 11th January 2009

Sunday afternoon found Judith sitting at the reception desk again with her head in her hands again. Really, for such a skilled accountant she had let herself become so over-stretched. Even with Henry Lloyd's cheque to pay off her tax bill she was struggling. She knew she had overpaid but didn't want the overpayment back although it would be handy, as she would need it for the next demand. The next one would be considerably less; that was one consolation. The problem was that the income from her business was not sufficient to cover all of her outgoings. Her mortgage was huge and the new car took nearly £300 a month on repayments. It was time for drastic measures. The car was too good to let go, but hardly anyone ever saw the flat. She considered selling it; it was in a beautiful building with stunning views across open countryside so it was unlikely to have lost value. If anything, she would make a bit of cash. She couldn't wait for her mother's house to be sold as all the legal stuff was taking forever. The estate agent would have to be her first call in the morning.

Monday 12ᵗʰ January 2009
Chloe felt very pleased with herself. She had sold a lot of her most recent stock and had arranged to go back to the dealer later in the afternoon to choose some more. She treated herself to lunch in Mrs. Peach's Cafe. She loved going there; the smell of Indian incense as you walked through the shop to get to the cafe was intoxicating and hinted at being illegal. She bought some sticks to take home and browsed the silk scarves on her way to an aromatic concoction of beans and spices on couscous. She was feeling better after a Christmas break and sales still being brisk. A lot of the worries of setting up a shop were subsiding and she had started to feel part of the town again. She was looking at the glass mobile hanging from the window and catching the light when she saw Judith walking through the shop. Her hands tensed slightly on her glass of water and she took a sip. Judith walked straight into the cafe and left Chloe no choice.

'Join me, Judith? What are you up to today?'

'Thanks. Decided to sell my flat so I've been round to the estate agent.'

'Selling? I thought you liked where you live.'

'It's lovely, but it's too big for me, and old. I fancy one of the small ones down by the river, you know, being converted from the old warehouse.'

'I've looked at the plans of those. They look gorgeous.'

'Yes.' A pause. 'Are you thinking of moving into town, then?'

Damn it, thought Chloe, *I always give too much away*. 'Only thinking about it. I can't resist looking at show homes, that's really what it's about.'

'The show home's open today. I'm going to pop down later.'

'You could walk to work from there. That's another good point.'

Judith laughed. 'Ah, now that's a bad point for me. I'd have less need to drive my beautiful car.'

Chloe joined in the laughter. Judith was alright when there were other people around, she thought, so why did she spook her out when she was alone with her? Strange. Anyway, better quit while she was winning. 'Right I need to get off. More stock to buy before the day's out.'

Judith stayed in the cafe for another half hour. She didn't notice the light catching the glass mobile. She was too preoccupied with her financial situation. Talking to Chloe had clarified one thing; she could easily justify wanting to sell her flat. Maybe it wouldn't look so desperate after all, especially if she could say that she had made a bit of money on it.

Back in the office there was a message from Henry Lloyd's solicitor. Judith called him straight back.

'It's in reference to the letter I sent you before Christmas,' he said, 'It was posted on the 19th actually.'

'I haven't seen a letter,' she said, 'but I know all about Henry's accounts. What do you need to know? I sent everything over, didn't I?'

'Yes you did. It's a strange one, actually. He made a payment to HMRC for no apparent reason. It doesn't show up in the accounts anywhere.'

Judith's left hand started shaking and her heart and her mind racing.

'Ms Dillon?'

'Sorry, yes, trying to think. No, I don't know anything about it. Sorry.'

'He didn't usually make any financial transactions without consulting you. Are you sure you don't remember anything?'

'I would have remembered if he owed any tax. He was meticulous about not owing any money to anyone.'

'Indeed. Well, if you remember anything will you let me know? It will save a lot of time and expense for the family if we can get it sorted out.'

She sat for a few minutes while her heart rate slowed to normal. The letter was sent on 19th so she would have been away when it arrived. Helen would have opened it. She knew what was in the filing cabinet, so started her search in the drawers of what had been Helen's desk. It only took a few minutes to find, and it was with a letter from HMRC regarding her personal account. Bugger! Helen must have made some connection otherwise she wouldn't have hidden them away together. Bugger!

Wednesday 14th January 2009

Most of Hexham closed on a Wednesday which usually meant that Judith's practice was busy with people who could leave their businesses and come for appointments. It was strangely quiet so Judith called the estate agent to bring forward the time to value her flat. It was a crispy, bright afternoon so should make him feel inclined to up the price. Shaws Lane had several beautiful old properties that had been converted to luxury flats, and Judith's building was thought to be the most prestigious, it having been a country house. It had extensive shared grounds, views over open countryside and even a tennis court. She loved the modern kitchen-dining room with white units and solid oak worktops, the central island with the gas hob, then Georgian sash windows keeping it classy and firmly of the period. She went home to tidy up a bit more; first impressions counted for a lot with these people.

David Clements arrived; senior partner of the business. That was a good sign. He worked quickly and quietly, measuring and comparing and making verbal notes on his voice recorder.

'You've maintained it really well since you bought it,' he said eventually. 'Even in this financial climate, I think we can ask £275,000.'

She stared at him. He seemed to be pleased with that.

'I paid £300,000 for it eighteen months ago. It can't have gone down that much.'

'I'm afraid it has. The good news is that anything else you look at will have been reduced accordingly. So, shall I put it on the market straight away?'

'Can't we try for £300,000 first, and accept an offer?'

'I wouldn't advise it. You'll probably have to accept an offer anyway.'

'Two-eighty then, please. I insist. Not lower.'

After he had gone, Judith broke her own rule of not drinking before seven. A loss of £25,000 in eighteen months! That equated to nearly £1,500 a month in value, and she paid over £2,000 a month in mortgage. No wonder she didn't have any money. The level in the wine bottle went down by another few inches as she came to terms with the concept of her being left with negative equity. Given that she sold it for £275,000, she would still owe £2,500, then there would be legal fees and commission to old Clements. She picked up the phone to call another estate agent and realised it was too late. Tomorrow she would get a more realistic valuation. She reached for her wine glass, missed it, and cursed as red wine dripped from the table onto the cream carpet. Bugger! And a carpet cleaning bill as well. She would have to get the balance of Henry's money back from the tax man after all.

With two more appointments made for estate agents to view her flat, Judith left the office in need of sleep. She walked slowly down to the car park and bumped into Chloe walking down to the station.

She tried again. 'Do you want a lift home? I'm having an early finish.'

'No thanks. I'll get the train.'

'Are you sure?'

'Judith, I hope you don't mind if I say this, but I would like our relationship to remain professional and not personal. Please don't offer me a lift any more. I don't want a lift, really.'

Judith's head was pounding as she watched Chloe march off down the lane. She felt rejected and miserable as well as worried about money, her dwindling clientele, lack of secretary, ill mother, dodgy cheque payment, her obvious bad judgement of character, bad judgement in buying property and generally everything. She drove home and opened another bottle of red before her self-imposed watershed. She sat in her favourite spot in the house; a sort of alcove on the first floor with nothing in it but a small table and a deep, comfortable armchair facing a window that reached from floor to ceiling and looked out over fields to hills beyond. There was no view this evening, of course, as it was dark, but she knew what it looked like and she knew she would miss it.

Friday 16th January 2009
At lunch time Judith took two ham sandwiches into Phoenix Antiques. Chloe looked a bit surprised.

'Point taken,' said Judith, 'let's carry on as we were. My turn to bring lunch I think, and time I had a good look at your new stock.'

She walked straight through to Chloe's office and started to unwrap the sandwiches. The front door opened, but instead of someone coming in, Chloe went out.

'I told her last night I wanted to keep everything professional and here she is bringing sandwiches. What do you think is going on?' Chloe spoke quietly into her mobile phone.

'No idea,' said Louise, appearing from the direction of the town centre, 'but I'm here now so go and chat about the shop and *nothing else*. Right?'

'Right.'

'Everything OK?' asked Judith when they came back in.

'Yes, I just wanted to catch someone outside. Too late.'

They ate and Judith chatted, then she asked to see all the new stock, then she studied all the paintings.

'You're going for these American artists, then? I've seen John Axton before.'

Chloe glanced at her watch, looked over to Louise, and raised her eyes to the ceiling. How much longer was Judith going to stay? In some ways it was handy having someone in the shop browsing; it seemed to draw more people in. It was noticeable, though, that whereas others came in and bought and left, she simply browsed with no apparent intent to buy. 'Yes, I bought a few at Newcastle, and more have come up since. It must be a trend.'

Eventually Judith glanced at the carriage clock tastefully displayed in near the window. 'My goodness, is that the time. Lovely stuff Chloe, I'll come back and make my final choice in a couple of days.'

'Great! See you then,' said Chloe.

'What do you think that was all about?' asked Chloe as soon as the door closed behind Judith.

'Not sure, but she looks like a woman under pressure. Did you hear that she sacked her latest assistant?'

'No, why?'

'Not sure, but it was sudden.'

'Last I heard she was really pleased with her.'

'I've told you; she's a funny one. Keep it professional and everything will be just fine.'

Saturday 17th January 2009

Judith's two estate agents visited within two hours of each other and confirmed what Mr. Clements had said. One even suggested a lesser valuation. She took her shining car out of the garage and drove to the Northumbrian coast for a long walk along the sand

Monday 19th January 2009

Chloe considered going to the bakery for a sandwich. She would only need to close the shop for a couple of minutes. She hung the sign on the door and was about to leave when she saw Judith approaching with sandwiches.

Chloe's stomach lurched. She quickly turned the key to lock the door, switched off the main lights and hid in the store room. She could see out of the dark room through the keyhole and watched as Judith stood for a while peering in. She moved a few steps away then suddenly turned back and looked in again. *She knows I'm here*, thought Chloe. *How long is she going to stand there? I'll be trapped in here all day.* She noticed that her hands were shaking.

Her telephone rang and she listened as the answering machine cut in. Judith's voice floated from the office to the store room, making Chloe jump.

'Hi there. I called round with sandwiches but you seem to be out. See you in a few days' time.'

Chloe thought it was probably a trick, and that Judith was standing outside waiting to spring out and say *Ah ha – I knew you were hiding!* She stayed where she was for another twenty minutes. She could have done some sorting out while she was there, but didn't. She needed to keep an eye on the door to make sure Judith didn't come back. The door handle moved. Chloe felt paralysed as she peered through, and then nearly sobbed with relief when she saw the elderly couple who had returned to pick up an item they had paid for earlier.

Tuesday 20ᵗʰ January 2009

Chloe sat in her doctor's consulting room. She was shaking again, and had been crying.

'And I haven't been sleeping well because of it all,' she continued. 'I felt stronger after a break at Christmas but it's all come back worse than before.'

The doctor wrote a prescription. 'These are very mild,' she said, 'but don't exceed the dose. If they're not working for you, come straight back.'

'Am I going mad? She's just a local business woman, after all. I hardly know her really.'

'Not mad, but it is making you anxious. You've discussed the boundaries you want to keep with the relationship so make sure you stay within them. These tablets will help you to keep it all in perspective, then you'll feel better able to deal with it yourself.'

Dr. Ellis reflected on the consultation after surgery with her colleague. She was worried because it was strangely reminiscent of a conversation she had had with Alison Hedges the year before. Shortly afterwards Alison had moved away from Hexham.

'Where do we stand ethically on this one?' she asked the senior partner.

'Impossible situation,' he replied, 'we can't break anyone's confidence. And anyway, what would you say to Judith Dillon? You're frightening people; stop it. She doesn't appear to harm anyone.'

'Not physically, no, but we can't let her go round frightening people.'

'There is nothing we can do. Look after your patient, that's the best that you can do.'

She didn't say it, but she thought she might do some research into similar cases. Maybe there was something she could do.

Friday 23rd January 2009

Chloe hated the dark evenings walking down to the station. The sooner she moved into town the better. She set the burglar alarm and switched off the lights in the shop. Before setting off she had a surreptitious look up and down the road. No Judith. Time to go now. She would be a bit early for the train today but she needed to vary her time of leaving.

What am I doing? she thought, *I need to keep the shop open regular hours. I can't afford to harm the business. Never mind, I have to do it for now anyway.* She took a deep breath, locked the front door and ran across the road and into the lane that led down past the car park to the station.

Judith appeared as if from nowhere and fell into walking beside her.

'Good day today?'

'Yes, look, Judith. I know what I said the other day, but please leave me alone. Completely I mean. No more lunches.

No more browsing. Nothing. Please, just leave me alone.' Her voice had been getting louder with every word and a couple turned around.

'Everything alright, ladies?' said the young man.

'Yes, fine. Thank you,' said Chloe.

'Mind your own business,' snapped Judith at the same time.

Chloe took another deep breath as instructed by Dr. Ellis and thanked her silently for the tablets that at least stopped her shaking and crying. She smiled at the couple again. 'Thanks.'

Wednesday 28th January 2009

Judith despaired at the standard of applications for the post of her secretary. She chucked them into the tray to look at again later. Maybe they would improve if she ate something. She had intended to make sandwiches to bring to work every day to save money but hadn't managed it for more than two days. She walked across to the bakery and stood patiently in line. The person getting served was three ahead of her and wearing a thick woollen hat and scarf. As she turned round she saw it was Chloe. Surely she would at least say hello. Judith opened her mouth to speak and tried to catch her eye. Chloe's eyes looked blank, almost as though she didn't recognise her. She walked past without speaking.

CHAPTER 11

Carlisle, February 2010

Monday 1ˢᵗ February 2010
At Spanish tonight Joanna seems to be back to her normal self. That's good. Whoever this person is with the car, I think they have been having a bad effect on her. We all go for a drink afterwards then she and I stop for a chat before going our separate ways.

'Park on Thursday?' she asks, 'Or are you bored to tears with that routine?'

'Not bored at all. It's lovely to see Ricky looking after the ducks that nobody else likes, well according to him, anyway.'

'Yes, and he'll be going to school full time soon so we won't have our Thursdays off together. I'll be able to get on with finishing my OU course instead, so I suppose that's the silver lining.'

'How long have you been doing it?'

'I started a marketing degree after a gap year, at nineteen, but got pregnant in the final year so came home. I'm really just finishing it.'

I privately think that I wouldn't have given up just for that. Loads of people carry on studying when they're pregnant; even when I was at uni ten years earlier. It was a nuisance actually; we all had to work round them. That just carries on into the workplace, though. Time off for any minor ailment the little darlings fall prey to.

'Oh, sorry, what did you say? I was miles away.'

'I said I was really ill. My blood pressure was dangerously low. They said I almost died and had to have complete bed rest.'

'Oh my God! Poor you.' I take back all that I thought just

now. 'Anyway our buses will be here in a minute; better go.' In truth I am starting to freeze to the spot. We say goodnight in Spanish and walk briskly in opposite directions.

Tuesday 2nd February 2010
Maureen's clear-out operation works with military precision; well, better than that really. She had tentatively asked whether I would stay on a bit later if we were falling behind with the packing and moving but it is all ahead of schedule when my shift ends at five o'clock. I put the cash I have counted and balanced into the safe and move the last few bits of my stationery items into a cardboard box with my name on it. Maureen is staying to the end, of course, and her stuff will be the last to go. Well, she is the most important person, after all. I put my stuff onto the trolley we have borrowed from the restaurant and offer to wheel it to the store room on my way out. Her natural inclination is to say no, but even she can see that it is sensible.

'Yes please, Judith,' she says in her usual stilted way. 'You will need to bring the trolley back here, though. We'll need it again later.'

I resist the temptation to be totally condescending; after all, I've caused the woman enough grief already. We're quits now and I'm determined that from now on we will work in harmony.

'No problem,' I say as I push the trolley into the lobby and wait for someone to release the outer door to let me into the store.

Wednesday 3rd February 2010
Ken and I are definitely closer now, but we have maintained our regular Wednesday evenings out. It's quieter in town so we can always get to see what we want at the cinema and can always get a table in a restaurant. His mum has invited me

round for Sunday dinner some time because they eat in the evenings. She's nice; they all are. I enjoyed the evening I spent there. Ken and I always work on a Sunday. It's part of the letting people with children have time off when they want. I don't mind really.

My phone rings mid-way through the morning. It's Ken and I wonder whether he has been asked to stay at work this evening because of the refurbishment of the offices. It's not that.

'Judith, it's me.' Why do people always do that? They know their name pops up on a mobile phone but they still say '*it's me*'.

'Hi Ken. Everything OK?'

'Yes, sort of, but Mary's asked me to call you.' Maybe Maureen was right and this fraternisation is frowned on by the powers-that-be. I sigh. 'She wants to know if you'll come in to work tomorrow and do the early shift.'

'Why on earth is the general store manager sorting out the shifts in the cash office? Hasn't she got better things to do? Like chasing you round the store?' I'm trying to keep this light but I can tell by his voice that something's going on.

'I'll tell you later. Will you? Come in tomorrow? She knows it's your day off.'

'Yes, of course, but I'll need my beauty sleep if I have to be up at six.'

'Thanks, Ju. See you tonight.'

He's started calling me Ju. It reminds me of Rosie calling me Auntie Ju. I quite like it. I spend the day wondering what's happened at work, and I suspect that Maureen has had a bit of a breakdown and is off sick.

In the middle of the afternoon he rings again.

'Ju, it's me again. If I pick up some steaks and stuff can we eat at yours tonight?'

'Yes, if you want to. Do you want me to buy something to eat if you're busy?'

'No, I'll do it. See you about seven.'

Something is going on. On the one hand I can hardly wait for seven to come, and on the other hand I really don't want to know. By eight Ken and I have cooked, drunk half a bottle of red and we are sitting down to eat.

'Are you going to tell me now?'

'I suppose I'm going to have to.'

I sit and wait, fork poised before popping the piece of sirloin into my mouth.

'You won't like it.'

'This much I have gathered. Just come right out with it.'

'Well, OK. Last night when the guys from Leeds were doing the cash office they loaded Maureen's desk onto their trolley to wheel it away. Well, they had to break it apart first, and guess what?'

'What?' I say, and as that one word comes out of my mouth, I know exactly what he is going to say. The succulent, tender steak that I've been chewing suddenly feels like gristle in my mouth and it takes every piece of will power to swallow it. Oh shit! I so do know exactly what.

'Two bank notes fell through the space where her drawer had been. It looked like they had been Sellotaped to the underside of the desk to be taken away at a later date.'

'Oh my God!' I whisper. 'Oh my God!' That was not supposed to happen.

'It was a ten and a twenty. That's what's been missing from the two times the store float wouldn't balance.'

'I know, Ken, I get it.'

'Yeah, sorry, I know you do. Well, it explains a few things, doesn't it?'

I suddenly see a way out. 'Does it, though? If she knew

they were there, why did she leave them there knowing the furniture men were coming?'

'It shows she's not functioning properly. She's a nervous wreck. You've seen her lately; she's snappy and she's been telling lies about you.'

'I suppose.'

'Eat up,' says Ken, and I force down a bit more food. The jacket potato goes down OK but I cannot swallow another piece of steak. I leave it and drink far too much wine for a work night.

'Take my steak home for your mum's dog,' I say. He looks at me and can see that it won't do any good to either make me eat it or ask if I want him to stay the night.

Thursday 4th February 2010
The cash office looks shiny and new, and our boxes have been neatly stacked on one of the desks ready for us to put away our papers, files and stationery items. Julie and I don't feel shiny and new. She normally works in the evenings and isn't familiar with the morning routine so I take charge and we are soon standing back in the cash office. We sort out what we need in order to count and balance the cash from the night before and leave the putting away until later. To be fair to Maureen, they had done an extra note lift last night and there wasn't too much for us to do. By the time Sal comes in at ten-thirty we have almost sorted everything out.

She sits down, ashen-faced. 'I don't believe it!'

'I don't know her as well as you, but I don't either,' I say. 'It can't be true. There must be an explanation.'

'You're clever, Judith. Can't you work it out?'

'What do you mean, I'm clever?' I ask, a bit taken aback.

'Anyone can see you're too clever to be working in here. Anyway, we need to try to help Maureen.'

I agree with her, actually, but feel I must remind her that Maureen was blaming me for the missing money. She looks horrified.

'How did you know that? Oh I suppose Ken told you.'

Actually you told me, I think but don't say, 'Yes, he did mention it. He thought I should know.'

'And you never said anything to us. You are a marvel, Judith. I think I would have gone mad if she'd been saying it about me.'

'Sal, I felt like she was feeling the pressure. I thought that if I made a fuss it would make things worse. I thought that if I just got on with my job that everything would settle down. I didn't expect this, though. It is such a shock.' I find that sticking with the truth is the best tactic in these situations, well at least not telling any lies.

The phone rings. It is Security asking whether we are doing a change run this morning, then the checkout supervisor buzzes to ask the same thing. How we let the systems fall apart if Maureen isn't here to keep us to time. We set about doing it right now.

My mobile rings.

'Hi, Judith. Are you here?'

'Oh my God. Sorry, Joanna, I was called in to work. There's been a problem overnight so I won't make it today. Sorry.'

'OK. See you soon,' she hangs up, but not before I hear Ricky asking where I am.

I work until Anita comes in at three, and we have the same conversation that Sal and I had earlier. Mary Morris catches me just before I finish to say thank you for coming in at short notice. I think that's the first time I've actually had a conversation with the woman. I go home feeling quite exhausted. So they think I'm clever, do they? I'm going to have to be very clever to get Maureen out of this without getting myself into it. Bugger. Why is the course of my pissing life never smooth?

Ken rings as he's finishing work a couple of hours later. I tell him I've got a headache and want to be left alone.

My phone beeps with a message. 'Call me if u change yr mind x'

My phone beeps again. God, Ken, get the message! This time it says, 'Hi J. Hope your crisis averted. Come to the cafe tomorrow night for a latte? J'. Oh, it's Joanna. I don't ring back; I've got too much to think about.

Friday 5ᵗʰ February 2010
I'm on the rota to be here early today with Anita so I'm back at the store at seven-thirty. After the change run at eleven, Mary Morris comes into the cash office to see the three of us; Sal has come in by now as well. She tells us that Maureen has been suspended from work pending the investigation into the money that was found. She stresses that this is not to say that Maureen is guilty of anything, but while there appears to be reasonable cause to believe it, it is better that she isn't here. She asks us to pass on this message to the other members of the cash office team by telephone as soon as possible. She also cautions us about going to see Maureen socially during this time.

I finish work at three, and it is about five before I get into town to Cafe Bar Sierra and order my latte from Liam, the skinny young man with his hair tied back. He says Joanna's popped out and will be back soon. I assume that she's gone to one of the shops that closes about now, and sit down to read the *Daily Mail* that someone has left. It isn't long before she comes back, looking a bit pink. I put that down to it being cold outside and warm inside. She gets a coffee and comes to join me.

'So, it's all happening at your place, then?' she launches straight in.

'My place?'

'At work. I hear Maureen's been sacked.'

'Who said that?' I ask. I don't know why I continue to be shocked at the speed of the grapevine. I suppose there's not that much that goes on in Carlisle normally. 'Anyway, it isn't true.'

'Isn't it? My cousin says she's gone.'

I decide that the real story needs to be established. 'She's been suspended, that's all, while they investigate. It's what happens. It's standard procedure.'

'You are very sweet and loyal to be playing this down, Judith, but if she's been stealing, she needs to be sacked.'

'Yes, I know. If she has.'

'What other explanation is there?'

'I haven't actually thought of a satisfactory one yet,' I say with complete honesty, 'but I am working on it.'

'You don't even like her. Why are you so worried?'

'I think it's out of character, that's all. Anyway, sorry about yesterday. It was all a bit of a panic and I didn't have a chance to call.'

'That's OK, but Ricky was asking after you.'

'Sweetheart,' I say. Mothers like it when you say things like that about their little angels. 'Anyway, let's talk Spanish. Senor Rossi is giving us a test on Monday.'

Monday 8th February 2010

Our Spanish test isn't very scary, and there is nothing at stake as we aren't going for a qualification. It is fun really; he makes us get into teams and test each other. Very clever. There are prizes for the best question, the best answer, most fluent answer, funniest question, etc. We all get a prize for something then we have to learn a Spanish song; I don't know what that's all about but it definitely is not my forte.

As nine o'clock approaches, Joanna looks a bit excited. She says she's not staying for a drink as her friend Danny is picking her up. She has her coat and scarf on in a flash and disappears with a cheery wave. Danny, eh? I must find out who he is.

Tuesday 9th February 2010

I seem to have inherited the early shifts in our reorganisation with Maureen being off so I'm finished by three again today. I walk into town, do a bit of shopping then call into Cafe Bar Sierra for a coffee before heading home. There is someone ahead of me being served so I take my time to walk up to the counter. He doesn't appear to be waiting for anything but stays and talks to Joanna anyway. I walk up to her.

'Oh Judith,' she says, 'this is Danny, you know, the one with the nice warm car.'

'She only wants me for my car,' Danny smiles, 'but that's OK. Soon she'll love me for who I am as well.'

This takes me somewhat by surprise.

'Don't take any notice, Judith, he's just messing about.'

'Am I? I don't think so. Anyway, I'm off. I'm going to take my mum and dad to see the house I looked at yesterday.'

'Have fun,' she says as he leaves.

She gets me a coffee and comes to sit down for a few minutes. I know where I have seen him before; he's the man in the photo in the drawer.

'So, how do you know Danny?' I ask.

'I've known him for ages, right back to school days. He was my best friend's older brother. I don't think he ever saw me then, though. I was just another one of his sister's nuisance friends.'

A group of four girls come in and she gets up to serve

them. She's working on her own this evening so there's no chance of a proper chat. I drink my coffee and get ready to leave.

'Are you still getting Thursdays off? With all the bother at work, I mean?' she asks. 'Ricky wants to know if we'll see you.'

'Yes, I am. I took a couple of half days last week but am planning to have tomorrow and Thursday off this week.'

'See you at the usual time then? In the park?'

'Yes, absolutely, see you then. And tell Ricky that I have lots of bread that I've been saving especially for the ducks.'

Wednesday 10th February 2010

I slept and slept earlier today. It's not working long hours that's making me tired, it's the fact that I can't see how to get Maureen out of this. I know I wanted to wipe the smugness off her face, but a criminal record is a bit too much. I have thought about it sober, and last night I thought about it with the aid of a bottle of medium-priced Rioja. That didn't help either. It contributed to the long sleep though. I've arranged to meet Ken later. There's a film he wants to see so that's good. I can apply my mind to the problem without having to talk.

We go to Le Gall for a drink before the cinema. I think a hair of the dog will be just what I need to perk me up a bit but it doesn't work and I feel sleepy. As the film goes on I feel my eyes getting heavy and end up almost nodding off with my head on Ken's shoulder.

'Did you enjoy that, sleepy-head?' he asks as the credits roll.

'Yes,' I lie.

'You didn't see any of it.'

'I know. Sorry. Not in the mood.'

'Shall we go for something to eat?'

'No, I think I'll just go home.'

211

Ken looks disappointed. Really, I can't be doing with this. I haven't decided what to do about Maureen and he wants to go out and be jolly, then he'll want to come back to mine. I need time to think. I need space to think it through.

'Is everything OK?' God, now he's doing the concerned look with his big, soft brown eyes.

'I'm fine, Ken, really. It's just that this business with Maureen…'

'I know you've been working a lot of extra hours. You must be shattered.'

'I'm not tired. It's just that it's affected everyone in the cash office. It's such a strain working in that atmosphere. There must be a way of helping Maureen but I can't seem to see what it is.'

'Why is that so important to you? She was accusing you of setting her up when it was her all the time. Can't you just ride it out and when it's done, it's done and you can all move on.'

'We've been through this, Ken. I can't explain but it seems out of character and I think there must be an explanation.'

Actually I think he is probably right, and unless I confess to everything, I might as well just forget it and move on.

'I don't see why you have to shut me out of your life because of it.'

I know I have been shutting him out, of course, but this is more important and urgent. I have to sort it out and I have to do it on my own.

'I'm not shutting you out,' I say feebly. 'I'm really not. Well just for now, maybe. Leave it, please leave it.'

'OK, but I'll walk you home.'

'No, don't. Just to the bus stop will be fine.'

He opens his mouth to say something else and realises it's pointless. He nods and we walk down to West Tower Street. He can get his bus from there as well. I don't know why he doesn't drive into town in the evenings as he hardly ever drinks alcohol. Maybe he's doing his bit for the planet. I'll ask him one day when I feel like conversation.

Thursday 11th February 2010
I meet Joanna and Ricky in the park as usual. I wasn't lying when I said I had lots of bread. My shopping and eating habits have gone up the creek since the Maureen stuff and I seem to have bits of bread and other food half-eaten all around the kitchen. Ricky is delighted and so are the ducks. It's lucky they're not fussy as most of it leaves a lot to be desired. Anyway, it's so cold that even Ricky is ready to retire to a warm cafe for some lunch as soon as his job is done.

We're munching away happily when Ricky looks at me.

'Danny takes us to the seaside,' he said.

'Yes, I know, in his nice warm car,' I reply.

'He's taking us there again soon.'

'Lovely.'

'Do you know Danny, Judith?'

'I have met him but I don't know him,' I say, trying to move the conversation to another tack, i.e. getting him muddled up in words.

'You must know him then.'

'Not really. I know what he looks like. But I still don't know him.'

Ricky looks at his mum to gauge whether I am being serious or joking with him. She doesn't give anything away.

'Why don't you?' he gives up.

'I saw him talking to your mum but I didn't talk to him so I don't know anything about him or what he likes doing or where he comes from or what he does for a job,' I pause for an exaggerated breath, 'or where he lives or what music he likes or what he watches on telly or what he like to eat or...'

213

Ricky gives me the sideways look and bursts into giggles.

'Shall I stop now? I could go on all afternoon telling you what I don't know about him.'

'Tell me what you do know.'

'I know what he looks like and that he took you to the seaside and that he gave your mum a lift home from Spanish on Monday.'

'Is that all? I know more than that.'

'I expect you do. Oh yes, I know he was taking his mum and dad to look at a house.'

'Is he going to buy it?'

'I have no idea. I don't know him,' I say expecting the conversation to go round again.

'Is he, Mam?'

'Yes, I think so. He said he liked it.'

'Good! That means we can see him more. I like him.'

She tousles her son's head and touches noses with him.

'That is a very good thing, Ricky, a very good thing.'

I look at her enquiringly, not sure that I want to know. Well I want to know but I don't want anyone to spoil our friendship and our routines.

'OK, OK, I like him too,' she says with a smile, then to me, 'I told you that I knew him at school? Well when I came back from uni after I was ill I met up with him again. He'd been away to uni too and was deciding what to do work-wise. He got a job in Manchester and used to stay down there during the week then come back at weekends. It suited us both really well. Ricky was smaller then, of course, but my mam was happy to babysit at weekends.'

'So what happened?' I prompt as she stops talking.

'He was made redundant from the job; youngest member of staff, least experience, cheapest to let go. He came back up here last summer while he looked for something else and we were practically living together. Then he heard from a firm in London that he had applied to ages before and they wanted him to go and work down there. He decided to go. I decided to stay.'

I suspect there is more to it than the plain facts but don't ask any more. I don't want to know anyway. I don't want him back in her life. We do stuff. I get on with her son. I haven't seen her mother since that afternoon last month but we seemed to be overcoming our differences.

'What does Gaynor think?'

'He's the one I told you about on Christmas Day, you know, the person who got close to the family then disappeared. She is a bit wary, to say the least.

'Mmmm.' Oh well, it might just shift her attention away from me if she has someone else to worry about.

'Is Danny staying here now, Mam?'

'Yes, he is. He's got a job in Carlisle so he's back.'

'Yeah, yeah, yeah,' Ricky bounces on the chair nearly tipping it over backwards.

'Oh no, the food has kicked in and given the little man a burst of energy. Time we went before he wrecks the place.'

We gather up our coats, scarves, hats, gloves and bags and make for the chilly air outside.

'Is Danny driving us home?' Ricky asks hopefully.

'No, sweetheart, he's at work. We'll catch the bus.' She looks at her watch. 'Actually we'll go to meet Nana from work and get the bus back with her.'

'Yeah, yeah, yeah,' Ricky bounces on the hard ground.

It's time for me to make a swift exit. We exchange farewells and I say that I'll pop into the cafe next week.

'It's half-term – again. Ricky hasn't got any school at all so I've got some time off and hopefully Danny is going to take us somewhere in his car.'

'Yeah, yeah, yeah.'

'I'll still pop in for a latte,' I say with forced jolliness, 'even without you the coffee is good.'

I walk slowly down through the underpass and up the hill, stopping to look at the river as I cross the bridge. I haven't seen the man with the dog lately; maybe something has befallen it. I don't care. I have enough to worry about without a three-legged dog's health. My phone rings. It's Ken. I don't answer it. It rings to alert me to a voice message and I switch it off. I simply cannot think. I need time to think. Tomorrow morning I'll be back in the thick of it all again. It isn't my conscience that's bothering me, I've identified that, it's the sense of injustice. It also isn't fair that Joanna's old flame is back to mess everything up.

Tuesday 16th February 2010

This week is dragging already despite the store being busy because of half-term. No Spanish last night, no Joanna and Ricky on Thursday and I've told Ken I don't want to go out tomorrow. Not a single (official) word has been said about Maureen other than to thank us all for doing extra hours and carrying on as normal. It doesn't feel like normal. The mood in here still hasn't lifted and everyone gives us strange looks when we go for our breaks. It's as though Maureen's under suspicion but nobody trusts any of us either. I go for a walk at lunch time, down to PC World. It's time I had a laptop and had some contact with the rest of the planet if only from the privacy of my half-house. I don't want to go to the canteen, not for the accusing looks or to bump into Ken.

He catches me as I'm leaving at three.

'Judith, hang on a minute.'

'Ken, please leave me alone for a while.'

'Why?'

'I've told you.'

'You haven't really. Is it really about Maureen?'

'Yes, totally. Please believe me. Anyway, I'm going now.'

'Have you changed your mind about tomorrow night?'

'No Ken, I haven't,' I say as I turn and walk away.

I pick up my new netbook on the way and spend the evening happily installing broadband and surfing the internet. I say happily, but that's not really true.

Friday 19th February 2010

It seems that I have had a shot of defiance. I decide that I will go for lunch in the canteen. Sometimes I go to the customer restaurant but the canteen is subsidised and I don't really see why I should pay more for virtually the same thing. I stop next to the store entrance for a look at the newspaper headlines before going up to the staff area then find myself yanked back by my hair.

'Ow!' I yell as I lose my footing and fall backwards.

'You bitch!' Maureen's voice screams out, 'You scheming bitch! Are you happy now? Are you?'

I cover my face as I see her foot coming towards it at speed and roll out of the way. She doesn't get close as the security man comes over and pulls her off. The emergency tannoy announcement goes out and suddenly the managers who are on the shop floor appear. Ken is one of them, of course. He helps me up then leads me through to the security office and gets me a glass of water. He puts it down then puts his arms around me and gives me a hug.

'What did you say to deserve that?' he asks.

I give him a weak smile. You've got to hand it to the man for trying. 'Not a single word. She came up behind me and grabbed my hair.' I rub my head and check that a clump hasn't disappeared. It feels as though it has.

'Mary Morris captured her and marched her off with the security man. I dare say she'll want your side of the story soon.'

'Yes, of course.'

'She might want to know if you want to press charges.'

'God, no, of course not. The poor woman is obviously on the edge.'

As Ken starts to tell me how nice I am, I feel an overwhelming weariness and almost feel like crying. I rest my head on his shoulder for a few moments, which I instantly regret doing as he will take it the wrong way and think we are back to normal. He gives me another hug.

'Come on. Let's go and get you something to eat.'

Someone in the canteen says that Mary Morris made Maureen ring her doctor and arrange to go and see him this afternoon and she sent the security guard to drive her there, presumably to make sure she went. I see her peering in through the door and when she sees us, she comes over.

'Judith, would you mind coming to see me when you've finished your lunch?'

'I'll come now,' I say pushing my half-eaten sandwich away. 'I'm not really hungry.'

'OK,' she says, picking up my coffee, 'but you can bring this.' She marches off with it and I follow obediently.

As Ken predicted, she asks me what happened and makes a note of what I say. She asks me if I want to press charges. She says it will be quite straightforward as a member of the public called the police while I was being attacked.

I say the same as I said to Ken, that Maureen was obviously under a lot of stress and that I don't want to make it worse. I do my normal speech about there being a mistake with the money in the cash office and she says, yes, maybe but as yet there is nothing conclusive. She asks if I need to go home and I say no, I will go back to work now.

Saturday 20th February 2010

The rumour is that when Mary Morris explained what had happened to the police they were interested in it all and have been round to Maureen's house to interview her. The rumour is also that they will want to interview all of us next week. It seems a bit much, but maybe it will put an end to it all as they won't be able to find her guilty either. I am strangely cheered by the news and think I might try to take a few days off next week when all the staff are back after half-term. I ask Mary Morris if I can have the three days off at the end of the week as well as my usual Wednesday and Thursday. I say I will talk to Anita about covering the shifts. She says that is a good idea as I am looking tired, but that I will have to have my police interview before I go. So that part of the rumour is true. Good.

I might even go across to Hexham and see my mother. I'll ring first and confirm a good time with Tina, so that I don't upset that hysterical girl again. I wonder whether I should contact Fiona. I'll wait until nearer the time.

Monday 22nd February 2010

I have been really looking forward to coming back to Spanish class, mainly to see Joanna, but it has been a bit of a let-down. Senor Rossi asked us all to talk about what we did in the half-term break. Well, I can hardly chatter on about missing money and police interviews and being attacked at the newspaper department, so I just say I have been working a lot and I have bought a new computer. That leads to a flurry of exchanging email addresses that I didn't expect. Joanna, on the other hand, never stops going on about her friend Danny who is back from London. She talks about the trips out in the car, the meals at her house and what the house he is going to buy is like, and how she has helped him to choose curtains. This is not what I want to hear right now. I was hoping for a bit of friendly support and noticing that I wasn't myself, but oh no, she is totally wrapped up in him. As soon as the class ends I leave without saying goodbye and walk home.

Tuesday 23rd February 2010
A police car is parked near the staff entrance as I arrive at work just after seven. It seems I am to be the first person to be interviewed. Mary Morris asks me to get the tills set up as quickly as possible then Sue and I are to report to her and have our interviews before starting work on counting yesterday's takings.

PC Plod has been afforded Mary Morris's desk and she is sitting to one side. She asks me whether I want anyone with me, other than another of the cash office staff and I decline. It takes nearly an hour by the time PC P confirms that I was at work on each occasion that the money had gone missing, he confirms that I am a fairly new member of staff, he asks about where I had worked before and concludes by asking me what I think the explanation is. I remind him that on the first occasion, there hadn't actually been any money missing and that on the last occasion we had a relief member of staff in who took quite a lot of Maureen's attention but apart from that, I couldn't see a pattern. He asks me to read back what he has written and sign to say that it is a true record. I stand up, but Mary Morris stops me leaving straight away.

'Just before you go, Judith, we have decided to take the fingerprints of everyone who was in and out of the cash office at that time,' she says.

'That's a lot of people,' I say. 'Are you including the office fitters from Leeds?'

'Yes we are,' says PC Plod, and opens his little kit.

'This all seems very old fashioned,' I joke, 'don't you just do DNA now?'

'We do what is appropriate to the situation, Madame,' says

Plod, 'and this is mainly for elimination purposes; nothing to worry about.'

I allow him to press each of my fingers and thumbs into the dye and roll them on the piece of paper with my name on. He asks me to sign it as mine. Mary Morris asks me not to relay any part of the proceedings to anyone else until everyone concerned has been interviewed.

Later she comes down to the cash office and thanks us for our co-operation. She tells us that Maureen has been signed off sick until the end of next week, by which time everything should be able to be sorted out. She wishes me a pleasant break from work.

Wednesday 24th February 2010

I go back to the car hire place I used before and hire what looks like the same car. I will ring Mill View some time but for now I think I will pack a few things and spend a few days in Scotland or the Northumberland coast. I don't really care where I end up, as long as nobody knows where I am. I drive home and spend a little while on the internet looking at B and Bs. I decide on Northumberland then I can go into Newcastle and get a bit of culture as well as blowing away cobwebs walking along the deserted beaches and sheltering in the sand dunes.

In a moment of impulse I ring Mill View and ask how my mother is. I am shocked to learn that she has deteriorated a lot and has been very ill. Tina says she would have contacted me if she had had a contact number for me. That woman knows how to make someone feel bad just by her tone of voice. I'm sure they're not supposed to do that in care homes. Anyway I agree to give her my mobile number, and she agrees a time that I can call in tomorrow morning so I decide to stay here for one more night and set off early.

Monday 2ⁿᵈ February 2009

'Mr. Clements please,' said Judith. 'No, nobody else will do. I need to speak to him now.' She waited for a couple of minutes then hung up and redialled.

'Mr. Clements please. Thank you.' This time she was put straight through. 'Mr. Clements, it's been three weeks since you put my flat on the market and nobody has been to view it. Where are you marketing it, apart from your shop window?'

'I told you that I believe it is over-priced.'

'And I do not!'

'Anyway, I do have someone who took the details last week. I am hoping they will request a viewing.'

'I hope so too. Will you chase them up?'

'Yes, Ms. Dillon. I'll do it today.'

Tuesday 3ʳᵈ February 2009

'How have you been, Chloe?'

'Much better, thanks Doctor. The tablets have been keeping me on an even keel and I've hardly seen Judith. I think I can stop taking them.'

'Finish the course, but try taking half a one a day for the next week and if that's still OK take half a one every other day until they're finished.'

'I don't want to get hooked on them.'

'You won't. Trust me.'

Saturday 7ᵗʰ February 2009

'Mum, do you think Auntie Ju's OK?'

'I suppose so. Haven't seen her for ages. That's normally a good sign. She's been to see Granny quite a lot as well. I think we won't upset things while they are going smoothly. It's easier that way.'

'Ok; just wondered.' She picked up the local paper and scanned it for what was on at the pictures and to see whether she recognised anyone in the articles. The property supplement fell out. 'Mum, look! It's Auntie Ju's flat.'

It seemed that Judith had frightened Mr. Clements enough to put a full page feature of her flat on the front cover of the property section.

'Well, well, well,' said Fiona. 'I'll give her a call.'

Judith's phone clicked to the answer service. 'Ju. Do you want to come over for lunch tomorrow before we go to see Mum? Just let me know.'

Sitting in the alcove, Judith listened to the message. She thought she should go round. Things were going horribly wrong and she needed her family; the trouble was that she hated to ask for help and hated to show weakness even to them. *I'll call them back later*, she thought, *when I've decided what to do*.

Monday 9th February 2009

'Ms. Dillon? Mr. Clements here. It seems the full page feature on your flat has brought back the person who showed interest before. How quickly can I take them round? You don't need to be there, of course.'

'As soon as you can, please,' said Judith, 'today if you like. It's all tidy.'

'Good, this afternoon then at about two o'clock, while the light is still good.'

Judith applied herself to the work she had to do so that she could get to the flat and meet her prospective buyers. She didn't trust old Clements to push them for the asking price, and felt that she could sell its features much better than him. She was delayed slightly and didn't leave the office until two, so arrived home at about quarter past. There were several cars in the visitors' car park and she couldn't tell whether or not she was too late. She left hers there too, for speed, and ran up the stairs. As she entered she could hear voices further in. Mr. Clements was saying, 'Yes indeed, that is described as the study area, but you can see that the present owner uses it as a place to sit and enjoy the view.'

She hung up her coat in the small cloakroom and tried to see who he was talking to. A woman was sitting on her chair. She felt a pang of jealousy in her stomach that soon it would be someone else's favourite place to sit.

'Ah, here is the owner now,' said Mr. Clements as he saw Judith. 'This is Ms. Parks.'

'Judith Dillon,' said Judith as she approached with outstretched hand and welcoming smile, then she froze as Chloe turned to look at her.

'Oh, no. No, no, no,' stuttered Chloe as she got up and backed away. Then realising that she was backing herself further into the alcove, she rushed past Judith and ran down the stairs.

Mr. Clements and Judith stood at the window and watched the red Seat Ibiza screech away down the driveway.

'I think we may have lost that sale, Ms. Dillon. Perhaps next time you will leave the selling to me?'

Thursday 12th February 2009
Judith posted her letter to HMRC requesting that they refund her overpayment. A few thousand pounds wasn't going to solve everything but would be better than nothing. She laughed to herself that she now thought of it as hers. Walking back past

her office to the car park, she saw Chloe locking up the shop and crossing the road at her normal place. She thought she would try to sort out the bad feeling once and for all and she ran across to join her walking down the lane.

'Chloe, about Monday, you didn't need to run away.'

'Please leave me alone, Judith.'

'I've obviously upset you and I'm sorry.'

'I need to catch the train.' She tried to pass Judith on the narrow lane but she stood in her way.

'What have I done to upset you, Chloe?'

She took a deep breath and spoke slowly. 'I don't know. I feel claustrophobic when you're around, like you're always watching me. Sorry. Let me past; I need to catch the train.'

Judith stood aside so that Chloe could pass. She watched her walk down the lane, and then she turned into the car park. She could see through the sparse winter trees that Chloe had stopped to speak to someone else. She would have one more try. She stopped by the car park entrance until she saw Chloe set off again, gave her time to cross the road into the station yard and then pulled out. Chloe turned and looked back at her, then walked more quickly towards the doorway to the station. Judith pulled into the station car park, jumped out of her car and followed Chloe through the ticket office towards the platform.

Chloe looked over her shoulder a couple of times. Normally she would have headed straight for the waiting room, the one with the big, black marble fireplace. Even when it wasn't lit, it seemed warmer than the other one. She didn't want to be trapped in there today. Seeing Judith at the door, she hastened on. She glanced back over her shoulder again, then stumbled and tripped over her own feet and fell from the platform onto the tracks. A horn sounded as the goods train from Newcastle to Carlisle trundled through, sending a blast of cold air around the building. Then there was a screech of brakes and an alarm sounded. Station staff rushed to the line and waiting passengers stood and stared at the spot where Chloe had been moments before.

Judith stood and watched the scene. It appeared to her that the world had suddenly become silent, a sort of calm before a storm or a picture frozen in time. She turned and walked back to her car where she sat for a few moments struggling to comprehend what she had just witnessed, then she switched on the engine. As she approached the exit from the station car park, she had to wait to allow the ambulance and two police cars through.

Fifteen minutes later she was back at her flat. She looked at her favourite seat in the alcove and remembered Chloe sitting there just a few days ago. Red wine wasn't going to be strong enough so with shaking hands she opened a bottle of whisky. She sat in front of the television and watched the local news report of a dreadful accident at the station.

Friday 13th February 2009
Judith decided that the only way she was going to cope with the day before was to apply herself to work. She had two people coming in for interviews and needed to read their CVs again; she couldn't remember a thing about them. She arrived at the office early, tidied up and tried to concentrate. She was making notes to remind herself of what to ask when she heard the outside door open downstairs. She glanced at her watch. Nine-fifteen; nobody would be that early for an interview. She thought it was probably the postman.

'Judith Dillon?' asked a man wearing a suit that looked as though it had been slept in.

As she nodded, he reached into his pocket and brought out an identity wallet. 'Detective Inspector Gibson. I need to talk to you about Chloe Parks.'

'I'm afraid it's not convenient right now. I am expecting some people for interviews this morning. Shall I come to the police station later?'

'I must ask you to come with me now. I am going to caution you. You do not have to say anything but it may harm your defence if you do not mention when questioned something which you later rely on in court. Anything you do say may be given in evidence. I think you know she died last night at the railway station.'

'Yes, I saw it on the news last night. It's tragic but why am I being cautioned?'

DI Gibson glanced over his shoulder at a woman who had appeared at the top of the stairs. 'DS Doggart,' he introduced her as she flashed her ID at Judith. 'You saw it on the news? I understood that you were there, at the station when it happened.'

'I must have been but I didn't know then what had happened.'

'We need to discuss this at the station. We need to ask you to make a statement and answer some questions.'

'I'll call in later.'

'Now, please.'

He signalled to DS Doggart who started walking around to where Judith sat. Judith glared at her, then sighed and stood up and put on her coat. She set the answering machine on the reception desk.

'Can I call my applicants and tell them I'll rearrange?'

At the station it was all a lot less chatty. Judith was sitting in a small office with the two police officers who set up two voice recorders. DI Gibson cautioned her again.

'Am I under arrest for something?' Judith asked. 'Can I call someone?'

'No, you're not under arrest but yes, if you would like to, you can call your solicitor.'

She was going to say Fiona but thought that would send her over the edge even if it had been allowed; her family solicitor was already over the edge. 'No, I don't want to call anyone. Just carry on.'

'I understand that you were friends with the deceased,' started DI Gibson.

'Yes, we've known each other since she opened her shop in September, Phoenix Antiques.'

'Yes. How did you become friends? Or was your relationship purely professional?'

'Well, mainly professional. I bought several items from her, but we have been to some of the same social occasions as well, the theatre and a concert.'

'Yes, indeed. Was that by arrangement?'

'What do you mean, by arrangement?'

'Did you arrange to go together or meet by chance?'

'By chance at the concert. I can't remember about the theatre.'

'What about the auction rooms at Newcastle? Did you meet there by arrangement?'

'Not exactly, no, but we knew each other was going. Why?'

'Why were you there? You're not an antiques dealer.'

'Why are you asking?'

'Ms. Parks kept a diary.'

DI Gibson stopped talking, and he and DS Doggart looked at Judith, watching for a reaction. She gave them none.

'Did you know she kept a diary?'

'No.'

'She wrote that she was feeling anxious; even a bit frightened.'

'We all feel like that. The recession is affecting everyone

around here. I would be surprised if she didn't feel anxious especially after investing in her shop. You are surely not suggesting that she committed suicide?'

'She wasn't feeling anxious about business. She didn't appear to have any money worries.'

None of us appear to have money worries, thought Judith. 'So what was she anxious about?'

'Her relationship with you. She thought that you were following her. She used the word 'claustrophobic' quite a lot. Were you aware that she felt like that, about you, I mean?'

'Certainly not; we get, got I mean, along very well. She invited me round for lunch on several occasions. She offered to bring a painting round to my flat to see how it would look. She came to look at my flat earlier in the week.'

'So you don't believe that she was afraid of you?'

'No. Not at all.'

The police officers started to ask similar questions in different ways, but Judith stuck to her story.

'So, yesterday at the station. What were you doing there?'

'I went there to offer Chloe a lift home. I was leaving at the same time as her. I often offered her a lift home to save her catching the train.'

'Indeed. How many times did she accept your offer?'

'Never.'

'Indeed. Did you not think that strange behaviour for a friend? Do you know why she always refused?'

'She preferred to catch the train, to have thinking time, she said.'

'So you never went to where she lived.'

'No.'

'OK, so you went right into the station to offer her a lift that you knew she would probably refuse?'

'Yes. Well, we had had words before Christmas and I

wanted to clear the air. Actually I didn't go right in, only as far as the door to the platform.'

'Words? About what?'

'I can't remember. Just a silly thing. It could have been sorted out if only she hadn't...'

'If she hadn't what? Thrown herself under a train?'

'I thought she tripped and fell.'

'Is that how it looked to you?'

'I suppose so. I didn't really see.'

'Why did you run away after the incident?'

It's reduced to an incident now, is it? thought Judith. 'I didn't run away.'

'You left without waiting to see the outcome. If you were such good friends, why didn't you wait and see whether there was anything to be done?'

'I saw the ambulance come and left the experts to it.'

'You were leaving before the ambulance arrived.'

'Yes, I suppose so.'

'Why didn't you stay?'

'It was obvious there was nothing for me to do.'

They concluded by Judith giving her account of how Chloe tripped, in her opinion because she wasn't looking where she was going and didn't appear to know how close to the edge of the platform she was. Judith dutifully signed the cassette tapes to say that she had given permission for them to be made and they were sealed into a plastic bag. She was allowed to go.

'Check the flat viewing,' said DI Gibson to DS Doggart, 'and recheck the diary entry that said that Chloe thought that Ms. Dillon followed her home.'

'Shall I get Louise Holmes to come and give a statement today?'

'No, leave her until tomorrow. She's really upset and we have enough to be getting on with for now.'

As Judith walked up the stairs to her office, she switched on her mobile phone. There were three messages from Fiona, two asking if it was Chloe who had been killed and one asking if it was true that Judith was at the police station. The message on the office phone was Louise, less intelligible through sobbing, but her meaning came through loud and clear.

In the early afternoon the two detectives came to take Judith back to the police station to continue the interview. They went through the same procedure as before, then started again.

'We have been in contact with Mr. Clements.'

Judith looked back at DI Gibson without comment.

'He confirms that he took Ms. Parks to view your flat on Monday afternoon.'

Judith continued to hold eye contact.

'He stated that Ms. Parks was startled and distressed when she saw that it was your flat, indeed when you arrived unexpectedly during the viewing.'

Judith still didn't react.

'Have you anything to say about that?'

'No. What do you want me to say?'

'Can you confirm that what Mr. Clements said was true?'

'Yes, I told you before. We had had words and I wanted to clear the air.'

'So why was Ms. Parks so afraid when she saw you at the flat? What did you do to frighten her?'

'I didn't do anything to frighten her. If you say she was frightened, she was frightened, but I didn't *do* anything to make her frightened. What do you think I did? What could I have done? What did she say in the diary I did?'

DI Gibson didn't reply straight away. Judith continued to maintain eye contact. It didn't make him uneasy but he wondered how anyone could not blink for such a long time. He blinked and continued.

'You said you hadn't been out to where Ms. Parks lived.'

'Correct.'

'But you followed her home one evening.'

'No I didn't.'

'She noted in the diary that a car like yours pulled out behind her and followed from a distance until she turned off to Haltwhistle.'

'Really? Then what did I do?'

'I don't know. What did you do?'

'I was on my way somewhere but didn't feel too good so I went back home. There is no law about being on the A69 at the same time as someone else.'

'No, indeed.'

'Did you go and visit your mother on your way back? Or your sister?'

'No, I told you, I didn't feel well so I went home.'

'We can check.'

'Please do.'

It was getting dark by the time Judith came out of the police station for the second time. This time there was a message from Fiona begging her to get in touch. She felt exhausted and drove to Fiona's house.

'Auntie Ju, you poor thing. Your poor friend.' Rosie threw herself at Judith as she collapsed onto an armchair.

Fiona brought in a mug of tea.

'Here. Where have you been all day? You couldn't have been at the police station the whole time.'

'Most of the time. They let me go at lunch time then came

232

back for me in the afternoon. They're saying horrible things. Haven't you got anything stronger than tea?'

'Yes, of course. But you'll have to stay the night. You look exhausted. You'll fall over if you have alcohol. Oh my God, Judith! Sorry. That was a really insensitive thing to say. I just mean, you look so tired.'

'It's OK, people always say things like that when someone dies.'

'So did she fall?'

'I suppose so. It looked like it to me.'

'You were there?' asked Rosie.

'I was at the station. She sort of stumbled.'

'So what are the police saying that's so horrible?'

'They suggested that she might have done it deliberately.'

'Do you think that?' asked Rosie from the kitchen.

'No.'

'Then neither do I,' said Rosie bringing Judith a whisky. 'Anyway, why would she?'

Back at the police station, DI Gibson and DS Doggart went back over the interviews with Judith.

'She doesn't look as though she's lying,' said the young sergeant.

'She doesn't look particularly bothered,' said her senior officer.

'No, she hasn't cried or got angry or any of the classic things that people do.'

'She's a cold fish alright. Do you find her scary?'

'No. But then, not a lot scares me. I know what you're asking though. I've never been stalked but I dealt with a stalking case last year in Newcastle. It was very unpleasant for the person concerned but nobody else could see that there was much wrong. The stalker was very clever about it.'

'I don't think Dillon was deliberately stalking Chloe, but it undoubtedly looked that way to her. I don't believe there was any intention to harm her. I don't think this line of enquiry is going to go anywhere at all.'

'I'll go and pick up Louise Holmes in the morning. Do you want someone else to sit in with you? I've known her for ages.'

'No, I'd rather you were here. She's more likely to open up if she sees a friendly face. I understand that she's devastated.'

Saturday 14th February 2009

The local paper had been geared up for Valentine's Day advertisements and declarations of love by the local population. It was completely overshadowed by the news of the young businesswoman who had fallen under a train. The CCTV cameras in the station had been used to create stills of Chloe's last few moments and in one of them Judith was clearly visible by the door with Chloe looking back at her over her shoulder. The look on Chloe's face was of fear, according to the journalist, and nobody studying it disagreed. Judith was shopping in Tesco and everyone seemed to be talking about it. She overheard a range of views about herself, some by people who didn't know her at all borne out by the fact that they didn't recognise her as she walked past. A couple of people offered condolences but most averted their eyes or nudged the person next to them and nodded to indicate that she was there. She did what she had to do and left as soon as she could.

Approaching the driveway to her flat, Judith noticed a lot more cars in the visitors' parking bays. In fact, they were double parked in most places. She drove round to her garage at the rear of the building thinking there must be a wedding or a funeral on. By the time she had unloaded her bags of groceries from the boot, she was surrounded. Cameras flashed, and voices called out at the same time.

'How well did you know Chloe Parks?' 'What were you doing at the station?' 'Do you blame yourself for her death?' 'Do you think she jumped under the train?' 'Why did she look so frightened when she saw you?' 'Can I have an interview? An exclusive? We'll pay?' 'Just a few minutes of your time, Judith.'

Judith fell back against her car. She stared at the sea of faces, lost for words in the noise of it all and thought she would collapse. She forced herself to get a grip and firmly closed the boot, locked the car then turned to face them.

'That is my friend you're talking about. No comment.'

She marched past them and through them, trying where she could to knock into cameras and voice recorders, and to avoid meeting anyone's eye. At the door to the flats, they stood back as though observing some unwritten rule that said there's a two foot force field around the entrance through which hacks could not pass. She had planned to drive to Northumberland later to get away but she knew they would still be there.

She called Fiona to say that she wouldn't be going to see their mother and to explain why.

'We've had them here as well, Ju. Two phoned and one came to the house. They were asking whether I knew Chloe and stuff like that.'

'Don't say anything. I didn't. I'm hoping they'll get bored and go away soon.'

'Are you OK?'

'Yes, just a prisoner here for now, that's all.'

Sunday 15th February 2009
The journalists had gone by mid-afternoon. It was bitterly cold and starting to frost over as the sun set. Suddenly the car park was empty and Judith felt able to venture out. She

thought that an hour sitting with her mother was just what she needed. They would probably either talk about times long past or just sit there. Either would do. She hoped that her mother hadn't heard or understood anything about this business.

The drive to Mill View was still and frosty, and the cold air cleared Judith's head as she walked up to the house. She got past the first door release, which worked on a buzzer from inside the building then found she was trapped in the large porch where she had to wait longer than usual before someone came to physically open it. Eventually Tina came to let her in. She led her straight to her office and shut the door. 'I'll get straight to the point, Judith, there is a lot of bad feeling here.'

'About what?'

'About the incident that you were involved in, of course. What did you think I meant?'

'I don't know, and I wasn't involved in any incident. A friend had an accident and I would like to see my mother, please.'

'I don't think that's a good idea. There's a lot of upset here.'

'What has it got to do with anyone here? Did someone know Chloe? Is that what it is?'

'No, but the train driver's sister works here. Well, she's off sick with it all. Her brother, the driver, is in a terrible state and the whole family is upset. All the staff are affected.'

'If she's not here, what's the problem? I'll go and sit in Mum's room.'

'No, Judith, I'm sorry but no, not today.'

Judith sat and looked at Tina but she was not going to be swayed. She played the waiting game back. It occurred to Judith that Tina was the only person who could out-wait her and she put it down to years of dealing with difficult residents and their families. Eventually she gave in and stood up to leave.

'Will you tell her I came in to see her please? When she's in a state to understand. I'll come back in a few days' time when things have settled down.'

'I'll call you when I feel that things have settled down,' said Tina firmly as she let Judith out of the building.

Five miles away in a small terraced house, Tommy and Ivy Shipton sat in their respective armchairs staring into the open fire. It was silent apart from the crackle of the logs. Upstairs, their son Tom, back in his old bedroom lay curled up and shivering despite the tablets to calm his nerves. He had been a train driver for fourteen years and this was his first fatality. He hadn't had time to call out, let alone stop, and it wouldn't have helped if he had. She just appeared there on the line then she was gone; out of sight and out of life.

Ivy went up to see him. 'Anything you want, love?'

He shook his head.

His sister, Shelly, came out of her room waving her mobile phone around.

'Bitch! That bitch Judith Dillon's been in to work. It's all her fault our Tom's like this. She should be locked up, not allowed to go round scaring people under trains. Tina sent her away and told her to stay away.'

Tom turned away and buried his head deeper into the duvet.

'Come on Shelly. Leave your brother alone for a while. Come downstairs.'

Tommy was still looking into the flames.

'You go and talk to him,' said Ivy.

He shook his head. 'Nothing you can say. He knows it wasn't his fault. That doesn't make it better.'

He didn't say much at the best of times, but Ivy knew that her husband was remembering when, on the Newcastle Metro, some drunken lads had pushed someone under his engine. One of the reasons they'd moved to Hexham was to get away from the memories and now their son was suffering the same way and probably always would. Tommy still did.

Monday 16th February 2009
Dr. Ellis sat in her colleague's consulting room.

'I knew I should have done something more.'

'It wasn't your fault, you know that. We can't be responsible for everything our patients do.'

'The police came round yesterday to ask about the tablets I prescribed. They'd read her diary. They knew as much about her anxieties as I did. There must have been something else I could have done.'

'You could have advised her to go to the police, but what would they have done? Just the same as you; advised her to keep clear boundaries and advised her to tell Judith Dillon how she was feeling. As far as we know, Chloe did those things and then she had an accident.'

'Yes, but…'

'But nothing. You are a doctor. You have living people to deal with today. Go and give your time to them.'

Dr. Ellis, just for a moment, wondered whether Dr. Sinhan's attitude to this was a cultural thing, but she knew he was very experienced and usually right, and was probably trying to make her feel better. The practice manager rang through to see whether she was ready for her first patient.

Judith hadn't slept well so had got up and was in her office by seven-thirty. By eight-thirty she was glad that she had, as a couple of the local reporters were outside giving it one last try.

If they'd done any investigative work they would have seen her car parked nearby, but as it was they hung around outside waiting for her to come in.

There were three phone messages asking for her to return people's accounts as they wanted to find another accountant, and when the postman arrived he brought three more such requests.

'Oh, you're here,' he said as he dropped off the bundle of envelopes. 'There are people downstairs waiting for you.'

'I've seen them. Don't tell them I'm here. They'll get cold and go away soon.'

He hesitated, as if debating whether to say anything, but decided against it. It was none of his business; that much he had learned since becoming a postie.

Louise sat in the police interviewing room. DS Doggart had hugged her when she picked her up and squeezed her hand as she handed her a glass of water, but once the interview started she was completely professional. It became clear to DI Gibson and DS Doggart that Louise considered Judith to be the cause of her friend's death but she couldn't tell them any more than the diaries or Judith herself.

'Did Chloe consider coming to the police?' DS Doggart asked gently.

'I suggested it but she said no. What would you have done, anyway? There wasn't much to go on.'

'No, indeed,' agreed DI Gibson.

'Actually I blame myself.'

They looked at her and waited. They knew that guilt was often part of the grieving process and they let her speak before reassuring her.

'I put the thought in her mind, you know, that Judith Dillon is a bit weird.'

'How did she react when you said that?'

'Dismissed it, really. It was later that she noticed it as well, but maybe she wouldn't have if I hadn't put the idea in her head in the first place.'

'Maybe and maybe not, but if she is 'weird' as you put it, then it's likely that she would.'

'Judith seems to be alright on a business level, but personally you never know what she's thinking or doing. She lies about her family, for a start.'

'In what way?'

'Pretending they're all happy-happy, and stuff like that.'

'Well, we all keep family secrets,' said DS Doggart.

DI Gibson flashed her a look that said 'keep to business, not chat'. She blushed, then continued, 'Anyway, I don't think you have anything to blame yourself for. We've read her diaries and she refers a lot to the support you gave. You were a good friend to her; no need to feel guilty at all.'

'What do I do about her shop? Should I open it?'

'No, not yet. We'll need to contact her next of kin. Perhaps you could help us with that.'

'Her father is still alive. He moved to Spain years ago, near Alicante. They're not close and I haven't got his address although I visited him with Chloe once. Her mum died soon after they moved.'

'No doubt we'll find the address in her house.'

DS Doggart drove Louise home and went in for a cup of tea but she was not able to get any more information. Louise just kept saying the same things over and over again. It was looking more and more like an accident.

Fiona came back from shopping, dumped the bags on the kitchen floor and reached for her anxiety pills. Rosie appeared, looking as though she had just got out of bed.

'Been shopping?' Rosie asked unnecessarily, then noticed what Fiona was doing. 'Why are you taking one of them? I thought you'd stopped.'

'You'd want one as well if you'd been with me.'

'What happened? Why aren't you visiting Granny? Has Tina banned you as well?'

'I couldn't face it. The comments I've heard about Judith are unbelievable. Some people are saying that she pushed Chloe under that train. Why would they say that? There were the pictures in the paper, for a start, but even so.'

'Didn't you tell them? Who was saying it anyway? People you know?'

'Yes, a couple, but most people I know were full of pity or embarrassment. They didn't know where to look. I felt guilty, and sorry for Judith, and really angry, and just plain embarrassed as well. It was horrible.'

Rosie put the kettle on in the universal gesture of making everything alright.

'Anyway, what do you mean, banned from Mill View?' said Fiona.

'You know my friend Moira who works at Mill View at weekends? She phoned and said Judith had gone to see Granny yesterday and that Tina wouldn't let her in. Something to do with the train driver's sister being upset. She works there as well.'

'Oh my God. I'll have to phone her. Oh my God, the poor train driver. I hadn't even thought about him.'

'I was planning to go out tonight but I think I'll stay in.'

'It's half-term, go out and enjoy yourself. None of your friends will be bothered.'

'Tash will, you know Louise's daughter. She never liked Judith and nor did her mum. Anyway, you don't look like you should be left on your own.'

'I'll go round to Judith's and drop you in town on my way.'

Judith wasn't very forthcoming. She wanted to confide in Fiona about her financial situation but couldn't bring herself to do it, so she drank wine and Fiona drank tea then Rosie called and said she was going home because Tash was talking about her to some others and making her feel uncomfortable. There didn't seem to be anything Fiona could do for Judith, as usual, so she went to pick up Rosie.

Tuesday 17th February 2009

Judith got to work early again. It seemed to be the only way to avoid the eyes of Hexham. Two more phone messages, one from Stoneleigh wanting to take their business away and one from one of the applicants for the vacancy saying she was no longer interested in the job. She bundled up Stoneleigh's file with her notes and copies of their tax returns and put it into a large envelope. She supposed she would have to go to the post office sometime, but then she had a better idea; she would drive out to Haltwhistle or even further away and post things there. She could shop somewhere else as well. She decided to let it all pile up then she would go to Carlisle on Saturday and make a day of it. She would be anonymous there.

The postman arrived.

'Not much for you today,' he said, trying to sound chatty but realising it was probably the wrong thing to say. Judith nodded but didn't reply.

There was another letter from Henry Lloyd's solicitor making enquiries as to the nature of Judith's last visit to Henry the day before the cheque was presented for payment. *Sod them*, she thought and shredded the letter. Half an hour later he phoned and asked the same question. She told him in no uncertain terms that she didn't know anything about a cheque made payable to HMRC and that she would appreciate being left alone to grieve for her friend. She decided that attack may yet be the best form of defence.

'HMRC?' he said, 'Did I mention that it was made payable to HMRC?'

'Yes you did,' said Judith, then suddenly unsure, 'last time.'

'I see. So you don't know anything about it?'

'No I do not. Good day.'

Judith wished she had kept the letters instead of shredding them. She wasn't actually sure whether he had mentioned HMRC before. Bugger! Her head was spinning with it all.

She opened another letter which contained a cheque for her tax overpayment. Some small mercy. Maybe she could open an account in a different bank and pay it in there, but would definitely need to go to a different town. She knew all the people in all the banks in Hexham and so decided to go to Carlisle on Friday instead of Saturday.

DS Doggart answered the phone and signalled to her boss that it was something interesting. She made notes as the caller spoke. DI Gibson read them over her shoulder.

'That was Langdale's Solicitors, Mr. Langdale himself. He wants to make some official enquiries about Judith Dillon's financial transactions and those of a late client of hers.'

'Well, well, well, very interesting. Let's give him as much assistance as we can.'

They arrived in Judith's office just before lunch time and escorted her back to the police station, this time to enquire about Henry Lloyd's final meeting with her, and to ask about a mysterious payment.

They asked Judith to sit where she had done last time, and they went through the same process of cassette tapes and signatures.

'What has this got to do with Chloe's death?' she asked.

'I thought I had made that clear,' said DI Gibson, 'this concerns the death of Henry Lloyd.'

'So it's a completely different enquiry?'

'Yes.'

Judith answered the questions in the same matter-of-fact way that she had answered the questions about Chloe. DS Doggart watched her face and her body language throughout. She noticed a slight clench of her hands when asked about her last meeting with him at Mill View; she noticed Judith's cheeks redden slightly when DI Gibson asked for the third time about the cheque to HMRC. None of that would show up on the tape, of course, and DS Doggart said afterwards that she thought Judith was definitely hiding something this time.

'I doubt it has anything to do with Chloe Parks' death, though.'

'No, me neither, but a juicy fraud case might make the town feel better.'

'There is obviously a side to you that I haven't seen yet,' laughed DS Doggart.

'Indeed,' he replied, then apparently out of character again, 'but you ain't seen nothin' yet.'

Friday 20th February 2009

Judith drove west along the A69 and reflected that nothing was likely to happen this day that was different to the last four. Thank God for the cheque. Once the mortgage and car payments went out next month there wouldn't be much left for anything else. She knew she had so few clients left that she wouldn't be able to meet the payments from then on. Getting right away from it all would help her think properly about it; to come up with a proper plan. She couldn't think in Hexham. With her mobile switched off and no one knowing where she was going, she had taken with her everything she needed to open a bank account with the £6,000 from the Inland Revenue. Langdale's were on to her, that much was clear, but it would be difficult for them to get access to her personal bank accounts and tax records. Henry had so much money when he died, they would probably write it off anyway. At least Martin Lloyd would be on her side. He would want everything to be sorted out and done with as quickly as possible.

Louise Holmes sat with a cup of tea. Tears ran down her face. She had just spoken to Chloe's father in Spain. He wasn't really well enough to travel but seemed determined to come back to Hexham for the funeral. Louise offered to make the arrangements on his behalf, which he accepted gratefully. She also told him that she would pick him up from the airport; well she had nothing else to do now. Tash came into the kitchen and hugged her mother.

'Is he coming back?'

'Yes. I'll pick him up from Newcastle on Wednesday then he'll have all day Thursday to rest before the funeral on Friday.'

'Will *she* be coming to the funeral?'

'I don't know. Why don't you ask Rosie?'

'I haven't spoken to her.'

'No, I suppose you haven't seen her, with it being half-term. Why don't you give her a call?'

'I have seen her, the other night, but I didn't *speak* to her. I don't want people to think I'm on their side.'

'Tash! That's not fair. It's not Rosie's fault.'

'Judith's her auntie. Everyone knows she's weird. I don't want to be, you know, *associated* in any way.'

'Stop that right now.' For the first time in over a week, Louise thought about someone other than herself.

'Mam, *you* said she was a weirdo as well.'

'Not in public, I didn't, and I don't want you saying it either. What we say here is between us. I certainly don't want you telling anyone else that's what I said.'

The look on Tash's face gave away the fact that she'd already told all her friends.

'It doesn't mean anything,' she said, 'everyone else is saying it too.'

'It's not fair on Rosie and her mam. They're lovely; and this is turning into some old fashioned witch hunt. We'll be running the family out of town soon. It has to stop.'

Tash shrugged and took her coffee up to her room. Ten minutes later she came back down.

'I called Rosie. I have been mean to her lately and I've said sorry.'

Ivy Shipton sat on her son's bed and rubbed his back. He had barely moved except to eat and go to the bathroom.

'I've heard from the police,' she said, 'the funeral's next Friday.'

He nodded.

'Do you want to go?'

He nodded again. 'I have to, Mam.'

'We'll come with you.'

Fiona went to visit her mother after lunch. She thought Rosie seemed a bit brighter, which was a relief. Teenage girls could be quite cruel to each other. If Tash was making a point of being her friend, then others would soon follow.

Mill View was an ordeal, though. It was clear that the care staff blamed Judith for Chloe's death and for the torment of the driver's family and although they didn't say anything to her directly, Fiona could feel their accusing eyes on her as she moved from one part of the building to another. Her mother 'wasn't very good', to use their terminology, so she sat next to her in silence for nearly an hour. On the way out she stopped to speak to Tina.

'Did you have to ban Judith?' she asked. 'She really is having a bad time with all this.'

'Your sister is not the only one having a bad time,' said Tina. 'Look, I know it isn't your fault, or Judith's probably, but that's the way it seems to Shelly Shipton. She's a strong character and makes her feelings known. It's best for Judith if she doesn't come here, especially until after the funeral. And the last thing we want is for your mother to get wind of it.'

'I suppose funerals have a way of settling everyone down. Shall I tell her that; that she can come back after the funeral?'

'Don't be too definite. Can you say not before the funeral then we'll see how everyone is?'

Judith opened her new account and paid in the cheque. At least she could afford to eat while she thought about how to manage the sale of her flat. She couldn't see where she was going to get any more clients from at the moment. This would all blow over soon enough and then she could pick up the pieces. She went for a coffee and a sandwich in a cafe in Carlisle. It called itself a 'cafe bar', whatever that meant. She was fairly sure that such an establishment didn't exist in Hexham. It was a bit tatty but the coffee was strong and fresh, and the brie and avocado filling absolutely delicious. It could do with a makeover, she thought, and then it would be a really nice place to eat. She stayed there as long as she could without someone demanding that she bought something else, and then drove up to Cost-Save to do a big shop while she still had credit on her visa card. They were advertising for staff; maybe she needed to get a job. She thought about who might employ her in Hexham, and couldn't think of anyone.

Judith pushed her full trolley across the car park and as she opened the boot, she noticed that someone had bashed into the passenger door. She cursed. If she had been in Hexham, she would have thought that someone had done it deliberately. Expecting to see someone she knew laughing at her out of a car window, she looked around. There wasn't anyone. That dent would cost money to put right, and she was nearly out of fuel; another fifty quid. Where would all this end?

By the time she got home it was dark and starting to get frosty. Judith sat in her car for a few moments before getting out in case any reporters were lurking there. They had clearly moved on to more interesting stories. *God, I am so paranoid*, she thought, and carried her shopping upstairs a few bags at a time. She had bought enough for a siege.

When everything was put away, she opened a bottle of Rioja. *I don't have to lower my standards quite yet*, she said to herself, and after half a glassful, switched on her mobile phone.

'Ju, it's me. I spoke to Tina. She thinks the funeral on Friday will settle people down so you should be able to see Mum soon after. Ring me if you want, or come round.'

So, the funeral is on Friday, is it? Time enough to decide whether or not to go to it. She pressed the flashing button on her house phone.

'Ms Dillon? DI Gibson. Please contact me as soon as you get this message.'

Bollocks, thought Judith, *not bloody likely*.

The next message was a woman's voice. The accent was more Geordie than local and she thought she recognised it.

'I hate you, Judith Dillon. I fucking hate you. If you could see my brother you'd hate you an' all. Don't come near me or my family – *ever*.'

Shelly from Mill View. She wondered how she had got her

home number. She was ex-directory. Tina would have to be informed about that.

Saturday 21st February 2009
Judith didn't feel like facing the wrath of Hexham on another Saturday morning so she looked at the headlines of the local paper on-line. Damn it, she was still in the news. To be fair it said that Chloe's death was officially an accident, but also that there was a groundswell of public opinion against a local accountant who was following her that afternoon. She supposed that was the best she could hope for.

Her doorbell sounded and she glanced at the CCTV screen by the door. It was the two detectives. Bugger; she had forgotten to ring them back. She didn't let them in, but put her coat on and went downstairs to see them. Sure enough they wanted her to go back to the police station for more questioning, once more about the cheque that Henry Lloyd had written a few days before he died. She stuck to her story of total ignorance and after an hour they brought her back home.

'We are making more enquiries,' said DI Gibson as he pulled up at the imposing building, 'and I will be seeking permission to have access to your bank accounts.'

'You won't get it from me,' muttered Judith.

'I didn't mean from you,' he said.

Back in the flat, Judith made a list of everything that was bad in her life, fully intending to counter each item with what she was going to do about it. She found it to be a depressing activity. It was likely that she would lose more clients who would not be replaced very easily. It would be a miracle if anyone around here were to offer her a job at the moment or in the foreseeable future. She wouldn't be able to pay the mortgage after next month, except with Henry's cheque, and couldn't force the sale of her flat. Even if she could she would be left owing money on it. She had no friends left in Hexham and her family were either embarrassed by her or oblivious to her. She could give up the office but would have to give three months' notice. She could return her car. Bloody marvellous.

It was only four o'clock but she opened another bottle of the Rioja she had bought in Carlisle the day before. By seven, she was part way through the next one, but with a new list written.

Sunday 22nd February 2009

Judith didn't wake up until after noon. Her head ached and she felt more than a little sick. Twenty minutes under the power shower helped, and after two strong cups of coffee sitting in the alcove looking out over the fields, she felt strong enough to read the two lists she had written the day before. Nothing had changed. She would have to go through with it. The phone rang. She ignored it.

She packed everything she could carry on a train. She wrote a note to Fiona and Rosie asking them to take all the food and drink, and anything else they wanted from the flat as she wouldn't be coming back. Fiona had a key; she would come round eventually. She wrote a letter to Mr. Clements asking him to arrange to have the flat repossessed.

By three she felt well enough to eat, so made herself a huge fry-up and more coffee. She also made sandwiches and packed them neatly in a plastic box along with a banana, a yoghurt and a Twix, then washed up for the last time in her spacious north-east wing of a grand country house and loaded up the car.

Judith didn't cry often, but leaving like this was ripping her heart out and it was all she could do not to break down. She drove down the long driveway, forcing herself not to look in the rear view mirrors.

She was in her office within ten minutes and she looked round critically. She couldn't really carry anything else, but there was nothing that she wanted anyway. She wrote a note to a rival accountancy practice offering them all her remaining clients and enclosing the key so they could collect the files. She also wrote to her landlord, the bridal shop downstairs telling them that she had gone and where the key was. She didn't leave a note for DI Gibson or DS Doggart or Langdale's Solicitors. If they wanted to press charges, they would have a way of finding out where she was.

So that was everything, except to look up the times of trains on Sunday evening and to choose whether to travel east or west. Fate could decide and she would get on the next one stopping at Hexham. She considered, just for a moment, jumping under the next one that didn't stop at Hexham but discarded the thought as quickly as it had come. Something had to be better somewhere; surely it did.

At seven o'clock Judith sat in her car in the station car park. The train to Carlisle would be there in fifteen minutes. She had bought a ticket and had one more job to do before dragging her two suitcases, back pack, holdall and handbag onto the station. She called the BMW garage and left a message.

'Judith Dillon here. I've left my car at the station. The keys are hidden on top of the front wheel on the driver's side. Please take it back.'

Friday 27th February 2009
The day of Chloe's funeral dawned crisp and bright but by the time of the service at the crematorium there was a light drizzle of rain falling. Chloe's father walked down the centre aisle following the coffin containing his only daughter. He leaned on a stick with his right hand and on Louise who had linked arms with him on his left side. He looked straight ahead with

no expression on his lined and tanned face, but his eyes look glassy and red.

The crematorium was almost full, mostly with people Chloe had known in Newcastle, but there were a few friends from Hexham as well. Tash sat on the front row with her dad waiting for her mother and Mr. Parks to join them. Pauline sat in the row behind with her mum and dad and some people that Chloe had met through her business. Fiona and Rosie sat near the back on the other side. They hadn't known Chloe at all but felt a need to be there to show respect, and in a way, to represent Judith. They were acutely aware of people looking at them then looking beyond them, as if to see whether Judith was there somewhere. A local reporter and photographer sat at the back, watching everything and making notes.

A bit further down opposite Fiona sat a youngish man who looked as though he hadn't slept for a month. He was with a young woman and a middle-aged couple. Rosie heard the reporter say to his colleague that he was the driver of the train. She looked over then nodded and whispered to her mother that the young woman was Shelly from Mill View.

As soon as the service was over, the reporter, a young man, approached Rosie. He looked at her and held her gaze, she thought, for a little too long for such a sad occasion then he said, 'So, where's your Auntie Judith today?'

Nice looking though he was, she suddenly felt repulsed by him, so much so that she didn't even answer. She turned back to Fiona and took her arm.

'Let's go, Mum.'

Fiona nodded, and with one last look round, walked towards the car.

'Better that she wasn't here,' she said.

'Yes, but I wish we knew where she was.'

'She'll tell us when she's ready. Shall we go to her flat this afternoon and decide what to do with her stuff?'

'Yes. Can we take most of it home so it's there when she's ready?'

'Poor Judith,' they said together.

CHAPTER 13

Carlisle, March 2010

Monday 1ˢᵗ March 2010

Back at work today and now back at Spanish. For once I have something to talk about. I tell the group about my trip to see my mother but without going into how shocked I was to see the state she's in, and about going to the theatre in Newcastle and walking in Northumberland. It all sounds quite jolly when told in halting Spanish; it was relaxing and a chance not to think about anything except where to go and what to do for a few days.

I did feel refreshed until I got back to work where the atmosphere has got worse since the police interviews and fingerprinting. Anita seems glad that I'm back; she's had to hold the fort for a few days on her own. That just goes to show that I should be second-in-command. Maybe that can be my next mission. Actually, maybe I should be the supervisor if Maureen doesn't come back; or even if she does. She's hardly been stable lately.

Anyway back to the here and now. I must stop this daydreaming as I miss what's going on. Senor Rossi is setting homework for next week. He has photocopied some articles from Spanish magazines and newspapers and is handing them out. We are to read our own then précis it to tell everyone about it next time. No problem; my spoken Spanish was actually quite rusty but I can still read it reasonably well. Nine o'clock comes round.

'How are you, Joanna?' I ask on the way out. 'We don't seem to have had much chance to chat tonight.'

'No, it gets more like a proper lesson all the time, doesn't it? I'm so glad you had a good break. That business at work was really getting to you.'

'Yes, thanks, it was good to get right away.'

'Mam suggested I ask you for dinner one night when none of us are working. How about Thursday this week? I have to change my shift and work the morning but I'll have the afternoon and evening off.'

Gaynor suggested I come for dinner. Well, well, well. Maybe she's fed up with Danny-this Danny-that the whole time as well. I haven't spoken to her since that afternoon in January so I suppose this is her making a gesture of peace. It might even be something we can bond over.

'That'll be lovely. Thanks. Shall I bring something?'

'No, just turn up.'

'Well I'll bring some wine, shall I?'

'OK, thanks. About seven?'

I nod and jump up and down on the spot. It's still cold enough for snow to be lying on the hills. 'I'm going to have to move. I'm freezing. See you on Thursday night.'

I decide to walk back home. It's a cold night but clear and frost-free at the moment. I did a lot of walking in Northumberland and started to feel a bit fitter again. I must keep it up. The River Eden looks absolutely beautiful as I cross the bridge. I love it when the moon is reflected right in the middle, kind of solid in the centre and ruffled around the edges. I must be feeling better if I'm noticing things like that again. Oh well, the only way now is up; metaphorically and actually as the road steepens here. That's OK; I've started to feel cold again by stopping to marvel at nature. Keep moving, that's the answer.

Thursday 4th March 2010
My little holiday wasn't expensive but I did spend more than I had intended so I decide to catch the bus to Joanna's house

tonight rather than get a taxi. I may get one back, I'll see how I feel later. The trip through Carlisle and out the other side is quite familiar to me now and there isn't much point in looking out of the windows anyway as it's dark. Just over three weeks until the clocks change again, thank God, I hate these dark evenings. The bus pulls into Cumrew Close and I get off and turn up the lane to her street.

Ricky throws himself at me as she answers the door. He's in one of his hyperactive moods. Joanna suggests that he and I do a jigsaw or read a story while she finishes cooking and before Ricky goes to bed. He chooses a jigsaw and a book. That suits me as I am able to avoid Gaynor's eyes and conversation for a while longer. She has a bottle of wine in hand as usual, and I think I am safe to accept a glass knowing what she's going to be like in an hour. She takes Ricky to bed after a while and after he has ceremoniously kissed us all goodnight. I sit in the kitchen and drink another glass while Joanna puts the finishing touches to rack of lamb, new potatoes and a selection of fresh vegetables. It smells lovely; obviously sprinkled with rosemary, and there's mint sauce and redcurrant jelly to go with it. I'm starving and am glad when Gaynor returns and we can eat.

'So, Judith, how have you been?' she says. She sounds friendly but I detect the inquisitor style she started with on Christmas Day.

'Oh, fine thanks, Gaynor. You?'

'Yes, I've been busy. I hear you have too, with Maureen being off – sick.'

I turn and give her a look that Joanna can't see that says *back off*, then turn back and smile sadly.

'Yes, poor Maureen. I hope it's all going to be cleared up soon and she can get back to work with a clean slate.'

'Do you?'

'Yes, I do. I am so sure there's an explanation for it all.'

'Judith's said that all along, Mam, that she doesn't think Maureen did anything wrong.'

'Yes, so I hear.'

'Do you know Maureen?' I ask Gaynor.

'Not well, but I work with her older sister. The family aren't happy about it all.'

'No, I'm sure.' I wonder where this conversation is going. Gaynor pours more wine, and to be honest I feel like I need it. Joanna gives her mother a warning look and I can't tell whether it is for the booze or for the line of conversation. We eat in silence for a while.

'This is delicious, Joanna,' I say, absolutely meaning it.

'Thanks. It's my favourite meal to cook for guests.'

'Where's Danny tonight?' Gaynor asks.

'He's at his parents' place. His brother is back for a couple of days so they're all catching up together.'

'Nice. Did you see your family while you were away, Judith?'

Here we go again. 'Yes, well I saw my mum.'

'Not your sister or niece?'

'No. Rosie's away at university now and my sister happened to be in Leeds visiting her when I was there.'

'When did you last see them?'

'I can't remember exactly.' I can, actually, remember exactly, but I'm not going to tell nosey Gaynor; Monday 16th February 2009 at about nine in the evening; over a year ago. It wasn't the happiest day.

'Roughly'

'Mam, stop it, you're doing it again. Stop asking so many questions.'

'I'm just interested. It's nice when someone's interested in you, isn't it Judith?'

Personally I hate it when anyone takes any interest in me,

but that is not the answer required here. Gaynor tops up my glass and I take a sip knowing I should stop drinking now. Where is she going with this? She tops up her own glass as well, and Joanna's, but she is clearing the plates and going to the kitchen to sort out dessert. Gaynor gives me a meaningful look before I can give her one.

'I'm really interested in people,' she goes on, 'maybe that's why I enjoy working in Marks and Sparks. I'm one of the few that actually like the customers!' and she laughs in a not-funny way. Joanna comes back over with apple crumble and I laugh along with Gaynor.

'That's better,' she says, 'you two laughing together for a change.'

I am not convinced. Gaynor is pleasant enough for the rest of the meal, but I am still on my guard. I thought I had relaxed over my holiday but now I think I am still a bit tense. Joanna goes to make us a coffee and she starts again.

'For example,' she says as Joanna comes and sits back down, 'I was really interested in that woman in town.'

'Which woman, Mam?' she asks.

'Oh, Joanna, I don't think I mentioned it to you. This woman burst out of the crowd of shoppers and started shouting at Judith. I thought she was going to strangle her at one point, didn't you think that, Judith?'

'No, it was nothing really. A misunderstanding.'

'Did she mistake you for someone else?'

'No, she didn't,' Gaynor buts in, 'did she, Judith?'

'No she didn't. But what she was referring to was a misunderstanding from ages ago.'

'Not that long ago, surely. Just over a year wasn't it? Just before you moved to Carlisle?'

'What are you both talking about?' Joanna asks, looking from me to her mother and back again. Gaynor holds my stare and I realise that she is not as tipsy as she has been making out and my head is starting to spin. I feel at a considerable disadvantage. I continue to hold her stare while I decide how to deal with this. I stick to a version that no-one can possibly dispute; the truth as I see it.

'It's something I've been trying to forget,' I start to say.

'I bet you have, too!'

'Is it about your dead husband?' Joanna asks me. 'If so, Mam, just leave it.'

'Dead husband!' Gaynor snorts. 'Which dead husband might that be, Judith?'

'Mam, let Judith speak!'

'A really good friend, someone I cared for very much, had an accident and was killed.'

'Oh no, Judith, how awful for you. Mam, leave her alone. How did she die, Judith? Were you there?'

'She was there alright. It was her fault.'

I look at Joanna and say with all the sincerity that comes with the truth, 'It was not my fault. It was an accident.'

'The police interviewed you,' says Gaynor.

'The police interviewed everybody who knew her. The police always investigate what they call an unnatural death. Of course they interviewed me.'

'They let you go, obviously.'

I sigh deeply. 'Obviously. I didn't have anything to do with it.' God, my head is swimming. I really don't feel too good but I can't run away from this now.

'That woman didn't think so.'

'No she didn't and still doesn't. Her son was involved. It wasn't his fault either, it was an accident, but he sort of blames himself.'

'What on earth happened?' Joanna looks at me, pleading to be let in on the story.

'Your sister blames you too, and your niece does.'

'They don't blame me at all. They're just upset about it. We all are. I left Hexham to get away from it. I wish I hadn't in a way; maybe it would all be sorted now if I'd stayed.'

Gaynor snorts even more loudly at this. 'Yeah, right!'

'Mam, stop it now,' Joanna sort of screams. The scream cuts right through my head that has started to throb in the last few minutes. I feel very hot. I feel that if I don't go outside and get some air I will faint or shout back. I have to get outside.

'I need the loo,' I say and stagger to the downstairs cloakroom. I splash cold water onto my red face then sit on the toilet for a few minutes to try to get myself back onto an even keel

God, what has Gaynor put in that wine? It really isn't that strong. Oh my God, conspiracy theories now. My coat is hanging on the peg. I wonder whether I can stay steady enough to calmly lift it down and put it on without any fuss. I wash my hands and face in cold water again and grab my coat as I make my way back to the table.

'I need fresh air,' I say as levelly as I can. 'That wine has given me a headache.' Gaynor smirks. Maybe she did put something in it or maybe she thinks she has won this round. Either way, by fair means or foul, she *has* won this round and I simply want to go outside and walk home even if it is a couple of miles on a freezing night. I have to work early tomorrow as well. I have to leave. I have to sober up. 'Thank you for dinner, Joanna. I'll see you soon.'

I walk out of the front door in fierce and angry defiance at Gaynor who is still staring at me. How dare she do this to me? How fucking dare she? I can't even get her back because she's Joanna's mother. How fucking dare she?

I start to walk down the street back to where the main road joins it. A car has just pulled round the corner and I see straight away that it is Danny. I step out in front of him from behind a parked van and he swerves into a car parked opposite. That sets off the car alarm causing its owner to come running down the path. He starts yelling at Danny who has climbed out of his car, albeit from the passenger door. The driver's door must be bent but he doesn't look hurt.

'It wasn't my fault, mate,' says Danny, 'she stepped out in front of me – from nowhere.'

'Yes, and you can go back to nowhere!' I scream at him.

'What?' He spins round and takes a closer look at me. 'It's Judith, Jo's friend, isn't it? What's going on?'

'Don't call her Jo! I don't like it!'

'What about my car?' the man from across the road says as his wife comes out with the keys and switches off the alarm.

Joanna and Gaynor come running out, and I can hear Ricky crying inside the house.

'Danny, what happened?'

'Jo! Judith ran out in front of me. I crashed.' He's started to shake a bit but just enough to make her concerned. Joanna gives him a hug.

'Go back!' I scream at Danny again, 'Just go back to wherever you came from.'

'What?'

'Don't worry about her, Danny,' Gaynor joins in. She had gone back into the house to get Ricky and she carries him like a shield from me. He is still crying.

'You stay out of this, Gaynor,' I hiss, 'it was alright until you started.'

'Started! Started what? To tell my vulnerable daughter what you are really like? I think she has a right to know, especially if she's leaving Ricky with you.'

'A right to know what?' Joanna asks. 'Nobody has told me yet what this is all about.'

'It's about nothing,' I think I am screaming again, 'except your mother's suspicious mind. Why can't I just get on with my life in Carlisle without *someone* dragging it all up again?' The *someone* was accompanied by a stare at Gaynor.

She turns back to the house, soothing Ricky and muttering that as long as no one was injured she was going into the warm to finish her coffee.

'What about my car?' the man from across the road says again.

A police car comes round the corner and two large policemen take charge. God, I'm a bit fed up with giving police statements. Danny and I are breathalysed. He's sober. I'm not. They tell me to wait in the police car and they would drive me home. Danny is able to drive his car back off the other one and park it safely outside Joanna's house. She stands next to him throughout, occasionally looking over to me uncertainly. They all agree the insurance claims and arrangements for repairs can wait until daylight. The police offer Danny a lift home as well, but Joanna says he can stay the night at her house and not to worry about that.

My phone rings. It's Ken. I almost don't answer it but have lost all rational thought.

'Judith, it's me.'

'I know, Ken, it says so on my phone.'

'Are you OK?'

'No. I'm sitting in the back of a police car. My friend isn't my friend any more. Gaynor knows everything. Everything is total shit. I am definitely definitely definitely not OK.' I know I am slurring my words, and that my attempt to disguise it is making me sound ridiculous.

'Where are you? Who isn't your friend? Everything about what?'

'Forget it, Ken. Not your problem.'

'It is. I'm your friend too. I'm your boyfriend.'

'No you're not. You never were, not really. I needed you for something but now that's done. That went wrong as well. It's all gone very very very wrong.'

'I was; I am. What do you mean? We can sort whatever's the matter.'

'No, we can't. I don't want to anyway.' I click the off button and slump back in the police car and wait for them to drive me home. I can hear my mother's voice. *You've done it again, Judith. You've really done it this time.*

Friday 5th March 2010

I get up for work on autopilot. The shower wakes me up a bit but doesn't help my headache. I take some aspirins and drink a cup of coffee about ten times stronger than normal. Walking to work I feel as though I have a block of lead on each foot. I make my way across the car park towards the staff entrance, my head pounding in time with my heartbeat. I see Anita and Sal getting out of Anita's car. I wonder why three of us are needed this early in the morning. Just as well they're both here, the way I'm feeling today.

Mary Morris and Lucy the personnel manager are waiting for me at the top of the stairs.

'Good morning, Judith,' says Mary Morris, 'please come straight through to my office.'

Bloody hell! When did it become a disciplinary matter getting pissed the night before work?

'I expect you saw the police car outside,' she goes on.

Bloody hell! When did it become a crime to get pissed the night before work? I remember the car crash, but still can't make the connection.

'No, I didn't actually,' I reply, although I don't really think anyone is expecting me to.

We go into her office and there is PC Plod who took our fingerprints.

'You remember PC Stone?'

'Yes, of course.'

'He took your fingerprints.'

'Yes, I remember.' I wish she would offer me a seat. I think I am going to faint with this hangover. I start to sway and grab the back of a chair to steady myself.

'You have obviously realised what we are going to say, Judith,' says Mary Morris.

Where does she get that idea from? 'No,' I say, 'I don't. It's just that I have a very bad headache and think I am going to faint.' At last someone pushes a chair behind me and I fall back into it.

'I am sorry that you have a headache, Judith,' Mary Morris goes on as Lucy hands me a plastic cup of cold water, 'but this won't wait. I'll come straight to the point. Your fingerprints were found on the Sellotape sticking the notes under Maureen's desk.'

I sip the water gratefully, and after a few seconds I realise what she has just said.

'What?' I whisper, 'This is impossible.'

'Not impossible, I'm afraid Ms. Dillon. They were there as clear as anything. There is no mistake; no mistake at all.'

Mary Morris gives Plod a look that says that she wishes to deal with this herself and he lowers his eyes. 'Maureen made an allegation that you, in her words, were setting her up for some reason. I didn't believe it at first but now,' she hesitates choosing her words carefully, 'now, I wonder whether you can convince me otherwise?'

She has obviously instructed everyone to keep quiet and that is exactly what they do. The four of us sit there in silence as the clock on the wall becomes first audible, then loud, then like a torture technique. I can see no way out at all. Somewhere through the ticking and pounding and swaying nausea I decide that my best chance is to get Maureen right off the hook, not through any conscience attack but because those that own up get lesser prison sentences, at least on television programmes they do.

'When I say impossible,' I say, 'I mean that it seems impossible that I should make such a basic error.'

'So you admit it?'

'When I did it, no one had mentioned refurbishment. I had intended for the notes to fall down in time then everyone would see that there was not, in fact, any money missing at all. It seems impossible that I didn't realise what would happen that night and simply move the notes to the safe to be found by someone else.'

They don't know what to make of this, of course. They weren't expecting me to say that.

'Why did you do it at all?' asks Mary Morris.

'Because she was getting on my nerves, because she was always so perfect, because she was my supervisor, because I am cleverer than she is, because she wanted me to hang on every word she said, because I was expected to be in her loyal gang, because, because, because. I don't know. I wish I hadn't started it.' I look up at PC Plod. 'Are you going to arrest me now?'

'That is up to Mrs. Morris.'

'I would prefer to accept your immediate resignation,' she said, 'on the understanding that nobody here will give you a reference when you apply for other jobs. I think it unlikely that you will be offered a job in Carlisle when news of this gets out.'

Here we go again. No charges pressed, although they could be this time. No chance of another job. No friends left who will speak to me. It would be out of the question for Ken to have anything to do with me even if he wanted to after this, and after last night. I sit in Mary Morris's office staring out of the window to the piece of grey sky above the bare tree, contemplating nothing at all. Void. Blank. No plans. Nowhere to go. No one to see. Nothing to do. No cash to speak of. It would probably be easier to get arrested and go to prison but knowing my luck, I wouldn't get locked up. I'd just get a fine and a police record and still be in the same situation. The clock starts to get loud again. They continue to sit in silence.

'Please can I have another glass of water, and a piece of paper and I'll write out my resignation now.'

Lucy the personnel manager jumps up to get me a drink. I take two more aspirin before picking up a pen and starting to write.

'Give Lucy your locker key and she will pack up anything you have to take with you,' orders Mary Morris and I do as I am told. By the time I have completed the short note of resignation she returns with a carrier bag with my comfortable shoes and the book I still haven't finished reading.

Saturday 6th March 2010

I wake up at six-thirty as usual and instantly remember that I have nowhere to go. I stay in bed and try to go back to sleep but within an hour the traffic has started to build up, the sun shines through my flimsy curtains and the heating switches itself off. I get up and make a cup of coffee then my phone rings. It won't be Ken or Joanna or Gaynor so I am at a loss to know who else it can be. It's Mill View. I don't answer it so Tina leaves a voice message in her caring but urgent voice telling me that my mother has taken a turn for the worst in the night and suggesting I come to visit as soon as possible. I know she means now. Bus or train? That is the most challenging decision I will have to make today. I consult the bus timetable and the train

266

timetable and decide on the train. It's still only eight o'clock so I slowly get showered and dressed and make my way down to the station. At least I don't feel sick and headachy today.

At Hexham Station I expect to feel something horrible or nostalgic as I walk along the platform, but I feel absolutely nothing. Nothing except cold and miserable, that is. I can't afford a taxi to Mill View as I have no idea where my next pay cheque is going to come from. I catch the bus that will take me to within about half a mile of it and look out at the roads I used to call home. Maybe I should have contacted Fiona. She might have picked me up. She might not have, as well. Better to stay independent.

Tina comes to let me in to the fortress. She ushers me through to her office and shuts the door. She dispenses with formalities.

'Judith, thanks for coming over so quickly. Your mother is really very unwell. She had a stroke during the night so there was a delay in getting medical help.'

'Can I see her?'

'Yes, of course, but I wanted to prepare you first. She has lost all feeling down one side and can't talk.'

'She hasn't been making any sense for ages. It's OK. I'll just sit with her.'

'Fiona has been here but she's gone to pick up Rosie. They'll be back soon.'

'Are you preparing me for that as well?'

'No, of course not. That's not my place, to comment on your family relationships.'

'No, I suppose not.' I sit quietly for a few moments. 'Is there anything to do? To be done, I mean? What is the prognosis?'

'It's not good. There's nothing we can do to cure her. We're simply making her as comfortable as possible.'

'How long?' I bet everyone asks that. She'll probably say she has no way of telling.

'She's unlikely to live beyond the weekend.'

'The weekend! I thought you were going to say… well, never mind, it doesn't matter. Can I go and see her now.'

My mother is in the room that I arranged for her, and let's be honest, forced her to take. She looks pale and thin and very fragile. I sit down next to her and hold her hand. She sort of acknowledges it with a flicker of her eyes so I squeeze it gently.

'Hello Mum,' I say, then put my head down to it and to my surprise the tears start to flow. She seems to make a huge effort to squeeze my hand back and when I look up I see tears making shiny lines down her face too and her mouth is slightly contorted. 'Oh, Mum.' I try to hold back the sobs. If she knows what's going on this won't be helping her. If she knows who I am it will probably upset her and if she doesn't it will confuse her even more.

She makes a sound that sounds like 'Jj jj'. She's trying to say my name.

'Mum,' I wail. And this is when Fiona and Rosie arrive. I didn't see or hear them come in but when I finally put my head up and rummage for a tissue in my bag, Rosie puts her arms around me.

'Auntie Ju, you're here. Thank God. How did you know?'

'Tina called,' I sniff and then blow my nose. I see Fiona reach into her bag but before she can do anything, I take a clean tissue and wipe the tears from our mum's cheeks. 'Sorry Mum,' I say, 'I didn't mean to upset you.'

'Jj jj,' she says again.

'She knows you're here, Ju,' says Fiona. 'She's really pleased you're here.'

How can Fiona be so nice? Are we really born of the same parents?

'Have you just got here? Shall I go and make us all a coffee?'

I nod and look at her. She blinks away tears and goes off to the kitchen. She knows where everything is. She probably comes here every day. Rosie sits next to me and puts her head on my shoulder and takes her granny's other hand. She is so still that I don't know which side she can't move. It doesn't matter. Nothing matters except that soon it will all be over. How did I let it come to this? Everything I touch turns out wrong. All the wasted time; and now I can't even have 'the' conversation, the one that would mend it all before it's too late. It's already too late; I know that. I start thinking of everything I don't know. I don't know much about my dad. I know he died, of course, but I was too young to know what drove him as a person. Was he even the driving force behind my parents' business or was it Mum? Does she care that it got bought out by a bigger company after she sold it, and that they closed it down in Hexham? Did she miss my dad, or was she happier without him all those years. Why don't I know anything? Why did she always favour Fiona? What did I do that was so bad even as a young child? Does Fiona know any of this? If she does, how come she knows and I don't?

She comes back with the coffees and I force myself away from self-pity and pay attention to my mother. One of the staff comes in and presses a button that silently summons Tina. Tina puts a finger to my mother's neck and holds it there for about ten seconds.

'I'm sorry,' she says to us all, 'I'm sorry but she's passed away.'

I expect Fiona to have hysterics and say it isn't fair that our mother should die while she is making coffee for me; for me who is never here and never helps with any of it. Instead she says to Rosie and me, 'I'm glad you two were here holding her hands,' and to my amazement she comes over and hugs us both as we all cry for someone we will never see again and never speak to again. The staff leave us alone. They take away the coffees and re-boil the kettle for when we are ready then they gently cover her face and lead us to Tina's office. *All in a day's work for her*, I think uncharitably, but allow myself to be consoled and talked to, and to have a part in arrangements for the funeral and the removal of belongings.

'Will you come and stay with us, Ju?' Fiona asks.

'Yes please,' I reply.

Monday 15th March 2010

I don't know where the last ten days have gone. We've been busy sorting out Mum's stuff from Mill View and from her house that Fiona and Rosie still call home. Rosie went back to Leeds during the week but came back again on Friday. Fiona and I have got along pretty well without her and Fiona has been surprisingly calm and organised. I expected her to fall apart, still do at some point, but she's been brilliant; much better than me. We have had a recurring conversation that goes:

She says, 'Don't you need to get back for work?'

And I say, 'No.'

Then she looks at me enquiringly and I carry on with what I am doing. I suppose I'll have to tell her sometime, but not yet. We've driven to the tip and back more times than I can remember and taken bags of clothes to the charity shops in the town. By Friday we had started to make an impression and the house was looking emptier. Fi starts to ask me what I particularly want for myself. There are quite a few things, actually, but I have nowhere to put anything. My rent in Carlisle is paid up to the end of April and I have no idea at all where I will go then. I can't transport the big pictures I really like, or the oak cabinet that has the glasses in it. I would like at least one of the old bedspreads we had as children. We haven't sorted out the books yet; there were loads that I'd intended to read as we were growing up but teenage life then business life got in the way. I know we are supposed to be throwing things out but there is suddenly so much I want to keep.

'There are loads of things,' I tell her, 'like the pictures in the hall and some of her crystal glasses. I have nowhere to put anything, though. My place is so small.'

'I'll keep it all for you until you're ready.'

'Are you planning to stay here? In this house?' I try not to sound as though I am making a judgement about this.

'No, of course not. You were right all the time. It's way too big for me on my own. Rosie's at uni most of the time, you'll never come back to Hexham to live and now Mum's gone.' She just sort of leaves it there. She really is doing very well. When is she going to break down and break this spell that seems to be enabling us to get through this with the minimum of pain?

Rosie comes in wearing black trousers and a green jumper. She asks whether we are ready to go.

'I don't think I'll ever be ready,' says Fiona, 'but the hearse will be here in a minute. Come on, Ju.'

Rosie keeps watch out of the window while we go to find coats and tissues and put on our shoes, and when she sees the cars coming up the road she links her arms with both of us and leads us from the house where we grew up.

The funeral at the crematorium is quite short and not overly religious. The bells in the nearby church tower chime twelve as we troop in which adds a nice touch. The vicar came round last week and told us that he knew Mum from Mill View. I nearly said, 'Well in that case you don't know her at all,' but who am I to talk? He told us what he planned to say, and Fiona added a couple of things. I am amazed at how many people there are at the service. I recognise a few of them from Mill View; staff and residents. There are some from the street where she lived for almost the whole of her adult life. There are some from the bridge club; surely she didn't still play bridge? I realise that all these people knew my mother so much better than I did. They all know Fiona and Rosie and a few ask how I am and what I've been doing these last few years. Maybe people round here have short memories after all. The vicar announces that everyone is welcome at the George Hotel for drinks and food and again, quite a few come back. The hotel has seen to all the catering. Most people don't stay long, and they certainly don't talk to me for long because I don't answer any of their questions. I suspect that Fiona has asked people to ask me what I am doing now as I still haven't told her anything.

I remember that it is Monday afternoon, and normally I would be looking forward to going to Spanish class. I wonder what everyone is saying about me and how much Joanna would have told them about that night. Everyone I know will know about the money I hid in the cash office by now as well. I expect that Maureen has been reinstated in her rightful place. I shudder at the thought and Rosie squeezes my arm. I am shocked that I have already stopped thinking about my mother and am back being preoccupied with my own life. Oh well, life goes on, as they say. I suppose I will tell Fiona and Rosie all about it tonight or tomorrow.

'How long are you staying, Rosie?' I ask.

'I'll go back later,' she says, 'but I'll be back every weekend for as long as Mum wants me to. How long are you staying?'

'I don't know. I suppose I'll have to go soon. I just don't know.'

'What about work?'

'If you stay tonight, I'll tell you and your mum together.'

She hesitates, and then nods. 'You must promise, though.'

I'll have to do it now I've said I will. 'I promise.'

Rosie seems to have it in her head that this is our last opportunity to talk together as a family, and as soon as we get home she says that she is going to draw up an agenda. She tells Fiona and me to go and put our feet up and that she will prepare dinner while we have a rest. After about an hour in the kitchen by herself she comes through to the lounge.

'I've done all the prep,' she says, 'so let me know about half an hour before you want to eat and I'll cook it.'

I look at my watch. It's nearly six.

'Any time for me,' I say, 'I'm not fussy.'

'Anybody want a drink?'

I would love a drink but the memories of that night are still haunting me. 'I'll wait until we're eating,' I say. 'It's not good to drink on an empty stomach.'

'Maybe not, but I'm a student and six o'clock is wine o'clock where I live now.'

'You carry on. Don't mind me.'

'OK. Mum?'

'Yes please. Red, please. Sure Ju?'

'Quite sure.' Especially if we are to have difficult conversations.

Rosie brings the wine and her list.

'This is the agenda,' she consults it even though she knows exactly what she has written. It turns out there are only three items. 'Granny's house, Mum's job – or lack of, and Judith's life. Any preference for what order we do them?'

'Me last,' I say quickly before anyone else can jump in.

'Granny's house first,' says Fiona.

'That's easily decided then,' says Rosie, then attempting a bit of humour, 'let's hope it all goes as smoothly as that.'

'I suggest we carry on sorting Granny's stuff. We can get one of those storage things for anything we want for later, then either sell or give away or bin everything else.'

Neither Rosie nor I can believe that Fiona is talking like this.

'That seems very, very, very something-but-I-don't-know-what,' I say, remembering a phrase we used as children.

'We need a fresh start,' she goes on. 'I don't want to be stuck in the past. The last two or three years haven't been that great. I've been stuck here. I don't want to be here on my own surrounded by memories of Mum getting worse and Rosie moving away and Judith, well, you know.'

'No-one will ever really know for sure,' I say quietly, referring directly to the incident for the first time since being back.

'So anyway,' Fi continues, 'then we can paint the place, get the carpets cleaned and get it on the market.' She looks at me, presumably for my usual comment about splitting the money and going our separate ways. I just nod.

'You OK with that, Ju?'

'Yes, I'm fine. Do we know whether Mum ever made a will?'

'Yes she did, and she altered it a few years ago, though what's in it, I don't know. She could have left everything to the dog rescue place.'

We laugh at this. She couldn't stand dogs; well dog owners I suppose. I wonder why she would change her will so late in life. *Que sera sera*. No point in worrying about it. I wouldn't be amazed if she had cut me right out.

'OK then. If you're sure. You can't do it all yourself though. Are you going to get a man in to do the painting?'

'Not while I'm not working, no. I'll do it.'

'And that brings us nicely onto item two. Mum, you need to get a job.'

'I thought I might go to university,' Fiona says after a slight pause for dramatic effect, and as we turn to stare at her she adds, 'I'll get a part-time job as well, like Rosie has.'

'Where? What are you going to study? Where has this come from, all of a sudden?' Rosie clearly had no idea about her mother's plans.

'Social work,' she says simply, then realising that we weren't keeping up with her train of thought, she continues, 'They're crying out for social workers. I've been an unpaid social worker for the last few years, well sort of, and I think I would like it. I'll work with elderly people helping to make sure they have a good quality of life. That sort of thing anyway. I can do it in Carlisle, at the university there.'

The irony of this is not lost on me. In fact, I wonder for a minute whether Fiona is taking the piss. I give her a look that says if she is, I'll know.

'What?'

She isn't. 'Nothing. Yes, they do a social work course in Carlisle. It's supposed to be really good.'

'How do you know that, Auntie Ju?'

My turn now; item three. 'Shall we eat first? My bit might take a while.'

'No,' they say in unison, and I start at the beginning and tell them everything. By about nine-thirty Fiona and Rosie have finished the first bottle of wine and we sit in silence while the enormity of my story sinks in. I'm ready for a glass now so go off to find another bottle and leave them to say what they will about the latest mess I have made of my life. I switch on the oven while I'm in the kitchen and put in the pasta bake that Rosie made earlier. I'm starving and I expect they are too by now. I go back into the lounge and they are still sitting in silence.

'More wine,' I say, and pour large measures all round.

Monday 5th July 2010

Manchester Airport: Terminal 1. 21:40 on a Monday night and the anoraks are still crowded around the big windows watching the planes being parked and towed. There are five middle-aged men with big bellies, grubby t-shirts, cameras, notebooks and pens, and an unnatural enthusiasm for aircraft. I can understand being interested if you're just about to fly, but they are clearly not going anywhere. What do they see in it? Apart from the logos painted on the planes, what on earth is so fascinating? The red light on the Air Malta A320 (I only know it's an A320 because one of them said it) flashes brightly against the dusky sky, its Maltese Cross white against its red tail. It follows dutifully behind Tompson.com, obeying instructions to the letter. I should be going to Europe. I like Malta and Spain. Abu Dhabi is too far away, even for me, but they're crying out for accountants there and it was easy for me to get a job. It's all pointless anyway because it doesn't matter where I go. I never escape from it; the memories and the mistakes and the upsets go with me everywhere. The luggage wagon trundles past the window towards the Etihad A330 (I only know it's an A330 because it's the plane I'm going on) and I think I can see my luggage. I haven't got much but with my inheritance at least I can afford decent leather cases. It's good to have nice things again and I vow never to have to lower my standards like I did in Carlisle.

My new job pays a lot of money so next time I fly it'll be first class. I daren't do it yet in case it doesn't work out. I must keep telling myself that it will work out. I'll make sure it does this time. I'll have to get used to not drinking in public but that's OK, I'll have wine in the flat. The company flat that I can have for six months looks lovely in the DVD they sent me. It's brand new and overlooking the sea. I think it will suit me very well, and will be great when Fiona and Rosie come for Christmas.

I go to the bar to get another glass of wine. Airports are easy for women alone. No one gives a second glance as I sit here on a red plastic seat at a round, grey plastic table with a large glass of Pinot Noir. It's not like Carlisle where, if you sit in a bar or a restaurant drinking on your own, you're either sad and lonely, or you've been stood up, or you're on the pull.

That was one of the many good things about Joanna's cafe bar; you could just sit there.